WE WILL BE HEROES

THE VIGIL AND ANTE FILES
BOOK 2

Whimsical
Publishing & Illustration

For Mom,
I love you.

PREVIOUSLY ON THE VIGIL & ANTE FILES...

by ~~Agent~~ *Consultant* Sam Hunt

———

(Spoilers...obviously)

So, you're an agent who forgot what happened a few months ago. Or you skimmed over that monstrous file. Either way, I've got you.

VIGIL & ANTE Studios has an entire fandom dedicated to the best superhero franchise of all time. But the rest of the world doesn't know the movies are made to cover up the government's biggest secret: *the superheroes are real.*

I used to work at Ketch-a-Burger with Rosemary Collins, a seventeen-year-old fangirl and theatre kid wannabe who lived in NYC with her terrible parents. She discovered that Ironfall—the coolest on-screen supervillain—was stalking her. At first, she thought it was a prank, but soon she learned the secret. I'm sure you can guess what happened from there. Either way, I'll fill you in.

Ironfall threatened to harm Rosemary's parents if she didn't cooperate, and VIGIL wanted her to work as a double agent. Coolest job opportunity *ever*. If she didn't spy on Ironfall, he would win, but if he learned of her betrayal, he would kill her parents. Very dramatic, I know.

Rosemary agreed to go undercover within Ironfall's operation, which was clearly the best option. I mean who wouldn't want to hang out with their favorite movie characters?

Enter, me: the real hero of this story. I got too close to the truth, and Ironfall, in all his coolness, tried to kill me. Rosemary saved my life by divulging my own little superpower: wizard computer skills. Impressive, right? I hacked the CIA in five minutes, which I'm sure seems straight out of an unrealistic movie, but I'm just that good. Long story short, I joined the super-secret supervillain team.

Back to Rosemary, our epic main character. Ironfall fell for her. *Hard*. ~~Rosemary totally liked him back, but she'll never admit it.~~ His trust in her grew. (Not in me, though. He was still kinda mad I accidentally shot him.) He even revealed his best kept secret: his real superpower was the ability to heal.

Rosemary, Ironfall, and I, stole a powerful device from a top-secret vault. Ironfall killed two guards, and Rosemary witnessed the whole thing. Obviously, she freaked out. Anyway, after that, Ironfall found out Rosemary worked for VIGIL. She battled for her life while begging him to spare her family, but he was too strong. In a moment of weakness—love? We all thought it—he let her go. VIGIL arrested him.

This was when it really started to get good, because at the same time, Rosemary discovered her parents were even worse than everyone thought. In fact, they were secret CIA agents loyal to ANTE, a corrosive terrorist organization prepping to emerge from the shadows and take over the world. Sounds fake, but it was true. Desperate to save their reputation (cowards), her parents tried to convince Rosemary to join them, but like the hero she was, she refused. So, they kidnapped her and trained her anyway. After weeks of captivity, ANTE sent Rosemary to kill us (the remaining VIGIL agents). Isn't that fun?

Rosemary rebelled, of course, and instead she exposed ANTE's dastardly plot. Sadly, ANTE took precautions against this exposure and flipped her kill switch. Ironfall—the lovesick boy he was (and still is)—begged VIGIL to let him heal her, and once again, he saved her life. How romantic, right?

Ironfall kind of joined the VIGIL team gang thing, and we went on the run with less than three days to thwart ANTE's attack on Congress. We found out that the dude running ANTE was Ironfall's dad. Surprise, surprise. There were a lot of intense parts I'm too tired to go into here, but basically Ironfall flipped sides a couple times before ultimately helping us save the day. Everyone is still confused as to whether or not he's good, but he's now helping us hunt ANTE down, so that's something in his favor. He also passed a lie detector test, so that's another.

Congrats, you made it through. Please proceed to the next file...if you dare...

(No, I'm not sorry for how cheesy that sounded.)

FEDERAL BUREAU OF INVESTIGATION
FILED BY **[REDACTED]**
DATES: **JULY 10—DECEMBER 12**
ALL RELEVANT DOCUMENTS INCLUDED
INCLUDES VIGIL REPORTS
CASE #: **[REDACTED]**

CHAPTER 1

OFFICIAL VIGIL REPORT
FILED BY AGENT ROSEMARY COLLINS
DATES: **JULY 10–DECEMBER 12**
ALL RELEVANT DOCUMENTS INCLUDED
CASE #: **[REDACTED]**

JULY 10 – *11:27 A.M. PDT*

Doors on all sides. Possible hostiles. My eyes widened as I kept my gun pointed at the floor, at the ready.

This was what secret agents were built for.

The hallway seemed to stretch on forever. Why did each door have a window gaping into the inside? Sure, it was helpful for me, but it also meant potential opponents could see into the corridor.

The CIA already knew I was here.

I gulped, putting on my bravest face as I shuffled forward.

Noise behind me. I whipped around. Someone grabbed my forearm, wrenching me to the side. My chest tightened, but I pushed through.

I knew what to do.

Punch, deflect, punch, deflect.

1

In one swift motion, I flipped the man over. He landed on his back, head lolling to the side. He didn't move.

I looked around, expecting Ironfall to appear around the corner, and an unbidden chill drifted down my spine. *Ironfall.* The villain. *The villain who came to life. Who said he changed. Who lied. Who*—

I swallowed my personal feelings to prevent my heart beating out of my chest. *Focus, Rosemary.*

The mission.

The fallen man stared back at me. I looked away, forcing myself into action by swiping the discarded gun. Someone would have heard the fight. I pointed the weapon in front of me like Manda instructed, then sprinted into a doorway for cover.

"Cut!"

A loud bell blared.

I sagged against the wooden set piece, stealing a rare moment of privacy as I caught my breath. Air filled my lungs as my mind raced back into the present. The fight scene had been carefully choreographed by Agent Manda, or rather her stuntwoman-turned-actress cover, Jana Anthony. I was safe on a sound stage. There wasn't even a ceiling on this "hallway." I was an actress, with a job to do, and I couldn't let the mess of VIGIL and Ironfall break through. My heart slowed, and I closed my eyes for three sweet seconds of attempted peace.

"Great job, everyone, let's reset the scene and go for another take."

I straightened, morphing into London Peters, my new alter ego. The show must go on.

Sam came up with my stage name, claiming it was perfect for a rising star such as myself. I'd rolled my eyes but agreed to it all the same, and I was finally getting used to answering to London on set. It took work to remember a name other than your own.

Taking a deep breath, I came around the other side of the fake hallway. One side of the set looked like a sleek secret agent HQ hallway against a green screen, the other was a city of crew, technology, lights, screens, and anything else you could imagine. This was my second week here and I still couldn't believe I was on an official VIGIL & ANTE Studios set. Despite the stress and reality of VIGIL behind it all, an almost permanent smile came to my lips as I took everything in once more.

I was here living my fangirl dream. And Sam was ridiculously jealous.

Cloaker, disguised as a random stuntman, got up from the floor where I'd left him and patted my shoulder. "Good job with that flip."

"You're the one who made it look real."

"That's the idea." He stretched out his neck.

Movement caught my peripheral vision, and I whipped around. Force of habit.

There stood the director, Sylvester Whitlock, a tall, broad-shouldered man in his mid-fifties who always seemed to wear intellectual glasses, a green-screen colored T-shirt, and blue jeans. He also had a mass of graying facial hair with even more on his head. Sam kept trying to convince me it was a toupee. A famous director would certainly have access to the best toupees and stylists, but I didn't quite believe Sam's conspiracy theory…yet.

"London." He looked directly at me. Sylvester Whitlock may be an Academy-Award-winning director, but he wasn't a VIGIL agent. He didn't know our secret. So I went by my stage name here. No one could ever know I was actually the character I portrayed. "We're going to do it again, but can I get a little more emotion from you this take? We're going for a closeup rather than a wide angle."

I nodded. "Sure."

He tapped a pencil against his temple. "Rosemary is conflicted here, so I want you to hesitate more. Go a little slower. Remember, this is her first mission, and she doesn't want anyone to get hurt. She's conflicted because she has to complete the heist to keep Ironfall on the hook, but also help ANTE."

Right, because he was an expert on Rosemary Collins. He wasn't wrong though. Those were my exact thoughts months ago. It was weird to have someone tell you how to act like yourself. My stomach turned at the thought of it, but I pushed it out of my mind to focus on the job at hand.

"Remember, this is not just a movie, it's a work of art." Sylvester was still talking. "You're the one that makes it shine. I really want to see that in these frames." He grinned. "I'm gonna make you a star."

I couldn't help but smile, even with his borderline narcissism on display. He always wanted everyone to know how great of an Academy-Award-winning director he was.

"Hey, can we get someone over here to touch up her make-up?" he shouted, pointing at my face in the sort of large circular motions that gave my old drama teacher a run for her money. "I'm not loving how the light hits it."

Before he was even finished with his sentence, someone was on top of me, brushing more powders onto my face. I closed my eyes.

To say I felt like a superstar in this moment was an understatement.

The makeup brush stopped attacking my face, and I opened my eyes.

Agent Liam stood on the sidelines dressed down in a hoodie and jeans. Much more of a Xavier Jay move. As executive producer and figurehead of VIGIL & ANTE Studios, he was the real one running this show (much to the Sylwhit's chagrin). He nodded as if telling me he was proud.

I smiled back, escaping the makeup artist as I moved toward him. I knew the crew wouldn't be ready to shoot for another few minutes since they were repositioning the cameras and lighting, and I wanted to take the chance to say hello while I had it.

"Don't mind the Sylwhit," he said as I approached. "He might be difficult to work with, but he's one of the best directors of all time."

4

"You know I've never actually seen any of his movies." I glanced over at the director to make sure he wasn't listening. He would absolutely give me homework to watch all his movies, and I didn't have the time (or patience) for that.

"Don't tell him that," he said. *Wouldn't want to damage his ego,* I could almost hear him say. That was something Xavier Jay would say, but not Agent Liam. And right now, he was talking to me as himself, not his actor persona. "Remember to separate yourself from the character. You might share a name, but you're different. It's our advantage."

"Thanks," I nodded. "I'll remember that."

"It's not you, it's a carefully branded image of you." His dark fingers straightened his shirt. "Made for your and VIGIL's protection."

"London!" Sylvester again. "I want you to rehearse the scene's stunts again with Jana. We may need to adjust your choreography for the camera angle."

I nodded, giving a small wave to Agent Liam as I made my way toward Manda. My body was already aching from all the stunt work today (and the fact that my call time was six a.m.), but movie Rosemary was exhausted during this scene too, so I guess I was method acting.

With another kick of excited adrenaline, I'd be fine. Or maybe I should start drinking coffee?

Manda walked over as I looked back at Agent Liam.

Ver walked on set at that moment too, looking like she fit right in. No one batted an eye. Even when she wasn't starring in a VIGIL & ANTE Studios movie, she enjoyed hanging out, and since Xavier Jay had given her permission, that was good enough for the rest of the crew.

But right now, Ver didn't look like she'd just come to hang out. She had a serious expression, and after she whispered something to Agent Liam, his face hardened as well. Seconds later they walked away with purpose.

Oh to be able to read lips. My spy skills needed work.

"London," Manda snapped, her long black braid swaying behind her as she talked. "Pay attention."

"Oh, yes, I am." I nodded. I was now, anyway.

"We're changing your assailant's entrance to the door across the hall." She pointed to the correct door. "He'll attack you on the same mark, but from behind instead of in front." She motioned to the disguised Cloaker. He jogged over and the three of us made our way to the set pieces to mark the scene.

Manda backed onto the set toward the piece of tape marking my blocking. "I want the same fight sequence, but he will come up behind you, holding his gun at your chest. You whip around, pull his arm forward, and dislodge the gun. Then you turn and go into the sequence."

I nodded. Okay, yeah, I could do that...hopefully without hurting Cloaker in the process.

"Let's do a run through in slow motion," Manda looked around, then pointed at us. "Can we get a mat down?"

Production assistants raced around, and before I knew it, a bright green padded mat covered the hallway's floor near my mark. Oh good, Cloaker would be protected by only an inch of padding when I tossed him.

I glanced at him, looking him up and down. "Sorry if this hurts." It definitely would.

He shrugged. "Nah, I know how to land." Then, in a lower voice, he added, "Can't be as painful as a gut shot."

I gulped. He'd been shot before? "Wow, okay, didn't know about that. Still, I apologize in advance."

"Okay, London, go to your mark," Manda said. "You're facing the door, gun out and at the ready." I acted out her narration. "And Assailant, go, raise your gun, Rosemary turn, yank his weapon, good, good. Now bring him up and then he lands." Her narration was slow, almost in a sing-song voice.

Cloaker gave me a thumbs-up from the floor. No broken bones, though I didn't do the full move. Couldn't really do that in slow motion, but at least we had the choreography.

Manda nodded with approval. "I think you both have it."

"We're going for a thirty-minute break." Sylvester's booming voice drowned out the soft chatter and clatter of the sound stage. "I want everyone back here on time and ready to go." He placed a hand on his hip and looked around.

The set came alive again, this time with people laughing, moving around, and flooding out of the stage, probably to snag some snacks and coffee from craft services.

Still, the break hadn't been scheduled beforehand, at least not on my call sheet.

I glanced over to see that Agent Liam had returned. He was motioning me, Manda, and Cloaker to follow him. What had Ver told him? What was going on?

We followed him out into the sunlight. I covered my eyes, squinting because everything was way too bright after the sound stage's strange dark lightness.

"I told him there are technical difficulties," Agent Liam whispered as we walked. "He shouldn't figure it out for a while."

Manda smirked as if she was happy to see Sylvester suffer. So far, they hadn't gotten along very well, but that wasn't saying much since she could probably count the number of people she liked on one hand.

"Ver and Sam found something." Agent Liam's voice was still low.

The air left my chest. Finally, after months. They found something.

"What is it?" Manda asked.

"Ver and Ironfall are waiting in Rosemary's trailer, and Sam is on the line." Agent Liam gestured us onward. "We'll brief everyone there."

JULY 10 – 11:50 A.M. PDT

Ironfall lounged on my trailer's couch like he owned the place, lying back, already dressed in his costume, dark hair styled so one wave slid across his forehead. The thought of fangirls going feral over that made me want to bang my head against the wall. That mixed with those brown eyes, a sliver of icy blue permeating his left iris.

I swallowed, not taking my eyes off him as we piled into the trailer's "living room." It was cramped, but we made it work. I took a seat at the table next to Ver. Manda and Liam sat across from us. Sam's face was projected through the TV on the wall.

Ironfall finally looked up, gaze falling on me of all people. "You're looking rough," he said, grinning. "You get beat up in your scene?"

It took everything in me not to demand he get off my couch. He needed to stop acting like he belonged. Stop wearing his stupid costume and his stupid grin and that stupid strand of hair curling delicately across his forehead. "If you read the script, you'd know." I grimaced, training my eyes back on Agent Liam. *If you're going to pretend to help us, then at least sit up and act like you're taking VIGIL seriously.* Five people packed in my trailer (yes, *my* trailer) made it feel small enough, but having him in here made it claustrophobic. My chest tightened.

"Why would you assume I didn't?" The ice blue in his left eye shimmered in the odd trailer lighting. Why did I notice that? "I'm a very committed actor, you know." He smiled wider.

"And you're too good at it," I said, looking away. So good I couldn't tell if he was working for VIGIL for his own nefarious purposes. Sure, he passed the lie detector test, but I was still waiting for the moment he'd change his mind and decide he didn't want to help us anymore.

And why was he still sprawled across my couch?

"We're not thrilled he's here." Agent Liam's eyes darted between the two of us. "I know. Let's get—"

"Hey guys," Sam said, a small picture on the TV screen. "It's me. How's set life for my favorite movie stars?" He looked way too happy to be here. "It's not fair you get to have all the fun." *Someone* was having too much fun. Ironfall. It was Ironfall.

"Combing through hard drive data isn't exciting enough for you?" Ver laughed, rolling her eyes. "Who would have thought?"

"You're lucky to be included in this meeting at all," Ironfall said.

"You're one to talk," Manda muttered, reading my mind.

I bit back my own angry retort and forced a smile. "We're happy to have you here, Sam. Even if it's only on video."

"Ugh, school and homework and stuff. You're so lucky you graduated," Sam said. I only missed the last few months of senior year, but VIGIL still pulled strings so everything tied up nicely. I was the proud owner of a high school diploma, a VIGIL badge, and a movie deal.

Not to mention a deal with Ironfall, the supervillain with questionable intentions.

Agent Liam cleared his throat, gesturing toward the TV as he pulled up a blue wire-y map of the United States as well as what was supposed to be a board of clues. But only one clue was there: we believed my…father…now led ANTE. That was all we knew.

"Ver and Sam have been combing through the data we recovered from the ANTE base where Cloaker was held. Most of it was destroyed when ANTE initiated the self-destruct protocols, but they cracked it." Agent Liam clicked another button, bringing up dots on the screen. "We now believe there are a network of four ANTE sleeper cells. We took out one during Cloaker's rescue. That leaves us the remaining three to find."

Ironfall sat up, finally deciding now was a good time to be professional. "Is that all we have? The number of bases?" Careful. Calculated. He was thinking. Was his mask lowering?

"ANTE was a little too thorough in covering their tracks. The data we recovered from the blasts was minimal," Ver said.

"Not even I could recover it, and that's saying something," Sam piped up.

"You're avoiding an answer," Ironfall said. "Which means I'm right." As much as I hated to admit it, he was correct. They were avoiding it.

"I'm still determined to get something...but yes, you're right," Sam said. "But that doesn't mean I'm admitting defeat!"

"Do we have leads on any operatives?" Manda asked.

"We're looking for groups of people embedded in government, Hollywood, and other key linchpin places in society. We believe they're hiding in plain sight waiting to be activated." Agent Liam turned, studying the map. When we rescued Cloaker, he warned us about how organized they were. They had backup plans upon backup plans. They had people waiting to mobilize in case things in DC went south.

"These bases could be branches, they could be separate cells, but we don't know," Ver said. "I know, it isn't the news we were hoping for."

"See if you can get anything off the hard drives. Check evidence from the blast too. I want you to comb through everything again," Agent Liam said.

"What are we looking for?" Sam leaned closer to the screen. "We were obviously very thorough."

"Just do it." Agent Liam straightened. "See if he knows anything he hasn't shared that could help." He glanced at his watch. "We only have a few minutes to be back on set. Anything else we should know?"

"The *Project Safeguard 3* premiere is coming up," Ver said. "Which is considerably less important—"

"YES!" Sam screamed so loud the speakers cut out for a moment. "Sorry. Am I invited?"

"Do you have an actor alter ego?" Ironfall rolled his eyes.

"Not yet," Sam said. "But I'm sure it's coming." In your dreams, Sam.

"Remember what you told me about the one time you tried

acting?" Ironfall said. "Something about puking?" I remembered him telling us about that back when…back when things were weird and normal and terrifying all at the same messy time.

"Whaaaat?" Sam's eyes widened. "I don't think I ever said anything like that. I mean it happened, but I'm a new man now ready to take on my role in the new movie."

"On that note, everyone head back to set. We have an action scene to film." Agent Liam waved his hands in a shooing motion.

"It's not even my call time yet and I need a nap." Ironfall turned toward me and laughed. Ugh, why was his laugh like that? And why was he so right? My eyelids felt like lead.

"Me too," I said, trying to keep any sort of emotion out of my voice.

"I also need a nap," Sam said.

"Oh shut up," Manda and Ironfall said in unison.

BESTVIGILMEMES.BLOGGINGLIFE.COM
FEATURING THE BEST VIGIL & ANTE STUDIOS POSTS
(DON'T @ ME)
– UNAVERAGEVIGILFAN2002

unaveragevigilfan2002:
This is my official petition to play literally anyone in I AM STARDUST. Please please please Xavier Jay or Noelle Atkins cast me. I beg you. NOtiCE ME.
Comments:
Ironfallismine4000: no because I'd give my right arm
givehimacameo: You deserve it fandom king
cloakercloakercloaker: MEEEEEEEEE
trying2act: I'll play a tree. ANYTHING

---

vigilagentmarie:

Okay but do you think the cast sees this? Bc that would be amazing

Comments:

unaveragevigilfan2002: yes of course

Replies:

chloechloechloe2004: source: trust me bro

makemeyourmovievillain: lol

clo4ker: I mean they should

shapeshiftingpet: and miss the best part of the fandom? They'd thrive here

degreesurge4pres: How do you know I'm not one of the cast??????

Replies:

unaveragevigilfan2002: and how do you know I don't have an in with them?

Replies:

shapeshiftingpet: A regular VIGIL agent

JULY 10 – 4:22 P.M. PDT

I shook my head at my phone. Oh, Sam, provider of peak entertainment. If these commenters only knew he was literally a VIGIL informant, that all of this was real.

That Ironfall was allegedly one of the good guys now...

I readjusted myself in the tall easeled chair with my name embroidered on it; I had one of my own now, and it really was the coolest thing. I sat alone in the greenroom tent (which was not, in fact, green) waiting on Ironfall to finish in hair and makeup. How was it that he took longer than me?

He could have himself ready in five seconds flat with all his disguises. The thought sent a shiver trickling down my spine. Who knew what his real plan was. He passed the lie detector test, so maybe he'd been sincere at that point in time, but things could have changed. Flipping sides was what he did.

We'd be fools to expect anything different.

A crinkling of plastic made me look up.

Ironfall.

I tensed, crossing my legs. The costume department needed to turn it down with his perfectly imperfect hair and midnight button-down shirt rolled just below his elbows.

That singular wave still swooped onto his forehead too. I looked away.

It was the costume department's fault that every VIGIL & ANTE Studios fangirl fell for him. Yep. Them and nothing else.

He took two steps inside before bursting the tension. "You see what Sam just posted to his little fan account?" Yes, and the dramatic irony was unmatched.

"I did." I nodded. Sam. Yes, think of Sam and not Ironfall's inevitable betrayal.

"Think I ought to shake things up a bit? Start an account?"

My head snapped up. "Absolutely not! You know what kind of scandal that would cause." Not to mention the PR nightmare. Was that his plan? No, he wouldn't reveal it so plainly. I needed sleep or caffeine in an IV, even though a single cup of coffee shot my anxiety to another level.

"Oh but it would be fun." The sliver of blue in his eye gleamed mischievously. "Maybe I already have."

He was just messing with me. I let myself relax, but not too much.

"You did not." I narrowed my eyes. "Ver is gonna kill you. *I'm* going to kill you." There. Now he wouldn't come up with any ideas.

He shrugged, striding all-too-confidently to the chair labeled

"Rhett Wickford." "Luckily you guys need me." Yeah, and I hated it.

"Cloaker's here. You're replaceable." I said it as more of a warning, one I would never stop giving him. *You're on a short leash. You slip up once, you're done.*

He either didn't catch my meaning or shrugged it off. "Am I?" Who was I kidding? He caught everything but pretended he didn't, and it gave him an advantage.

Two could play those mind games.

Just then a production assistant popped her head in. "Ready for you on set."

"That's our cue." I hopped off my seat, shooting Ironfall one last warning glance before leaving the tent.

Federal Bureau Of Investigation
Transcript Of The Interview Proceedings With

AGENT LIAM BLAKE, DIRECTOR OF VIGIL
SOME NAMES AND LOCATIONS REDACTED FOR SECURITY
INTERVIEW CONDUCTED ON JULY 23
LOCATION OF INTERVIEW: **[REDACTED]**
CASE #: **[REDACTED]**

PROPERTY OF THE FBI

SPECIAL AGENT LAUDE: You filmed *I Am Stardust* from June 27 to July 17, is that correct?
AGENT LIAM BLAKE: Yes. Multiple people on set can attest to it.
SPECIAL AGENT LAUDE: You called a meeting while on set on July 10, is that correct?
AGENT LIAM BLAKE: Yes. I claimed there was a technical issue to cover it up, then had everyone meet in Rosemary's trailer.
SPECIAL AGENT LAUDE: Tell me about the trailer's security precautions.
AGENT LIAM BLAKE: Before every meeting, we swiped it for bugs and made sure our lines were encrypted.

SPECIAL AGENT LAUDE: You're sure no one hacked in?
AGENT LIAM BLAKE: My people are the best. If anyone tried, they would know.
SPECIAL AGENT LAUDE: Tell me about them—your people.

CHAPTER
2

OFFICIAL VIGIL REPORT
FILED BY IRONFALL
DATES: **JULY 10–DECEMBER 12**
ALL RELEVANT DOCUMENTS INCLUDED
CASE #: **[REDACTED]**

JULY 10 – *4:35 P.M. PDT*

Getting away with murder should have been enough to make me happy. I chose VIGIL and avoided punishment. My past self would have called that a win as I soothed the sting of loss by calculating how to weave this into my long game.

But my master plan was gone, and the pain of losing felt more like guilt as I wrestled with what I'd done. How many people I'd hurt. How many lives I'd taken.

You're weak.

It was an echo of my father's voice, and I hated it.

I let the sounds of the lively film set wash over me. The crew thought I was Rhett Wickford, a seasoned actor from the blockbuster VIGIL & ANTE Studios franchise. Yet I wasn't even him. Rhett was a persona Cloaker had formerly portrayed.

Still, all I had to do was turn up the charm and no one questioned me.

I glanced at Rosemary, her hair as radiant as ever against her white leather suit. She almost glowed in the studio light, inwardly and outwardly. Her goodness was contagious, the opposite of me. What I did to her...it was horrible. I gulped, plastering another smile on my face, biting back a sarcastic comment about how my costume rubbed against my skin.

"Lock it up, we're going for picture," Sylvester shouted from across the room, eyes trained on the screen strapped around his neck. The film set slowed, a hush falling on the room.

"Camera speeding."

A boom mic hovered over my head. "Sound ready."

Time for some movie magic, my specialty. I smirked, breaking character for an instant. Though can you truly break character if you are the character in question?

"Side by side?" I whispered to Rosemary.

"Guess we have to," she said, face blank.

"Right." Ice slipped through my voice as I focused on the false wall ahead. She didn't trust me.

I wouldn't trust me, either.

How can you use your enemies to your advantage? I shoved my father's voice from my mind.

"Scene 16 alpha, take one," said the first assistant director. He smacked the slate together, making a loud noise, then scurried out of the camera's view.

I turned to face Rosemary like I was supposed to. Her coolness was gone, sending a shiver down my spine.

"Action!" the director shouted.

Time to act.

The film set disappeared as the pretend world became real before my eyes. All I could see was a Rosemary who I thought trusted me. A time before I knew she worked for VIGIL.

And it was my everything.

July 10 – 6:45 P.M. PDT

"Cut!" Sylvester shouted. I looked at the chaos forming around me. Stuntmen rose from their "unconscious" states splattered on the ground, small amounts of fake blood pooled around them. It didn't quite reach the level of realism, but this wasn't a horror movie.

"I can't get that stupid line right," Rosemary laughed, the glorious sound echoing through the fake walls of the set. "'Allocated' keeps tripping me up." She repeated the phrase a few times without tripping over her words. I watched her as I stood there, drinking from the water bottle someone handed me.

Her brown eyes flicked to mine, and I jerked away, focusing on something—anything—else. The crew swarmed the area to sop up the red syrupy liquid.

"Sorry, guys," Rosemary said. "It's my fault you have to keep doing this. Do you need help, Timothy?" She knelt and reached for a towel. I just stood there, watching. How did she remember his name? I hardly knew anyone besides the VIGIL agents, yet she made a point to show kindness to everyone.

He giggled (which put me off for some reason), moving the towel from her grasp. "It's really fine, don't worry about it. It's my job."

"I—I could help too," I said. Rosemary looked up at me, then back down to Timothy. I made a mental note to remember names from now on.

It's what a good person would do.

You were born to be a villain. Why couldn't I get my father out of my head?

"Leave it to the pros." Someone else I failed to remember laughed. "Wouldn't want to get your costumes dirty."

I glanced down at mine, partially to avoid looking back at

Rosemary. The buttons of his shirt had never been more interesting.

"Well, gives her more time to say 'allocated' to herself." I smirked, slipping back into myself.

"Hilarious," Rosemary said. Was she pretending the tension between us didn't exist, because of crew members not privy to our secret?

"Unless you'd like to say it to me." I winked, crossing my arms. Two could play at this game. "I could be your allocated person."

"Designated, you mean?" She rolled her eyes.

"I was trying to use the word. Appreciate the humor."

"Ha. Ha," she said, now turning to walk away.

Nothing was the same as it was, and I doubted it would be again. What would make her believe I truly wanted to be different?

JULY 11 – 7:28 A.M. PDT

Through the TV screen in my trailer, I watched Sam crack his knuckles before readying his hands at the keyboard. "You and me working together. Just like old times."

"Just like old times," I said, still thinking of my last conversation with Rosemary. Sam might be quick to go back to normal, but Rosemary wasn't. Did I want to go back to normal? I didn't want to be the same, so what was normal?

"Hey! Focus."

"I am, Sam."

"Thinking about Rosemary?" The smug look on his face made me want to slap him. I knew exactly what he was trying to do.

"I'm sorry?" My eyes widened. Time to play dumb.

He smiled sheepishly. "Nothing."

"That's what I thought," I said. Time to deflect.

"Let's get to work. These hard drives won't decrypt themselves."

"I thought they were mostly destroyed by the explosion."

"Well yeah, but what I said sounded cooler," Sam said. It really didn't, but I was gracious enough not to point it out. "No one appreciates art when it comes to words." That, however, was not off-limits.

"No one has ever put you and art in the same sentence." I sat back in the seat. The Sylwhit really could have gotten me a more comfortable couch. Or at least some pillows.

"I just did."

"No one besides you then. Who's distracted now?" I smirked.

"Right," he said, then smashed away at his keyword. "I know you have all kinds of daddy issues, but what do you know about your father's systems? Did he keep backups?"

Resisting the impulse to throw something at the screen, I lay back further. "That's something I can answer. Yes, he kept backups of his backups. He was meticulous, always striving for perfection." Perfection he pushed on me. My teeth clenched before I continued, "I would guess he kept multiples of the same thing on the drive, as well as separate versions of the hard drive in different locations."

"Now there's something I can work with," Sam said. "Give me a sec." Sometimes he meant a literal second, sometimes he meant an hour. So, I reached for my script (you really thought I was going to get up and go get it?) and focused on being a responsible actor.

I nodded, not that Sam noticed; he was already in his own virtual world. I looked down at the script, studying lines for a later scene. Another one where Rosemary was close with me. We'd be filming in our "old hideout," planning the heist. I smiled a little, remembering the good parts before guilt washed over me once more.

You should have killed her. My father's relentless voice. Of course, sparing her life was the right thing to do. I should have spared everyone's lives.

I sat up, shoving the script away from me like I wished I could do to my memories.

"How are you doing?" I asked. "Progress report?"

"Deep-fried hard drive, remember?" Sam massaged his temples. "By a sec I mean...well..." He drifted off again into his own world.

I shifted positions, resting my chin on my hand. I needed to distract myself.

"Wait!" Sam stopped.

I jumped. "Did you find something?" This could be big. I could help him present it and maybe VIGIL would finally start to think I'd changed.

Maybe I would think that I had changed.

"No, I was just thinking. You know, you can't really call yourself a supervillain anymore."

"I'm sorry?" Not the thing I wanted to dwell on.

"You're one of the good guys now, so you can't call yourself a supervillain."

I blinked. "Wait a second, you trust me?"

"Heck yeah. You're awesome." Sam grinned. If this was another one of his jokes... Still, a smile tugged at my lips, and not the one I used to deflect.

"That said, what's your real name?" Of course...he was trying to compliment me into giving him personal information.

"Ironfall?" How was he still typing?

"Not your supervillain name, your real name."

"That is my real name." It was the truth. My father had me for a single purpose: to be his supervillain. He didn't see the point in gracing me with a normal name.

You failed, Ironfall, my father whispered harshly. He rarely shouted, instead opting to reprimand in a low, commanding voice. Close to my ear so I *didn't miss a word.*

"I definitely wasn't expecting that. That's really what your father named you?"

"Yes. He trained me to be a villain. It was more efficient. Do you have a problem with it?" Maybe too much edge in my voice, but he needed to stop prying into my private life.

"No, no, I think it's awesome," Sam said. Yeah, sure. "Bad if you're trying to be covert though."

"Thankfully it's easy to make up names," I deadpanned. "And that's much more covert than using a real name."

He lit up. "Maybe I should come up with a superhero name for myself. You know what, I think I'm going to."

"You do that."

Just then my trailer door burst open. I didn't flinch, instead looking up. My father had taught me not to flinch years ago. It was a sign of weakness. It was paramount to always look at ease, even if your heart raced.

It was just Ver. Today she had her short blonde curls sleeked into a ponytail to keep it out of the way as she bounced from set to her computer and back again.

"Found anything?" she asked.

I could feel Sam's eyes widening in horror at being caught goofing off. "Not yet." Even I knew it was useless trying to fix the hard drives, and I knew nothing about computers.

She raised an eyebrow, not having any of it. "You haven't been working, have you? You know I can tell when you're hiding something." It didn't take a genius to know it. Sam wore his heart on his sleeve, for better or for worse.

"He was helping me with something." Why was I defending him? "While taking a break." The words slipped out naturally as if it were the truth, followed by a pang of guilt that wracked my chest. I never used to feel like this.

Lying is one of the most valuable abilities. Stop. It.

"Yeah, Ironfall—"

"I needed him to research something for my character before I was called back to set. Can't be too prepared," I said, shooting

Sam a warning look. If he wanted to get away with this, he needed to shut it.

"Okay then." Ver shrugged. "Well, you're wanted back on set, Ironfall. Or should I say Rhett? Sam, get back to work. Let me know the moment you find something."

"I'm guessing you won't be helping," Sam said. "Poor me, left to do all the heavy lifting."

I rolled my eyes.

"I'll be on set, but I'll check my phone often. Shoot me a text if you make any progress," Ver said, not giving in to Sam's pretend pity-party.

"Yeah, that's unlikely. This hard drive is fried—" Sam said. It was our only lead.

"Beyond repair, I know. This is like the fiftieth time we've tried getting something off it. In my opinion it's hopeless, but Liam did ask for it, so I'm following orders," Ver said, half laughing.

"I'll get back to you if I find more ideas," Sam said directly to me.

"Right. Good." I nodded as if it were a perfectly normal thing.

JULY 11 – 1:33 P.M. PDT

Lunch. Finally. My stomach growled as I made my way over to where the food was being served.

Thank goodness for craft services.

After being on set for six hours, to say I was starving was an understatement, even though a lot of time was spent sitting around waiting to act. The amount of acting in a movie was much less than in theatre. Also, things were filmed out of order, so that was something else to get used to. Today was burger day from the cast's favorite east-coast fast-food chain. Thankfully the director was legally obligated to listen to us. Which I definitely didn't take advantage of. It was something the man I was and the man I was desperately trying to become were both happy about.

I grinned at the thought.

Oh, Sylvester Whitlock. He was so innocent in all of this.

Innocent and way too demanding.

I walked up to the lunch table and picked up my delicious burger order and extra fries.

"Burger days are the best days," Rosemary laughed. "Thank you," she told the craft services crew.

"Thanks," I mumbled, following her lead, then went to sit down.

Much to my surprise, Rosemary followed me. Though, I suppose it would've been strange if she purposely sat across the makeshift cafeteria since we were the only ones here. The tables were empty all around, so for now it was just us. Agent Liam, Manda, and Ver would follow after with the rest of the crew as they weren't actors today.

Perk of being an actor: you eat first.

I sat down, unwrapping my burger.

"Having fun today?" I asked. Probably not the best thing to lead with, but she already threw me off my game.

My phone buzzed in my pocket, but I ignored it.

"Yes." Her eyes shone as she brushed back a copper strand. "I can't believe you actually did an impression of Sylvester in front of him."

"Would you expect anything less?"

"No, not really," she giggled.

"Have to impress the great Sylwhit."

My pocket vibrated again.

She shook her head as she finished unwrapping her burger. "More like make him sad he didn't have the power to fire the beloved Rhett Wickford."

"You know, I really don't like the name Rhett," I mused. "It's the worst."

"Too bad you were busy being a supervillain when Cloaker chose it." She smirked. "Should have thought that one through and been one of the good guys." Was that a jab or just a playful poke? It was hard to know with her. She was hot then cold, and I couldn't tell when it was genuine.

Those were the most dangerous people of all.

"I'm trying to be." Delicious burger smashed into my mouth. So, so good. "Every day I'm grateful for the second chance."

"Mm," she said before eating again.

Crew started trickling into the tent, grabbing plates and burgers. I looked at mine, halfway eaten. My phone buzzed in my pocket for the millionth time. I knew it was Sam without even looking at it. Wasn't Sam supposed to be working on that hard drive? If he was busy trying to find himself a code name...

I brought it out, looking at the screen.

Sam: name ideas! Lol this is the best idea ever

"Who keeps texting you?" Rosemary's face hardened.

"Sam. It's nothing."

"Sam? Why would he need you this much?"

It was clear she didn't believe me. "He's...working on a project for me."

"Really? What project would that be?" Her eyes narrowed.

"It's nothing bad," I said. "I know that's what your mind instantly jumps to."

"You know we have your phone bugged? We can see everything you do on there," she said. "Can't be too careful."

"I know," I said. "I assure you, I have nothing to hide."

"Okay." She nodded, but still didn't seem satisfied. "Because though you might be on the team now, if we even suspect you have a hidden agenda, you're done, Ironfall." The way she said my name versus the way she used to. I hated it. Hated myself.

I nodded. "You don't have to remind me. I know what I've done."

"Good," she said. She was scared I'd go back, not that I blamed her.

"For the record, I don't entirely trust you either," I said.

"We both betrayed each other." She shrugged. Yet she looked hurt. Why couldn't things just be better? Every part of me longed to wrap my arms around her until she was convinced that I wanted to be different. But she would never forgive me. I didn't deserve it.

I looked at Sam's barrage of messages. I stuck a fry in my mouth, chewing as I read.

Sam: The Coolest Hacker Ever

Sam: wait that's too long lol

Sam: The Hack

Sam: meh

Sam: ughhh why is this so hard

I grabbed another fry, stuffing it in my mouth to keep from laughing.

"What is it? You look happy."

I tore my eyes from the phone. "Do I?"

"What does it say?"

I shook my head. "Nothing important, and I always look like this."

"Right." She sat back in the folding chair, wiping her mouth.

Federal Bureau Of Investigation
Transcript Of The Interview Proceedings With

IRONFALL
SOME NAMES AND LOCATIONS REDACTED FOR SECURITY
INTERVIEW CONDUCTED ON JULY 23
LOCATION OF INTERVIEW: **[REDACTED]**
CASE #: **[REDACTED]**

PROPERTY OF THE FBI

———

SPECIAL AGENT LAUDE: Sam…Hunt?

IRONFALL: The one and only.

SPECIAL AGENT LAUDE: Would you say he trusted you?

IRONFALL: That's what he told me.

SPECIAL AGENT LAUDE: What about everyone else?

IRONFALL: No, they didn't. I was constantly being watched. By Rosemary especially.

SPECIAL AGENT LAUDE: Rosemary Collins, is that correct?

IRONFALL: Yes.

SPECIAL AGENT LAUDE: The two of you are close, right?

IRONFALL: It's not what you think.

SPECIAL AGENT LAUDE: Explain it to me then.

CHAPTER

3

ROSEMARY

JULY 13 – *2:54 P.M. PDT*

Sylvester Whitlock bent down closer to the floor. "Next time look a little more conflicted when you're facing away from Ironfall. It's too subtle for the camera to pick up. I don't want theatre big, but I need a little bigger." Conflicted about Ironfall. That was an easy one, not that I was conflicted now.

I nodded, adjusting the computer on my lap, swiveling to face Ironfall once more.

We were filming scenes for a heist preparation montage, or what I assumed would be one. This seemed like a scene that would end up in deleted scenes, but what did I know of filmmaking?

"Another take?" Ironfall said.

"We're striving for perfection, so absolutely!" the Sylwhit said.

I glanced Ironfall's way before pulling my laptop closer. How could he look so at ease sitting here among his enemies?

I shook my head.

It was time to focus, time to get back into the character of

Rosemary Collins from months ago. A Rosemary who felt like a different person entirely. That Rosemary hadn't betrayed Ironfall. She hadn't discovered her parents worked for an evil organization. Her mom hadn't tried to kill her. Ironfall hadn't saved her life. Twice.

A Rosemary who didn't have to re-enact her life… Tomorrow, we'd be filming my betrayal scene. A pang struck my chest as the Sylwhit told the set we were going for picture.

I looked down at the blue glowing screen of the computer.

Focus on the heist.

Before I knew it, the cameras started rolling and the scene was slated.

Movie character Ironfall nudged my arm. "Hey, you see that?"

I looked up at him, leaning a bit closer, heat radiating from his arm. "See what?"

"The staircase behind those offices. That could be our way in." He pointed at the blueprint on his screen. But I wasn't looking at the screen, I was looking at him. The curve of his jaw; the intensity of his concentration. The way the sliver of blue in his left eye seemed to glow.

He was like a different person when he wasn't masking his real self by joking around. Who was the *real* Ironfall, and why did I sometimes think I knew it?

"Right." I bit my lip, snapping my gaze away. The heist. Right. Was I supposed to follow along or stop because it was the wrong thing to do?

My parents. The thought jerked me from my character. Back then I did everything I could to try to save them from Ironfall. As it turned out, they were the reason for it all—and my mom tried to kill me. Now she was dead, and my dad might be the one pulling ANTE's remnants together.

"Are you okay?" Ironfall's voice jolted me back into the scene.

"Oh, yeah," I said. "Just thinking, that's all." Our eyes met for a moment, and for an intense heartbeat, I was lost in his haunting gaze. I pulled away again, looking back at the screen. Why didn't I want to pull away though?

I wanted—needed—to know what went on behind those puzzling eyes.

He turned, our eyes locking once more, my chest tightening as he said, "We can do this, you know. Side by side?"

I nearly choked on the lump rising in my throat. He wasn't supposed to say that. "Side by side." I hadn't said that back to him since…since he thought I was on his side.

Stay in character.

He blinked, turning back to the computer, shattering the spell.

"Well, what's your progress report?"

"Seeing as I'm not a hacker, nothing much," I managed to squeak out even though I couldn't breathe.

His hand brushed against mine as he turned the screen towards me. I swallowed.

"I think you have something here, Rosemary." His eyes lit up, the sliver of blue in his left eye shining extra bright. "We're doing this." Then he flashed his signature boyish grin.

I said nothing more, face burning as I kept eye contact.

It felt like an eternity before Sylvester Whitlock announced, "Cut! That was great! Let's bring that kind of chemistry to each shot. This is art, people. Art!"

I looked away, pretending to fiddle with the computer. The pressure in my chest started to dissipate. What had just happened? Why couldn't I hold myself together? I sucked in a deep breath to ease my burning lungs.

Agent Liam entered, beelining it straight for our happy director. "We're having technical difficulties again," he said. "We're going to have to finish filming for today, unfortunately. Be ready to be on your best game tomorrow."

Sylwhit did not look pleased.

Ironfall stood first, offering me his hand. I looked at it for a second, hesitating before taking it. Then for some reason, I did. I could hardly breathe again, but the moment I was up on my feet, he dropped it, walking towards Agent Liam. All I could do was follow.

Agent Liam abandoned the now complaining director, ignoring his protests as he moved toward us. Speaking in a hushed voice, he said, "We have something."

JULY 13 – 3:47 P.M. PDT

Our LA base was larger than our New York City one. With white walls and even more updated monitors and equipment, it looked more like something straight out of the movie. A large glass conference table engraved with VIGIL's logo took up the center of the room, surrounded by office chairs. Ver usually adopted it as her workspace, but her normal mess of hard drives and paperwork had moved to a counter on the far wall so our team could actually see each other across the table. Sam, of course, was calling in from New York, his face plastered on one of the many monitors covering the wall across from me. Honestly, the varied glow of the screen wall and the constant whir of computer fans was enough to make my head spin. I was exhausted, and this hadn't even been a full day of filming. It was week two of nonstop twelve-hour days on set. Sure, a lot of the time was spent sitting around waiting to film scenes, but the emotional energy was even greater. I always had to be on, hiding the truth of—well—everything.

I fought back a yawn just thinking about it. If only this chair reclined…

Sam must have caught me through his computer screen because he said, "You guys look dead." Still tormenting us, even from across the country.

Without missing a beat, Ironfall said, "Thanks, you too." He swiveled in his chair, shooting me an amused glance, but I shifted my gaze back to Sam. *No, Ironfall, I don't pay attention to you unless I have to.*

"Filming a movie isn't as glamorous as you think, Sam." Ver leaned back. "I mean it kind of is, but I'm exhausted."

I sank further into my seat, blinking away the desire to curl up on the floor and sleep.

Manda pressed her palms onto the glass tabletop, directing her eyes toward Agent Liam at the head of the table. "What do you have for us, Liam?" Clearly, she didn't want to be here any more than we did.

Cloaker stroked his dark five-o'clock shadow. "He has something good, from the looks of it."

Agent Liam stood, tablet in hand. I hoped he had good news. "We found the identity of a potential sleeper agent." He fiddled with the device, pulling up the image of a man on the large screen next to Sam's hilarious concentration face.

The suspect was tall with graying hair and pale skin. With a black suit, blue tie, and an American flag pin on his lapel, he looked like a politician.

Agent Liam pointed at the screen. "You're looking at Norman Spencer, a prominent California congressman. He lives in Northern California, and has been in politics for a long time."

"Sam and I found his name floating around the hard drive duplicate," Ver said. "We aren't certain he's involved, but it's worth checking out. I'd estimate he's a financial backer. He comes from old money: oil, transportation, things like that. Fifteen years ago, his daughter went missing. It was reported she was held for ransom and was returned exactly fifteen days after the date."

I glanced from her to Sam. "You think it was ANTE?"

"It's possible that's how they got to him." Agent Liam nodded.

Ironfall pressed his lips together. "It's a smart move. Something my father would do." Or something he would do himself. His face betrayed nothing.

"It's mot like political leaders aren't already corrupt," Manda said. Ver snorted in agreement.

"We're looking at all the options." Agent Liam pressed more buttons on the tablet. "Sam actually has another theory."

Sam nodded. "His son was recently diagnosed with a terminal illness. Given ANTE's track record with"—he glanced at Ironfall so hard you could tell from the screen—"creating powers, I think he could be a candidate for some sort of super soldier serum. Maybe that stuff would heal him."

Ironfall could heal him in an instant, but I kept the obvious to myself and said, "You think both his kids are the reasons he agreed to join ANTE?"

"It's possible." At this, Agent Liam sat. "The only concrete evidence we have is his name on the hard drive. He could have just been mentioned as a future target, but somehow, he's connected, and it's worth finding out whose side he is on. These sleeper agents might just be buried deeper than we think."

"Wouldn't he have been on the Congress floor during the attack a few months ago?" Manda narrowed her eyes at the table as if trying to solve a puzzle. "Why didn't he join ANTE then?"

Ironfall shrugged. "They probably weren't all activated. My father was a perfectionist with backups to his backup plans. It's probable he had sleeper agents there who didn't reveal their allegiance."

"Everyone there was cleared," Ver said. "Background checks, interviews, the whole nine yards."

"Sleeper agents could be anyone." Ironfall drummed his fingers across the table. "By definition you won't know who they are until they're activated." My parents were sleeper agents. So many were… I wrung my hands under the table.

"Why? Are you a sleeper agent, *Ironfall*?" Manda now looked up, staring darkly at him. She had a good point. My hands balled into fists now, just in case.

"I passed your lie detector tests, remember?" Ironfall quipped. "Or do I need to go back in there again and tell you where my loyalties lie?" He glanced at me, but I averted my gaze.

He hated me.

Agent Liam raised a hand. "That's enough."

Only the hum of the computers filled the air.

"Hey guys," Sam interjected. "Looks like our beloved congressman won't be home tonight."

Agent Liam crossed his arms. "How do you know that?"

"I may have taken a quick peek at his calendar." Sam grinned sheepishly.

Agent Liam only sighed before turning back to the rest of us. "Rosemary and Ironfall are going to take the helojet and search the good congressman's house tonight. This is just intelligence gathering, so be as stealthy as possible. See if you find anything suspicious. We don't know what you're walking into, so be careful. I want a full report when you return."

Great, off on another mission with the man who hated me. Why would he even think I trusted him anyway? He lied. He *murdered*.

I nodded, though everything inside me screamed for sleep. "Yes, sir." Would Ironfall finally see his opportunity to betray us?

"We have to find the remaining three ANTE bases, and this is our only potential lead right now." Agent Liam looked pointedly at Ironfall. "Make it count."

JULY 13 – 9:01 P.M. PDT

Under cover of night, we lifted off in VIGIL's helojet, another invention from the movies the world didn't know existed. It was a sleek black cross between a helicopter and an airplane, complete with an advanced autopilot and cloaking system. No, the inside wasn't like a private jet, just plastic seats lining the walls of the small cargo bay that led to the open cockpit.

Both Ironfall and I wore black tactical suits that matched the helojet's interior. Easy movement and as much protection as possible. Of course, Ironfall's had places for his daggers. He still insisted on them over a gun.

At least I could see his daggers coming. Put a gun in his hands and…well, I didn't know what would happen.

I arranged my duffel under the cargo area seats before stepping into the cockpit and sinking into the passenger seat, which was only slightly more comfortable than the cargo seats. At least this one had a bit of padding. My eyelids were already heavy. Thankfully it wasn't a long flight.

Ironfall took what would be the pilot's position if the thing didn't run on autopilot.

He looked so much more sinister when preparing for a mission. For now, his charisma was gone. "You ready?"

I nodded. "Yes." Was I?

He turned on the autopilot, and soon enough we rose into the air. At least autopilot wasn't something he could mess up.

"Looks like we have an hour until touchdown," he said, reclining in his seat. "Time to get some rest. Try not to slit my throat while I do it." His voice was ice, but his face relaxed as if he was already almost asleep.

My fingers clenched the armrests. Being alone with him was stifling. It felt like I was standing at the edge of a cliff, waiting for him to push me off.

When we were filming, things were different. It was both easier and harder, but on a mission, everything was life and death.

It would be so much easier if my feelings about him were black-and-white.

JULY 13 – 10:09 P.M. PDT

Something shook me. I opened my eyes with a gasp. Oh no, I'd fallen asleep. My heart rate skyrocketed as I blinked up at Ironfall. His eyes seemed to glow in the dimly lit cockpit before I looked frantically around, searching for something out of the ordinary. No warning lights. No blaring alarms.

The engines seemed quiet. Too quiet.

"We're here." He stepped back as I rubbed my face. "Sorry, I didn't mean to scare you. Are you okay?"

I looked at him sideways while wishing my heart would slow. My fingernails dug into the armrests.

"I didn't do anything, if you're wondering." He smirked. "We're at the congressman's house, Rosemary. For the mission."

I blinked more, then tried to scrub the exhaustion from my eyes. How I wanted to curl up in bed. "Right." I brushed a strand of hair behind my ear and made sure my ponytail was secure. "The mission." Everything was fine. He hadn't betrayed us.

Unless… The cloaking shield. Had Ironfall messed with it? Would a neighbor be able to see that a spy plane sat in the congressman's vast backyard?

"Do you need a minute to collect yourself?" he asked. Wait, that was actually a thoughtful thing to say…

I stood up, straightening my suit. "I'm good. Let's get ready." Then get home so I didn't have to worry about him for a time.

I looked down, checking the switch to ensure the helojet remained invisible. I sighed with relief as I saw it was on. The soft hum it emitted soothed my nerves as much as something could before a mission.

I geared up alongside Ironfall, strapping my gun and extra ammo to my waist. I also put in my comms.

"Comm check," I said after turning it on.

"Hear you loud and clear." I heard Ironfall's voice in person and through my comms.

"Sam, you copy?" He'd be the one to get us through the security system.

"I copy you loud and clear," Sam answered cheerfully.

"Let's move." I pointed toward the exit. The cargo bay's floor lowered into a ramp. It was dark outside, but my eyes quickly adjusted, and the congressman's dimly lit mansion came into view.

I took a few deep breaths to slow my heart.

I'd trained for this. Ironfall was trained, and he knew what would happen if he didn't follow orders.

He also knew my weaknesses, but I couldn't think about that. We were ready.

Time to bring ANTE down, once and for all.

JULY 13 – 10:15 P.M. PDT

"Security's down." I'd never been so glad to hear Sam's voice. "Now keep the device attached to the box while you're inside."

I hugged the wall tighter as my breath caught. Why did I have to be the one to scale the house and install Sam's magic device? All I could see was myself losing my footing and tumbling down to splatter across the concrete. Why couldn't I wear a harness?

The ground teased me as my vision went blurry. I blinked it away, taking a deep breath.

"Can I get down now?" I tried not to sound terrified.

Sam snickered. "Why? Are you scared? It's only the second story."

"You try climbing up here without a harness and then we'll talk," I groaned. Don't. Look. Down.

"I'll catch you if you fall," Ironfall said.

My grip slipped. What did he just say?

Laughter blasted through my earpiece. "Romance at its finest." *Hilarious, Sam.*

Ironfall said nothing. Not acknowledging it was the best move.

I shuffled down one foothold, but my stomach dropped as if I was falling. Just a few inches down and a whole lot to go.

"The goal is not falling," I breathed. "So if you could both be quiet that would be great." One foothold at a time, I clung to the wall until my feet hit the ground.

"Don't ever make me do that ever again." I gulped air as my heart threatened to break out of my ribcage.

"Okay, Ironfall, you're up," Sam said.

Ironfall had the front door unlocked within seconds, which again reminded me of how dangerous he was.

I drew my gun, training it on the ground in front of me, then nudged the door open. Seconds later we swept into the quiet house.

It was large, as was to be expected from a wealthy politician. Pictures of him and his two grown children lined the entryway. No wife. Ver never mentioned one now that I thought about it. I tucked that information away for later. The interior design was modern and a little too perfect. Not that I knew much from being the daughter of a fake interior designer.

Mom.

I shoved the old pain away as the entryway widened into an expansive living room with a stairway at the end. Nothing suspicious here, but anything ANTE-related wouldn't be in plain sight.

"I'll take the upstairs, you search down here," I whispered to Ironfall.

He just nodded as he started creeping around. I didn't stay to watch him. This was a big house, and we had no choice but to split up. Plus, I wanted out of here as soon as possible.

No one was supposed to be home, but we still had to be careful and quiet, just in case.

I held my breath, gingerly taking a step up the stairs. The lack of creaking wood was better than I expected. Whew.

Couldn't get too comfortable though. Soft and slow.

I readjusted my grip on my weapon.

Deep breath, Rosemary. You trained for this.

This happened every mission, and I'd been on multiple. I was a full-fledged secret agent now, but the anxiety never abated. It was always there to push through, my constant companion.

Did everyone else feel this way?

Focus.

The top of the stairs branched into a hallway. But with a thorough search of each one, all I saw were unoccupied bedrooms. Empty closets. Bathrooms. The typical things you'd find in a big house. One bedroom seemed decorated for a teenage girl, the other for a teenage boy. Probably his kids' bedrooms, left the way they were before they headed off to college a long time ago. Lots of boy band posters, movie posters, and stuff like that. That's it though. Nothing suspicious.

"Nothing upstairs," I said in a low voice. "Just two time capsule rooms from the early 2000s."

"Nothing so far downstairs."

"I'll head down and help." I pressed a finger to my ear, then descended the stairs. Holstering my gun, I met Ironfall in the kitchen.

"Wait a minute, something weird is happening," Sam said through the earpiece.

Ironfall and I looked at each other.

"It's like this weird spark went through my feed. Like something else is climbing into it," Sam said. "Give me a second."

I drew my gun again, just in case.

Ironfall balled his fists.

"Some sort of signal is coming in, but it's not something like cable or wifi or whatever," Sam said. "This is something different."

"ANTE different?" Ironfall asked.

"Could be."

"Can you tell what part of the house the signal is going to?" I whispered. "That'd be really helpful."

"One sec." I could hear the clacking of the keyboard over comms, that's how hard he was typing now. "It's going somewhere beneath you, I think."

"There's no basement," I whispered. "We checked the blueprints."

"Well, apparently there is." Ironfall opened a large cabinet in the kitchen island. "And I think I just found the entrance."

I turned. Sure enough, there was a small doorway leading to a staircase.

"Did you just find a secret passage?!" Sam screamed. I flinched. My poor ears.

"Shh!" Ironfall hissed.

"Right, sorry," Sam said.

Ironfall's form descended into the darkness. After a deep breath, I followed. The passage quickly opened into something larger. It turned a corner, revealing a large windowless room. The walls were a glossy white, and bright lights reflected off the sides in strange rippling patterns across the tile floor.

"Guys? What's—" Static filled the comms before dying out.

And there stood Congressman Norman Spencer. He faced the opposite wall, touching a screen that covered the entire far wall.

I stifled a gasp, looking at Ironfall before locking back on the congressman. He wasn't supposed to be here. Yet he stood behind a circular metallic table positioned in the room's center. Engraved in the center was an *A*.

A for ANTE.

A shiver ran down my spine.

ANTE. My parents.

Focus.

I pointed it out to Ironfall, who nodded. If this wasn't proof of our sleeper agent, I didn't know what was.

Ironfall drew his daggers, then motioned for me to take the other side of the table. We'd flank the suspect so he couldn't run.

I sure hoped I could trust Ironfall.

"Don't move!" I shouted.

The man froze.

"Put your hands up and turn around slowly."

"Don't think about trying anything, Spencer," Ironfall said. "That won't exactly go well for you."

I kept my eyes trained on him, trying to slow my thundering pulse so I could get a clean shot if I needed to.

The congressman raised his hands in the air, slowly turning around. Funny enough, he didn't seem afraid or upset. He seemed…calm. We were missing something.

For a moment, I took my eyes off the congressman.

Ironfall. Was he in on this?

I looked behind me.

And that's when I saw him.

A man, tall, wrapped in white and gray linens. His face was completely covered as well, almost like he was a mummy. The top of the linens came over his head like a cloak, and a solid white mask covered his face up to his eyes. But his eyes were so deep in shadow (and probably dark makeup) I couldn't see them.

A low, menacing hiss seeped between the draping fabric of the form, and ice coated my veins. Who was this? *What* was this?

I did not sign up for horror movie villains.

Noise from Ironfall and the congressman. They were fighting now and it jerked me back to reality.

I fired the gun at the mummy man, but the figure leaped out of the way and slid across the table, launching his feet towards me. I jumped back, preparing to fire again, but my assailant was already in front of me, knocking the gun from my hands. I cut my arm back across him, but he leaned back deftly, bringing another arm across as I counterattacked. Our arms connected—

I was falling…

Falling…

Falling…

Into blackness…

Such…

Blackness…

"…Rosemary—"

…Nothing…

Federal Bureau Of Investigation
Transcript Of The Interview Proceedings With

AGENT ROSEMARY COLLINS
SOME NAMES AND LOCATIONS REDACTED FOR SECURITY
INTERVIEW CONDUCTED ON JULY 23
LOCATION OF INTERVIEW: **[REDACTED]**
CASE #: **[REDACTED]**

PROPERTY OF THE FBI

SPECIAL AGENT LAUDE: Would you say any of the crew suspected VIGIL was real?

AGENT ROSEMARY COLLINS: No. They couldn't have.

SPECIAL AGENT LAUDE: What about when Agent Liam Blake shut down the set for the mission?

AGENT ROSEMARY COLLINS: He explained there were technical difficulties, and the crew bought it. Do you think someone knew?

SPECIAL AGENT LAUDE: That's what I asked you.

AGENT ROSEMARY COLLINS: Right, but there must be a reason you asked.

SPECIAL AGENT LAUDE: Just making sure this interview is thorough.

AGENT ROSEMARY COLLINS: Of course you are. Sorry. [chuckles]

SPECIAL AGENT LAUDE: Let's move on to Ironfall. Tell me about him as you left for your mission.

AGENT ROSEMARY COLLINS: Right, um, he was a bit cold, but I was cold to him first.

SPECIAL AGENT LAUDE: Why was that?

AGENT ROSEMARY COLLINS: I was suspicious of him. Not that he gave me a reason to be, I just was, given his past. I made sure he knew I'd stop him if he betrayed us.

CHAPTER

4

DOCUMENT FILED BY AGENT ROSEMARY COLLINS
PROPERTY OF VIGIL

THE FOLLOWING report documents my experience under the unknown supervillain's powers:

Fuzziness.

Then light.

Then details sharpened and blurred all around. A figure came into view. It was dark, surrounded by light.

"...holding ANTE together..." The voice wobbled in and out of earshot. A man? A woman? It couldn't be said.

"...but with our sleeper cells in position, it should be..." another voice called out.

Everything moved in slow motion, vibrating, shifting, twirling.

Everything and nothing.

"No!" The figure's voice rose. Anger. "I won't..."

The voices lowered again. Nothing understood.

"...I want you positioned..." the figure continued.

"Yes, sir..." said the other disembodied voice. So the other figure was a man. "I will gather our..."

The image slipped, slipped, slipped away into—
" —revenge…"

Federal Bureau Of Investigation
Transcript Of The Interview Proceedings With

AGENT ROSEMARY COLLINS
SOME NAMES AND LOCATIONS REDACTED FOR SECURITY
INTERVIEW CONDUCTED ON JULY 23
LOCATION OF INTERVIEW: **[REDACTED]**
CASE #: **[REDACTED]**

PROPERTY OF THE FBI

———

SPECIAL AGENT LAUDE: When was the first time you saw this other powered person?

AGENT ROSEMARY COLLINS: In Norman Spencer's ANTE bunker.

SPECIAL AGENT LAUDE: Did you immediately know he had special abilities?

AGENT ROSEMARY COLLINS: No.

SPECIAL AGENT LAUDE: Tell me what happened.

AGENT ROSEMARY COLLINS: He came for me, knocked the gun out of my hands. But as soon as he touched me, I blacked out. You'll have to ask Ironfall what happened after that.

SPECIAL AGENT LAUDE: How hard did he hit you?

AGENT ROSEMARY COLLINS: He hit my arm. He attacked, I blocked. It shouldn't have knocked me out.

SPECIAL AGENT LAUDE: So what rendered you unconscious?

AGENT ROSEMARY COLLINS: His powers.

CHAPTER 5

IRONFALL

JULY 13 – *10:23 P.M. PDT*

"Rosemary!" My voice was hoarse as I watched her collapse under the hologram—or something that looked like a hologram —that flickered to life over her. The blue clock spun through the air, the minute hands rotating backwards as if counting down towards something. What was it?

The shrouded man towered over her, letting out a creature-like growl.

What had he done to her? Some kind of technology? Power?

What would happen when the clock reached zero?

My fists clenched. I threw the congressman against the wall. His head cracked. That would hurt later, but not as much as the fist I smashed against his head next. He crumpled, and I whipped back around to Rosemary.

"What have you done to her?" I gritted my teeth together, pulling out my knives, tossing my blades in the air threateningly.

The shrouded man said nothing.

So beat it out of him. Yes, if there was ever a time to listen to my father's advice, it would be to get my girl back.

My girl? Where had that come from?

The weight of my dagger slipped against my palm. You mess with my partner, you mess with my blades. In one swift motion I reared my arm back, whipping a blade toward him.

He clawed the knife from the air before tossing it to the ground. No. I stared him down while readjusting my grip on my remaining knife. So this guy knew how to deflect. Time to change it up and hope it worked.

Must. Save. Rosemary. The one voice that wasn't my father's.

I launched myself toward him, balling my empty hand into a fist. He was ready for my attack, dodging me. He twisted me around, but I wrenched myself from his grasp, somersaulting on the floor away from him.

At his touch, my vision blurred, the world swirling as my muscles gave way.

Just like Rosemary…

His touch…

The warmth of my dreaded healing powers swelled, filling my chest with air. I straightened, the exhaustion gone.

The figure turned his head sideways as if surprised, a low hiss echoing against the solid walls.

"Surprised your sleep trick doesn't work on me?" I smirked. "Looks like you'll have to take me down the old fashioned way."

Still he said nothing. I stole another glance at Rosemary's seemingly lifeless form. The strange blue block still floating above her chest. Was it a projection?

Was she okay?

She had to be.

I couldn't lose her.

I whipped my remaining dagger across the man's chest. He wrenched it away, attempting to cut my legs. I leapt out of his way, taking another swing with my left hand. He dodged as if it was nothing. Someone trained him well. Who?

I gritted my teeth. Oh, this man was going down. *For Rosemary.*

I kicked a leg out, twisting as I brought the man to the ground. He threw me off. I swiveled, now facing the fallen congressman.

Only he wasn't fallen. Blood streamed across his face, mixing with his few strands of hair. Gun.

He had a gun.

And he was pointing it at Rosemary.

"No!" I tried throwing the other supervillain off me, but he held firm. Too strong. No. No. No. *No.*

I wrestled, adrenaline pumping through me because I couldn't lose—

The shrouded villain raised an arm, now holding a gun too. What was—?

My ears rang out, but I didn't flinch. I was trained not to flinch.

The congressman collapsed, the villain's gun smoking.

What? Why had the mummy shot him?

He then tossed the gun to the ground, sliding it across the room. I twisted, finally pinning him to the ground. Who was in power now?

"Who are you? Why did you shoot him?" My jaw flared as I breathed hard from the fight.

Still, he said nothing.

"Answer me!"

Make. Him. Talk. That voice was all my own.

He brought up his feet, kicking me back. I stumbled into the table before somersaulting to the other side. Long enough for him to grab another gun from within his shrouds, pointing it at me.

"Don't move." His voice was garbled, disguised. It was clearly electronic, but set to sound like an underworld creature.

"Ah, he does have a voice," I said, keenly aware of the weapon aimed at my head. A lethal shot, and this man was good at everything. I eyed the desk between us. I wouldn't be able to wrench the weapon from his hands before he fired.

My teeth clenched.

I raised an eyebrow, standing frozen, but not lifting my arms in surrender. I wouldn't give him that luxury.

He leaned down towards Rosemary, still pointing the gun at me. With one arm, he scooped her up. Then he slowly backed toward the door.

No.

I rushed him. Stupid plan. He fired, but I managed to dodge, bringing an arm back up to knock the weapon from his hands.

The shrouded villain dropped Rosemary.

I swiped at him with my knife.

He clutched his abdomen as red seeped through the linens. Good thing I couldn't accidentally heal him.

I stepped over Rosemary. "Don't. Touch. Her," I warned.

"Self-destruct in T-minus thirty seconds," a computerized voice blared. I knew that voice. It was the same one that went off moments before the New York ANTE base blew itself up when we rescued Cloaker a few months ago. We needed to get out of here.

The masked supervillain fled.

Rosemary!

The clock still counted down. I scooped her up, vaulting up the stairs with her head buried in my chest. Thrusting Rosemary through the open door into the kitchen, I burst out after her, picking her up again once we were both clear.

Fifteen seconds.

I bolted through the living room to the front door, yanking it open.

"What's going on?" Sam piped through my ears. "You went silent for a while."

"Shut up, Sam!" I snapped, running across the front yard, Rosemary's limp form pressed against my chest.

BOOM!

I flew forward, gripping Rosemary tighter.

Ow.

Ow.

Ow.

Ears ringing.

A tingling warmth radiated through me until I could hear and see clearly again. The heat of the flames burned like the sun on my skin as I watched them devour the congressman's mansion.

Rosemary still slept under me, her breathing rapid but even.

I rolled over onto my back, staring at the stars while I caught my breath.

Sam was no longer in my ear, the device probably fried from the blast.

We needed to get out of here. The entire neighborhood would be here soon, and was that a siren I detected in the distance?

Once more, I scooped Rosemary into my arms, sprinting for the helojet. I didn't know what was wrong with Rosemary, but she was alive, and as soon as I got her to safety, I would heal her. I sprinted up the ramp, slamming the button to close the hatch before settling Rosemary in the other chair in the cockpit. I stroked her cheek, warmth traveled from my fingers into her.

She was safe.

The clock above her sputtered and vanished.

She gasped awake. Oh thank goodness. She was okay. Relief washed over me as I braced for her questions and accusations… well deserved ones at that. Things hadn't exactly gone according to plan, and she'd assume it was me.

I would assume me too.

I turned, frantically pressing the helojet's buttons to get the dang thing in the air before we ended up on Sam's meme page.

"What happened? Why are we back on the helojet?" she said. Then her eyes darkened. "What did you do?" There it was.

"I didn't do anything. The supervillain attacked and somehow made you unconscious. It seems he can put people to sleep." My head whirled with more questions, things I didn't dare explore out loud until Rosemary was safe. Who was the villain? How did he get his powers? Had my father known about him? Did ANTE make more supervillains after me?

And why did he try to take Rosemary? He killed the alleged sleeper agent for her. That meant something.

"How do I know this wasn't a plot to join ANTE again?" she demanded. "Knock me out and plot."

"It wasn't, Rosemary. I would never do that. He tried to take you...the supervillain."

Her brow furrowed, but she said nothing of it. "Where's the congressman?"

"Dead. He tried to kill you, but our mummy friend took him out before he could. Then he tried to take you." It all sounded so suspicious when I said it aloud. Would I believe it if I were her?

"Why? That doesn't make sense." She narrowed her eyes. "You really expect me to believe that?"

"No." I straightened. "But don't worry, VIGIL has a lie detector to prove I'm right."

Her chocolate eyes flashed against the kaleidoscope of cockpit buttons. "I'll take you up on that. What about evidence? Hard drives? Did you get anything?"

"The house was rigged to explode. I barely got us out." Just barely. I could have lost her. I couldn't imagine that. She was the only person I had, even if she hated me.

I straightened my shoulders. We had more pressing matters at hand than our personal feelings, however.

"Seems convenient," she said. Yes, it did. If I were behind it, that's how I would hide it.

"I know, but it's true. All of it."

"We'll see." She shuffled in her chair like she was still trying to shake the sleep from her body. I couldn't read her face though. Was she hoping I'd lied?

"If you think I'm guilty, just arrest me." I stepped closer, crossing my arms. Yet this time, I wasn't. At least, I was trying not to be.

"I'm thinking about it."

"You know how easy it is to slip out of handcuffs. Just a few seconds and poof." I wiggled my fingers for effect. "I'm gone."

"But you need us for your game, whatever that is." She smacked my hand away. "Don't think I'm oblivious. You're up to something."

Something about her ever-innocent look made me retreat from her challenge. "I know, you notice everything."

"I don't like lying," she said.

"I may not trust you with much, but I do believe that," I said. "You always try to do the right thing. That's the one thing about you I trust."

She blinked. "Is that a…compliment?"

"If you wish." I shrugged. It was, and she deserved it.

"Right." She nodded stiffly, before turning away. "Well, I'm reporting in."

"I'll join you," I said. "And don't worry, I'm not doing it to gather secrets." Why had I said that? I should have kept my mouth shut.

Federal Bureau Of Investigation
Transcript Of The Interview Proceedings With

IRONFALL
SOME NAMES AND LOCATIONS REDACTED FOR SECURITY
INTERVIEW CONDUCTED ON JULY 23
LOCATION OF INTERVIEW: **[REDACTED]**
CASE #: **[REDACTED]**

PROPERTY OF THE FBI

———

SPECIAL AGENT LAUDE: So you got nothing from the sleeper cell?

IRONFALL: That's correct. There wasn't time.

SPECIAL AGENT LAUDE: ANTE has a habit of blowing things up before you can gather information from them.

IRONFALL: Are you trying to say something?

SPECIAL AGENT LAUDE: Just trying to get at the truth.

IRONFALL: Look, you already interviewed Rosemary, Agent Liam, and everyone else under the sun. I'd say you probably already have it.

SPECIAL AGENT LAUDE: Do we?

IRONFALL: Yes. They are some of the best people I know. You'd do well to trust them.

SPECIAL AGENT LAUDE: Agents go back and leak information all the time.

IRONFALL: You're referring to the time ANTE came out of the shadows and tried to take over, not the VIGIL team fighting for what's right.

CHAPTER 6

ROSEMARY

JULY 13 – *10:35 P.M. PDT*

The phone only rang once before Agent Liam picked up, his voice reverberating through the helojet's cockpit. "What happened?"

"You went silent and there was a loud noise! I thought you were dead!" Sam yelled through the speaker. Good thing I didn't have it pressed against my ear.

"There was an explosion. We lost everything, but we're okay," I said, clasping my hands together. "Norman Spencer was definitely ANTE."

"Was?" Agent Liam sounded surprised.

"He's dead," Ironfall said without looking at me.

"Which means the eyes of the world will be on his house," Ver groaned. "That complicates things."

I stepped closer to the speaker. "There's something else."

"How could things get worse?" Sam whined.

"Hush." I could almost see Manda rolling her eyes.

"There's another powered person at play," I said. "He can put anyone to sleep with just a touch. I'll let Ironfall explain his side of the story." I shot him a warning glance.

Ironfall's brows raised as if surprised I would let him speak. "He can knock someone unconscious with a touch. A clock floats above the sleeping person, presumably counting down to how long they have under his artificial anesthesia."

"Ooh, a nap king," Sam laughed. Call me exhausted, but I really wanted to punch him through the phone.

"We are not calling him that," Ver snorted.

"Not the time for jokes," Manda said. "We have a big day tomorrow and I'd like to get more than two hours of sleep."

"He rendered me unconscious, and I was asleep while Ironfall says he fought him." I tried not to sound too accusing, but I couldn't help myself. "Sir, he could have used that time to make his move. He could have destroyed evidence or set off the bomb himself."

"Nice theory." Ironfall glanced at me sideways before turning his attention back to the speaker. "But you're wrong. Our powered adversary showed up just after we found Spencer in his bunker. He touched Rosemary, and she collapsed. I fought him, but Spencer tried to put a bullet in her head. The villain must have wanted her alive because he shot Spencer. Then he escaped, and I barely had time to carry her out before the self-destruct system went off."

"We only have his word for it," I said.

"I'll prep the interrogation room." Manda sounded a little too excited about that.

"And this time I willingly submit." Ironfall crossed his arms, leaning against a chair like this was his personal private jet. "You know, why don't we make this part of our daily routine? Interrogate Ironfall. It'll be fun."

If looks could kill, the one I shot him would.

Someone cleared their throat.

Agent Liam said, "If what Ironfall says is true, it's interesting the villain—"

"The Sedator!" Sam suddenly exclaimed. "Let's call him that. It's a pretty cool name."

"Fine. It's interesting that the Sedator killed his sleeper agent to take Rosemary," Agent Liam finished. No one had the energy to argue with Sam over irrelevant things right now.

Why was everything about me? It's not like I was the chosen one. It all happened because of my parents.

Parents.

My dad.

"Do you think my dad wants me for something?" My voice trembled.

"It's a good possibility." Agent Liam hummed like he was thinking.

"Next time we need to send more people." Manda's tone became more forceful. "Outnumber the Sedator and bring him in. Ironfall couldn't get away with anything then."

"I am listening, you know," Ironfall deadpanned.

"Smart plan." Agent Liam paused. "I'll see what I can do. Is there anything else you noticed? Anything you saw that could lead us to another base?"

I shook my head. "No."

"No, sir."

Great. Back to square one. How fantastic. My throat ached but only because I was so exhausted. The Sedator's forced nap had done nothing in that regard it seemed. Plus, we failed our mission—and I was just emotional…

"One last question before calling it a night. Can I please have a cameo in the movie?" Sam pleaded. "I would *die* to be in it. I could be a tree or a cactus or an expendable civilian. I will do literally anything." He would. I was sure of that.

Oh, Sam.

Agent Liam sighed. "We'll have this discussion some other time. For now, we need rest. Tomorrow's a big day."

Tomorrow we went back to filming.

And tomorrow was the scene where I betrayed Ironfall. My

stomach constricted. That was one of the worst moments of my life, and I'd have to relive it. *Try not to think about it.*

I couldn't do this.

I couldn't do it.

"Ver, have Cloaker head to the crime scene and get anything he can before the police take it," Agent Liam said. "Whatever is left is all we have. Ironfall, when you get back here, let's have a chat."

We said our goodbyes, then sat in silence. As we flew, my mind kept running over what happened, trying to make sense of it. Had Ironfall betrayed us? What was that dream I had while I was unconscious? The new supervillain? I wasn't awake to make sure Ironfall did the right thing.

I readjusted my position.

"Do you want to go over lines?" Ironfall broke the silence. "Or something?"

The way he could manipulate conversation into something so innocent yet not innocent at all was infuriating. Because the script depicted an emotional, dramatized version of the last few months.

And tomorrow's scene.

Oh man.

Don't think about it.

I swallowed, not able to sit in the deafening silence for a moment longer. "Sure."

"No biting remarks. No jabs about me not knowing my lines?" He let out a low laugh. Another manipulation attempt, no doubt.

"I'm too exhausted for that," I said. "Which scene?" *Not tomorrow's. Please. Not that.* Just the thought of it made me feel like I was choking.

"It would make sense to work on tomorrow's scene first, am I right?"

No. Absolutely not. Did it not affect him the way it did me?

I shook my head, looking away. "That one's mostly action." It was a lie, and he knew it, but I couldn't let him see how I was affected by it. "I changed my mind after all, I'm going to try to rest," I mumbled.

He nodded. "Probably better that way." Maybe he was relieved too? I was okay with that because I already felt like I was about to throw up.

At the moment I just wished I could go back to the time before I knew all of this was real, when the VIGIL & ANTE Studios movies were just movies, and the only excitement I had to look forward to was watching a comic con panel when I got home from work. Why couldn't I at least go back to that time I brought him to Central Park and we went over lines? We could just be two teens rehearsing a school play. No pressure from the red carpet. No deadly nighttime missions.

Just us.

Us? I shook my head. There wasn't an us. There never was and never would be.

Goodness, I needed sleep or a caffeine IV.

I sagged in my seat, looking up at the stars. When did my life become so hopelessly complicated? The stars were brighter here than they were in New York City. Actually, there weren't many stars in the sky at all there, they were outshined by city lights and smog. But up here, in the air...they were clear.

The minutes crawled until Ironfall radioed VIGIL. "Helojet to base, looks like we have an ETA of five minutes."

"Copy that," Ver said. "I'll prep the roof."

"We'll be there soon," he said.

"Thank goodness." Did I say that out loud? Oops. Apparently my filters disappeared when I was sleep-deprived. Who trusted me on this mission again?

The LA city lights came into view a moment later, and soon we were rushing over the city. An orange glow emanated from all the city's lights, even though it was the middle of the night.

When everybody but stupid secret agents were asleep.

Go us.

All we had to do was land and sleep.

JULY 14 – 12:13 A.M. PDT

The apartment door clicked shut behind me, and in the darkness, I leaned against it with a sigh. As much as my body screamed for sleep, the quicker I gave in, the quicker tomorrow would come. And then I'd have to…

I closed my eyes. Just one moment. I took a deep breath, trying to calm my erratic pulse.

I opened them again right when a light flicked on.

"You're nervous for tomorrow, aren't you?" Ver said.

I stood straight, moving towards my room. "I'm fine. Just tired." Tired and not in the mood to talk about the one thing that made me sick to my stomach.

Maybe Agent Liam would find out Ironfall was guilty, and we would cancel filming.

"You're not fine," Ver said. "We may have only been roomies for a couple months, but I know you better than that. And anyone would be dreading tomorrow in your situation."

I stopped. "Really, I'm okay." My voice cracked.

"Okay, if you say so," Ver said. *Stop panicking, Rosemary.*

Before I even knew what I was doing I spilled everything without even turning. "I can't do it. I can't go back there."

"Hey, you can do this." She rushed toward me and placing her hands on my shoulders. "Remember, it's not real."

"But it was." All of it was. Remembering back to that cursed memory I could still feel his knife against me. How my heart raced. The look in his eyes.

"I know."

Nauseous. So nauseous.

"And what if he goes back to those feelings and just—" I

66

couldn't even speak the words. *Kills me.* Hates me for betraying him.

Turn on VIGIL.

Join ANTE.

Destroy the world.

"He's not going to." She patted my shoulders. "I promise."

"How do you know that? We can't trust him."

"I may not trust him, and he's probably up to something, but I do trust that he would never hurt you."

"But he could flip, remember what it felt like to be betrayed. Finish what he tried to do that day."

"He won't."

A sob wracked my chest. "I'm scared. I can't go through that again."

She wrapped her arms around me in a tight hug. The hug of a big sister I never had. "We will all be right there with you. You don't have to do it alone. Not like last time."

I squeezed her back, soaking her shirt with my fast falling tears. "Don't make me do this."

"I would do something if I could. It's out of our hands. Fans can become 'secret agents' of their own sometimes. Maybe they saw you and Ironfall in New York a few months ago. They saw you 'in character,' but something doesn't line up with the movie. If it matched the movie, they will now assume it was us laying the seeds for our signature publicity stunts. But if something doesn't match up, they start digging. This scene was pivotal in the events of a few months ago, so it's crucial it stays. It defined every moment after. We live in the precarious balance between fiction and reality. One mistake could tip the scale and put our whole organization in danger."

"I can't face him like that again. I just can't…after what he did to me."

"I know. I know," she said.

I cried more.

Ver continued to hold me.

After a little while I moved out of her arms. My heart rate slowing and the nausea abating, some. "I don't know if I ever can. Looking at him, all I see is betrayal. I hate myself for the moments he makes me laugh or forget what he is. It makes me feel dark inside. I hate it—because I'm afraid...I don't know... maybe I'll accidentally trust him like I almost did a few months ago..."

"It's like looking at your worst nightmare every day," she said.

I nodded.

"I know it's hard, but we'll both feel better after we sleep," she said. "That's what my mom always told me."

"Because there's plenty of sleep to go around," I said, sarcasm bleeding into my tone.

Before Ver could reply, we were interrupted by both our phones.

My stomach turned, again. Oh no. If we were needed back at the base I thought I'd die then and there. Or burst into tears again. Or both.

Ver pulled out her phone, while I stood frozen. The screen glowed onto her face.

"Liam's convinced Ironfall was telling the truth about the attack," Ver said. "He passed the lie detector test."

I blinked, processing her words. He didn't betray us. Why was there a small glimmer of hope inside of me waiting to be squashed? "Oh." It was all I could manage.

"Why do I get the feeling you're a bit disappointed he didn't switch sides again?" Ver said.

Because it would be easier. We wouldn't have to do this strange dance of light versus dark.

"No, I'm glad he didn't," I sighed. "I don't know. Maybe it'd just be easier. Then we wouldn't be on the edge of our seat all the time, constantly waiting for his inevitable betrayal." I hated that we needed him. When I joined VIGIL, it hardly existed anymore. We were a little stronger now, but we still needed Ironfall's inside information. Besides, it was helpful to have his fighting and disguise skills on our side.

"Hmm," Ver mused. "Maybe he won't betray us."

I shook my head. "No, he will. It's who he is."

"I know he has a terrible track record, and I trust him less than I trust a sketchy website, but maybe he'll surprise us," Ver said. "He does seem to admire you, so maybe that will rub off on him. He claimed it did, anyway. And the lie detector proved it."

"I know." I rubbed at my wet eyes. "I just don't know what to believe."

"Well, believe this. Tomorrow, you're going to go on set and do your thing. Agent Liam, Manda, and I will be right there supporting you behind the camera. Well…Manda's not great for emotional support, but she'll kick Ironfall's butt if he does anything stupid. We have your back."

I laughed. "Thanks, Ver."

"Anytime." She smiled. "Now let's get like an hour of sleep."

Federal Bureau Of Investigation
Transcript Of The Interview Proceedings With

AGENT LIAM BLAKE, DIRECTOR OF VIGIL
SOME NAMES AND LOCATIONS REDACTED FOR SECURITY
INTERVIEW CONDUCTED ON JULY 23
LOCATION OF INTERVIEW: **[REDACTED]**
CASE #: **[REDACTED]**

PROPERTY OF THE FBI

———

SPECIAL AGENT LAUDE: Seems convenient the entire ANTE base exploded.

AGENT LIAM BLAKE: Are you saying my people let it happen?

SPECIAL AGENT LAUDE: Well, one of your agents was asleep.

AGENT LIAM BLAKE: Things happen in the field. They were attacked by a supervillain who can put people to sleep. Sounds like an unfortunate circumstance, not treason.

SPECIAL AGENT LAUDE: This is just the first curious mistake by your team in a long string of them.

AGENT LIAM BLAKE: We handled everything to the best of our ability with our limited knowledge.

SPECIAL AGENT LAUDE: The FBI will be the judge of that.

AGENT LIAM BLAKE: You don't see the decisions we make every day.

SPECIAL AGENT LAUDE: Which is why we're the best judge. We can be objective.

AGENT LIAM BLAKE: When can I speak to my team?

SPECIAL AGENT LAUDE: After you've all been thoroughly vetted and interviewed.

AGENT LIAM BLAKE: It's been days.

CHAPTER 7

IRONFALL

JULY 14 – *9:42 A.M. PDT*

"Ironfall!"

I awoke with a start. Ver stood over me.

"How on earth did you wedge yourself in there?" She looked me up and down.

There I was, curled up on the floor in the corner of a film set, stealing sleep while I could.

The only thing I stole nowadays.

"That's a great question," I laughed groggily. I rubbed at my eyes, probably smearing the tedious work of the makeup team. I didn't care. I hadn't slept a wink last night, thinking about today.

"Well, you're on soon," she said. "So you might want to prepare yourself."

Nodding, I climbed out of the small hole, my senses flooding back as the sights and sounds of the film set washed over me. Crew setting up the cameras, gaffers doing whatever gaffers did (I still wasn't quite sure), and lighting people adjusting various equipment.

And straight ahead stood the film version of our old hideout. It looked old, but smelled new. Paint cracked on the walls, peeling and scratched as if the production design team hadn't only painted it weeks ago. The open space was broken up with scuffed furniture arranged like a small, abandoned living room.

"I'm always prepared." I flashed Ver a grin, turning away to find Rosemary.

She stood off to the side, glorious in her white-and-gold suit, hair hanging in bright red curls that almost seemed to glow. I took a deep breath, then walked over to her. She hadn't tried to leave yet, so she must not have realized I stood right there.

"You ready?" I couldn't say I was ready, so no doubt she wasn't.

She glanced at me before quickly fixing her gaze on the ground. "No."

"Hey, whatever happens, it's all acting," I reassured her. "It isn't real." But it once was, and nothing I said would erase that.

"Right," she breathed. She almost looked ill, her face even more pale than usual.

"Do you need a minute? I can stall them." I looked around the room for someone who could do just that.

She hesitated, straightening herself. Now she met my gaze, mask up. "I'm fine."

"The offer still stands if you need it." Anything to soften the memory of what I did to her... The urge to draw her into my arms, to make her feel better, to take away the memories of the past, almost overtook me. Instead I stood frozen, watching her walk toward the director.

Nothing could prepare me for this. None of my past training. Nothing. This was a whole new world of feelings.

Sylvester's voice filled the studio. "Okay, I want my actors in position for the start of the scene."

I moved to the lit portion of the set. It was like walking into a time machine, a blast from the past. And now we'd have an audience. Dread followed me with each step. Oh, Rosemary, I'm sorry for what I did to you...

I glanced up at Agent Liam, Manda, and Ver standing just behind the camera and sighed.

"Can I get more light on Rhett?" the cameraman said. "He's a bit dark."

After a few more adjustments, it was time. I shuffled just off set, hidden behind a pillar, ready to walk in on Rosemary making a phone call to VIGIL. I just about shuddered at the memory of how betrayed I felt, but I kept my composure.

It's only acting.

"Lock it up, we're going for picture."

"Sound rolling."

"Camera speeding."

"Scene forty-five, take one, mark." The slate came down with a sound so sharp I almost flinched.

"Action!"

I forced myself into the scene, into who I never wanted to be again, ever.

Into *Ironfall*.

Rosemary looked around the room, terrified. Was that how I made her feel? She was that scared of me? She took out her phone and hastily dialed a number. Again, she looked around as if waiting for me to pounce.

"You have to come." Her voice was low and shaky. "I know his plan. He...he's about to take over the world. He stole a machine from the vault—"

Pause. They'd add in Agent Liam's side of the call later.

She glanced over towards me. "Yes."

Another pause.

"Okay," Rosemary said. I could tell she was fighting to keep her composure, to stay in character as both a double agent and an actor in the scene.

The phone was still at her side, VIGIL's number still up on the screen.

It was how I found out the first time.

I straightened.

"Ironfall enter," Sylvester called.

This was it.

I thought of how I felt in that moment back then. Happy. Excited. Exhilarated. And way too excited to see Rosemary's costume on her.

I walked in. "Okay, everything's ready to go!" Then I saw her face. Terrified. Everything came flooding back. "Is something wrong? Was what I said back there okay?" I rushed to her side but refrained from touching her.

She nodded, but it was clear that was false.

"I don't think you're telling me the truth." I gingerly placed a hand on her arm, my gaze now meeting hers. "You can trust me, I promise." Here I was, ready to do anything for her.

She didn't speak.

"Rosemary?" My voice came out in a whisper as I searched her eyes for clues as to what was wrong.

Her breathing came faster, blood rushing from her face until she resembled a ghost.

Something clattered to the floor. I looked down to see VIGIL's logo on the screen.

No.

This wasn't…it wasn't true. I trusted her. I cared about her. I loved—

"You know what you have to do." My father's voice echoed in my mind. I gathered myself, jaw flaring as I stared at her.

"You." I narrowed my eyes. "You betrayed me."

She said nothing, still frozen with terror.

"You betrayed me," I repeated. "You're with VIGIL." And I knew what I had to do.

I'm sorry, Rosemary. It slipped through all the acting feelings. I'm so sorry I did this.

I lunged. She dodged, and I somersaulted, landing on my feet, slipping out my daggers.

I hate this.

"Please…" she pleaded. I steeled myself against her pleading. She betrayed me. And traitors must be—

I'm so sorry.

I deflected her punch and sliced my dagger across her. She grabbed my arm, yanking me off my feet, pinning me to the ground. Arms tied down, I thrust my legs upward, throwing her off me. I leapt to my feet, readying myself again.

"Ironfall, please." Her voice broke.

Traitor. She betrayed me.

I attacked her, repeatedly, unleashing everything I had inside with a carefully choreographed violent dance. She stepped back, moving closer and closer to the wall.

She cut across my hand, sending one of my daggers flying across the room.

The clang of metal hitting the ground was drowned out by the sounds of us fighting.

But then she was pressed against the wall. I raised the knife, ready to strike.

I'm so sorry. So sorry.

She held her arms against my fist, stopping the knife from finding its target.

She struggled, a tear falling down her face. "I can't beat you." Her voice was low and shaky.

I fought to keep eye contact. "I…I have to kill you." *Rosemary, I'm sorry. I never wanted to hurt you. I hate who I was.* "I have to." No.

"Please…Ironfall. I'm sorry I lied to you." Not as sorry as I was. She did the right thing and all I did was murder people. "Don't touch my family. You can't…please." Another tear slipped down her cheek. "I'm not strong enough to beat you."

I couldn't stand looking at her like this. So broken, forced to relive the awful things I'd put her through. "How did I miss this? I thought we—"

"I'm sorry, I had to." I wanted to scream that I knew and

understood why she did it. That I would never do it again. That I desperately wanted to be different. But her arms gave out.

My knife stood frozen midair. Because even the past me couldn't bring myself to let it find its target.

To kill the woman I—

I leaned forward, pinning her to the wall. Just like it had been choreographed.

Just like I did to her months ago.

"How long?" I pressed the blade to her throat. *I'm sorry.* "How long have you been a double agent?" It was too much, too much. The lump in my throat was suffocating.

"J-just after you forced me to join you," she whispered.

Tears streaked down my cheeks and a sob wracked my chest. I couldn't even say my next line.

She closed her eyes as if accepting that I was about to kill her.

I can't. All I wanted to do was apologize, comfort her, the urge was so strong it felt like it was clawing its way out of my chest. "I—" I choked. "Rosemary, I—"

I couldn't do it. I tossed the knife away. It clattered to the ground. Her eyes opened, questioning, searching my eyes.

We were so close, faces just inches from each other.

I'm so sorry.

And I kissed her. A hand found the crook of her neck as I cradled her, pouring all of my sorrow into this one gesture.

I'm so sorry, Rosemary.

I pulled back, her eyes opened, wide and searching. I brushed a hand across her cheek. "I can't do it. I can't finish this." I couldn't finish the scene.

And I whispered, "Go."

What did I just do?

She didn't move, she just stared at me in a way that took my breath away, tears streaming down my cheeks. No one on set said a thing. Everything was dead silent. It was as if we stood on the edge of a cliff, waiting to fall over into an unknown abyss.

"Cut?" Sylvester had lost his zealousness with this announcement.

Rosemary sagged against the wall, and I stumbled back away from her.

"I'm sorry," I whispered. "For everything."

"In my twenty years in the film industry, I've never seen a scene that powerful." Sylvester finally broke through the astonished silence of the film set. "The way you took it and made it your own, almost as if you were living in the scene."

I shot daggers at him. If he knew the scene was me reliving my greatest trauma, he'd understand why it was so realistic.

I looked over at Agent Liam, who was just staring in shock between the two of us.

"That kiss wasn't scripted, but it's perfect," Sylvester said. "The passion, the emotion. Flawless. A work of heartbreaking art."

I gulped, backing away from Rosemary who looked like she was about to sprint from the room.

"Let's take a break. I might need to rework some things with the script and storyline. I'll call you back to set when I'm ready for you," Sylvester said. "Bravo, everyone!"

While he stalked away excited that we'd win him an Oscar, Ver ran for Rosemary, who now looked like she was about to faint.

I rubbed my forehead.

I'm sorry, Rosemary. For everything.

Federal Bureau Of Investigation
Transcript Of The Interview Proceedings With

IRONFALL
SOME NAMES AND LOCATIONS REDACTED FOR SECURITY
INTERVIEW CONDUCTED ON JULY 23
LOCATION OF INTERVIEW: **[REDACTED]**
CASE #: **[REDACTED]**

PROPERTY OF THE FBI

———

SPECIAL AGENT LAUDE: Why did you go off script?

IRONFALL: I don't know what to tell you.

SPECIAL AGENT LAUDE: That's a first.

IRONFALL: You really don't want to be here, do you?

SPECIAL AGENT LAUDE: There are other more productive things I could be doing than talking to a supervillain who should be incarcerated.

IRONFALL: Maybe you should find another job.

SPECIAL AGENT LAUDE: Just answer the question. The quicker we get to the bottom of this, the quicker I can get on with my life.

IRONFALL: As if anything will ever be the same.

SPECIAL AGENT LAUDE: I'll ask once more. Why did you go off script?

IRONFALL: Personal reasons.

SPECIAL AGENT LAUDE: You're talking to the FBI now. Personal reasons isn't going to cut it.

IRONFALL: Fine.

SPECIAL AGENT LAUDE: Good to see we're on the same page. Now answer my question.

IRONFALL: I was sorry for everything I did to her, and I couldn't stand to see her reliving what I put her through.

SPECIAL AGENT LAUDE: So you kissed her? Made them change the script?

IRONFALL: What is your problem?

SPECIAL AGENT LAUDE: National security. Now answer the question.

CHAPTER 8

ROSEMARY

JULY 14 – *10:01 A.M. PDT*

He kissed me.

I stood alone in my trailer shaking, bracing myself against a chair as another wave of tears slipped down my face. The scene flashed back through my mind, haunting me even when I closed my eyes.

I wanted this to go away. All of it. So desperately.

Sobs wracked my chest and I sank to the floor, gasping for air as I clutched my knees to my chest.

Why did it have to be this way?

Why couldn't I wipe my memory and start over?

I lay on the floor and cried.

Maybe it was minutes, maybe an hour, but when the trailer door cracked open I didn't look up. I just buried my face further into my knees so they couldn't see how broken I was.

"Rosemary?" *Him.* Hesitant, voice low.

I didn't move.

"It's Ironfall," he said.

My chest felt like it had a thousand bricks inside.

"I just wanted to say that I'm sorry," he said. "For everything. I hate that they made us do that."

What about the kiss—the *unscripted* kiss? The one that felt so wrong, yet so right, and like an apology unto itself. Still, I said nothing, waiting to let the floodgates loose once more.

"I know I don't deserve your trust and forgiveness," he said. "I never will. What I did is unforgivable. That's all I wanted to say."

"Tell me today wasn't real," I mumbled. I needed to hear it from his lying lips because it felt more real than it had the first time. I was just as terrified. I picked my head up to find him kneeling beside me.

"It wasn't real." He wrinkled his eyebrows. "I promise it wasn't real, and nothing like that will ever be real again."

His face looked as honest as it had the day in the lie detector when he promised he was on our side.

I coughed, the next wave of ugly sobs taking over.

"D-do you want me to leave?" He sounded like he was in pain.

Did I? *It wasn't real.* But at one time it was, and I couldn't trust him, but here he was trying to comfort me, apologizing.

Was I buying it? Should I be buying it?

"I don't know," I choked out. I didn't know anything. I could still feel the chill of his knife against my throat but also the shocking warmth of his lips against mine.

He placed a hand on my back, and I melted. Soon his arms were around me, holding me securely. He said nothing, but I felt his own hot tears on my shoulder and the sharp rise and fall of his chest.

Was he just as upset as I was? Could I trust this?

"I will never stop telling you I'm sorry," he whispered.

We cried until there were no more tears left, until I was numb and the pain of reliving the worst day of my life dimmed to a dull ache, ever-present but no longer forefront.

I pulled away, wiping the remaining tears from my swollen eyes.

Ironfall chuckled through his still flowing tears. "You know I came here to see if you were all right, not to fall apart. Sorry about that."

His smile was contagious, though mostly because I was so exhausted; things always seemed funnier when you were tired. "It's okay. I needed it." I laughed this time. "Besides, everyone needs a good cry every now and then." I swallowed as the room once more seemed heavy.

"Right." He nodded, pressing his lips together. "See you later." He knew I still didn't trust him, I could hear it in the tentative tone of his voice.

"Yeah," I breathed.

Then he was gone, and the air was let back into the room. I could breathe again, and I actually felt—better. More free.

A knock sounded on the trailer door again. Oh no. I glanced in the mirror to see my mess of a face before running to the sink to splash myself with water. Still red from my breakdown, but it was the best I could do.

"Come in!" I tried to sound cheerful.

Agent Liam entered and I breathed a sigh of relief. Just him, no one I had to pretend my life wasn't falling apart with.

"How are you doing?" he asked. "I know today was rough for you."

I nodded. "Better now." Better after I cried all over Ironfall? His arms wrapped around me and mine around him.

"I'm sorry you have to do this," he said. "It's out of my hands."

I nodded, forcing a smile, which was easier after the emotional release. "I know. It's not your fault."

"Remember, it wasn't real. You were safe the entire time," he said. "And the story is just that, a story. It may be based on true events, but it's telling a story of characters. The Rosemary on-screen isn't you."

"I know, sir. It felt real though. Always does."

He stepped closer. "If it helps, Ironfall is pretty upset too."

"Yeah, he just left here a few minutes ago." I gestured towards the door. "He apologized."

"Are you okay with that?" His brow furrowed in concern.

"I think so." Something I never thought I'd say. Was I starting to trust him again? *No.* I couldn't let my guard down. Never with Ironfall.

"If you need me to shut down filming for another 'technical difficulty,' just let me know."

"Dad Liam strikes again." I smirked.

"Hilarious."

"Thanks for looking out for me," I said. "It means a lot. You guys are the only family I have."

"Anything for my agents. You know that," Agent Liam said. "Glad to be of service. Now, get cleaned up the best you can. I'll send a makeup team in here to fix you up."

JULY 14 – 12:08 P.M. PDT

Making my way back to set wasn't as scary this time. I think I was too tired to feel much of anything anymore, and that was a drug in itself. I also didn't look like I'd just had an emotional breakdown thanks to the makeup wizards. What would a traumatized secret agent/actor do without them? Cry more, I supposed.

A production assistant let me on set, and I already saw Sylvester making grand gestures while he explained the next shot to the cameraman. When he turned around, he focused in on me. *Here it comes.*

"I need all my actors right here." He waved his arms again. "We're making some changes to the story thanks to the brilliant

creativity of Rhett Wickford. Forever grateful for his genius."
What about keeping things consistent with what happened?
Ironfall hadn't kissed me when he let me go all those months
ago. Though we were so close to each other with his arms
wrapped around me and his head buried in my neck.

"We are going to focus more on the romance of the story.
Focus more on enemies-to-lovers in the struggle of good vs. evil.
I'm working on making adjustments to the screenplay now,
which you will hopefully get tomorrow. But for today, I want to
do the last scene again, focusing more on that. Rosemary, I want
to see more tension. That's where our money is gonna come
from, so that's what I want to see," Sylvester said.

"Is Xavier okay with the change?" I glanced at him standing
in the sidelines. "I thought it was really important we stuck to
the script."

"He will see my side. Besides, the tension throughout the
script was palpable, so the changes will be minor. Honestly,
we'll be bringing out what was already there." Sylwhit
shrugged, looking between us like he was about to make us kiss
again. "And I'm the director, so you two have to do as I say."
Please, no.

"Can I speak to you about that, Sylvester?" Ironfall said.

Sylvester really did make a valiant effort not to look annoyed,
but he still did. "What?"

"In private." Ironfall glanced at me. What did he want to say?

"Fine. The rest of you are dismissed, just stay close by," said
the director.

I escaped to Agent Liam and spilled the Sylwhit's entire plan
before he could get a word in. He stood patiently, nodding, eyes
downcast.

"I already know." He pressed his lips into a thin line. "As
much as I hate to admit it, Sylvester is right. It doesn't compromise the integrity of the story arc. It will also draw in an audience. It's a delicate balance, and I think this is one battle we
won't win."

"But we weren't...together," I whispered, looking around to make sure no one was in earshot. "In real life."

He spoke in the same hushed tones. "Trust me, Rosemary, this is the best decision for the film and VIGIL's image. It's going to be okay."

As much as I hated to give in, I did trust him. "Okay, I'll do it." *This is what's best,* I told myself.

Agent Liam placed a reassuring hand on my shoulder. "Thank you. I know how hard this is for you."

As I made my way back onto the set, the Sylwhit motioned me over. Oh great. What lovely torturous idea had he decided on now?

"Yes?" I tried to keep the worry off my face.

"Rhett is worried you're not comfortable with filming the scene again," Sylvester said.

I glanced at Ironfall. He said that? For me?

"I know it's a taxing scene, and your performance during the first take was quite emotional," Sylvester said. Was he actually being nice and thinking of his actors?

"I don't want to do it again if it's going to negatively affect you," Ironfall said. My stomach flipflopped...butterflies fluttering. Oh no, absolutely not. I shoved the feeling down. "It's a traumatizing sequence."

"It is," I said. "Brings up a lot of hard feelings." Our eyes locked. We were having a secret conversation in the subtext.

"How about we break it up some? I love the footage we have of the beginning part. I just want a couple closeups of Ironfall's face, and a couple of yours," Sylvester said. "And I'd really love at least one more angle of the kiss."

My eyes widened. Oh crap. "Th-the kiss?" The unplanned one I was still very confused about?

"Yes. That's going to be one of the strongest points in the story," Sylvester said. "Are you okay with breaking things up? You won't have to feel all the emotions of the scene the entire time. We can strategically place angles to give you breaks too."

I couldn't look at Ironfall this time. "Yeah, that's fine." I could do that. I didn't have to go back into the headspace. I could do that.

The kiss? That was another story.

Sylvester nodded, walking back to talk to the crew about the changes, I presumed.

"Thanks," I told Ironfall, still avoiding eye contact. Because eye contact and the mention of another kiss sent my stomach into somersaults.

"I never want you to go through that again," he said.

I finally looked at him, our eyes locking once more. My heart pounded in my chest, thumping in my ears.

"Okay, let's get ready for the second take! We are going to get a shot of Ironfall coming in to talk to Rosemary. London, I just need you to stand there. You're hardly going to be in it."

I nodded, stepping away from Ironfall. He was trying, even though I didn't know what to make of it. Either way I was thankful.

JULY 14 – 4:11 P.M. PDT

Filming was slow but broken up by lighthearted behind-the-scenes moments. Ver brought me a sandwich she'd smuggled from craft services. Sam sent me a compilation of "Illuman being a dork for 2 minutes straight." Good things to break up the story.

But now it was time for the kiss again and no amount of meme compilations could help.

As the Sylwhit went over the next shot with the DP (our director of photography), Ironfall came up beside me. I folded my arms to feel like I had some kind of barrier between us.

He laughed, looking at the fake hallway ahead. "Sam is gonna rate this you know." Great, he had to put it like that.

"I need a stunt double." I certainly didn't need the blush caked on my face right now. "If he could not do that, it would be great." The last thing I needed was him to talk about this. Ever.

"If he makes a meme about it, it's game over for him."

"Get in line," I said. I would strangle both of them or melt in a pile of embarrassment if this went on much longer.

"There is quite a long one, isn't there?" His eyes flashed. "It's a shame he's so good with computers." Phew. Something to distract from the fact that we were about to kiss. On camera. For the world to see.

Someone shoot me.

I chuckled nervously. Awesome, now I even sounded stupid, giddy, and embarrassed. "Yeah, someone needs to take his ego down a notch or two."

"Or fifteen."

I looked over, raising an eyebrow. "You're one to talk, Mr. 'body of a Greek god.'"

A smile crossed his lips, showing his way-too-perfect teeth. "You know what...?"

I smirked. "What? I'm waiting." Best to keep things light.

"This would be a really good time for Sylvester to be ready to say action." He glanced over at Sylvester, who was still chatting it up. If he could take about five years, that would be great.

"Need him to save you because you don't have a witty enough response?" Why did I say that? Why didn't I just end the conversation and sit here in even more suffocating silence?

He shot me a wry look. "I didn't say that."

"No, you just heavily implied it." *Stop it, Rosemary. You're not supposed to talk to him like this.* Not back how we used to before... When everything was still a mess, so I wasn't sure why I kept idealizing it.

Maybe because it was less of a mess than it was now.

Sylvester broke through and I both thanked and loathed him. "Okay, get back in positions. Ironfall, knife to her throat. Remember, you're both very upset."

"Let's get this over with," I muttered as I moved into position, pushed up against the wall. Ugh, this was the most awkward thing. Especially now that this was the third time I'd kissed this man.

And every time I didn't know how to feel.

You're just acting. It's fine. People do this all the time.

What about when fiction blurred with reality?

Ugh, I needed to stop thinking.

"Ready to go for a take?"

Sylvester nodded. "Let's do it!"

"Picture's up. Last looks. Camera ready?"

"Camera ready."

"Sound ready?"

"Director ready?"

"Ready."

"Lock it up, we're going for picture."

"Roll sound."

"Speeding."

"Scene 135, take five bravo." Here we go. I brought myself into character, staring at the villain just before me. His knife was at my throat; my back was pressed against the wall. He was so close that I could feel his breath.

"Camera speeding."

And yet this time I felt safe. Because now this was acting. Just a scene.

A small portion of the scene.

His face hardened as he also got into character.

"Marker." The slate came down, sending a shockwave of sound around the room.

"Frame."

"Action!"

"How long?" Ironfall said, eyes darkening. "How long have you been a travel agent?" I'm sorry, what? He burst out laughing, then turned to the camera and made a face.

Now I was laughing. Relief washed over me.

He rarely messed something up like that. Was he purposely trying to make me laugh? No, that was ridiculous.

"Keep the camera rolling, let's do it again," Sylvester said, also laughing, though he was trying to hide it and be professional. Wow, maybe Sylvester wasn't all business, fame, and unmatched stardom.

We calmed down, and Ironfall pressed the prop knife against my throat once more.

"Scene 135, take five Charlie. Marker." The slate came down once more.

"Action!"

"How long?" Ironfall's eyes searched mine. "How long have you been a double agent?"

"Just after you forced me to join you." I spoke in a low voice, keeping my eyes wide to seem afraid. He was close, so close.

A tear streamed down his face.

"Rosemary, I—" His voice broke. He tossed the knife away, still never taking his brown eyes off me. His gaze lowered to my lips. He looked confused, torn between what he knew he was supposed to do and what he wanted to do. Whether or not to kill me.

Stay out of the moment.

The moment where I knew he was about to kiss me.

"I—" he choked out again. And then he grabbed the side of my face, thrusting his lips against mine.

I froze, supposed to have been surprised by this. But the way his hands cradled my face, his warm lips crushed against mine, fireworks seemed to burst in the air as the world set to right. I leaned into the caress of his hand. I melted under his touch.

It was so right. So right.

Wrong. It's wrong.

He still couldn't be trusted.

He broke away. "Go," he whispered. He stepped away, and I ran behind the camera, still dazed from that kiss.

"Cut!" Sylvester said. "I'm going to review the footage, but I think we're ready to move on. Great job, both of you."

I nodded in thanks.

I didn't dare glance back at Ironfall.

Just acting.

Federal Bureau Of Investigation
Transcript Of The Interview Proceedings With

AGENT ROSEMARY COLLINS
SOME NAMES AND LOCATIONS REDACTED FOR SECURITY
INTERVIEW CONDUCTED ON JULY 23
LOCATION OF INTERVIEW: **[REDACTED]**
CASE #: **[REDACTED]**

PROPERTY OF THE FBI

SPECIAL AGENT LAUDE: Let's talk about your relationship with Ironfall at this point.

AGENT ROSEMARY COLLINS: I still didn't trust him if that's what you're asking.

SPECIAL AGENT LAUDE: Was it anything more than that?

AGENT ROSEMARY COLLINS: No.

SPECIAL AGENT LAUDE: Tell me what happened after filming the betrayal scene.

AGENT ROSEMARY COLLINS: It was awful. I went back to my trailer to be alone and broke down.

SPECIAL AGENT LAUDE: But Ironfall showed up.

AGENT ROSEMARY COLLINS: He came to apologize for the scene and everything he did.

SPECIAL AGENT LAUDE: Did you believe him?

AGENT ROSEMARY COLLINS: I didn't exactly know what to believe.

SPECIAL AGENT LAUDE: Explain what happened.

AGENT ROSEMARY COLLINS: We cried together for a while.

SPECIAL AGENT LAUDE: Just cried?

AGENT ROSEMARY COLLINS: Are you trying to catch me in a lie? You have my report. You have everything.

SPECIAL AGENT LAUDE: I'm doing my job, Agent Collins.

CHAPTER

9

IRONFALL

JULY 15 – *11:46 A.M. PDT*

I should never have kissed her. The taste of her lips against mine consumed me. I had thought of nothing else since it happened.

I leaned back in the chair, resting my feet up on the countertops of my trailer while waiting to be called to set to see Rosemary again. The TV droned on in the background.

Her kiss...

If I didn't distract myself soon, I'd start making mistakes in acting...or worse.

Your mistakes will be your end.

I ran a hand through my hair to silence my father's neverending string of advice and the memory of Rosemary, then I shut my eyes, focusing on the monotonous sound of the reporter's voice.

"It's been confirmed that California congressman Norman Spencer has been killed in the explosion that destroyed his home on July 13."

I planted my feet on the ground, reaching for the remote tossed onto the counter. I turned up the sound.

"The FBI still hasn't released a statement, but neighbors are speculating that a gas leak caused the explosion. Remnants are still being searched through, but it is believed Congressman Spencer was home. It is not known at this time if any foul play was involved," the news anchor said. The bright colors she wore contrasted with the somber announcement of her words.

So they found him. The FBI wasn't releasing details, probably because they noticed something that didn't show up on the blueprints. Not that the FBI was forthcoming about anything under the best of circumstances. Had Agent Liam been in contact with them to explain how we were involved? Did Cloaker get anything from the scene? He'd better have. Taking down ANTE depended on it. No doubt ANTE was alerted and already retreating deeper into hiding.

"Maria Santiago is on scene with more updates. Maria?" The TV screen changed to the scene. It was now surrounded with caution tape and police and FBI perimeters.

"Thank you, Sarah. Neighbors were awoken in the middle of the night by a loud explosion. They came out to see Congressman Spencer's house in flames. We are still waiting for updates, but we were assured the FBI in cooperation with local police will be holding a press conference at the White House today."

"Are other houses on that street in danger?" asked the main news anchor.

"They have already been cleared. The area is safe," said Maria Santiago.

So the FBI really was staying close-mouthed. I wondered if they found an explosive device. Or maybe Cloaker had found it. I hoped the latter was true, because at least that would be something to start with.

No such device had been discovered in the ashes of the New York ANTE base, but maybe this one would be different since the structure was different. This one was in the basement of a building, whereas the other was filled with underground tunnels that collapsed in on themselves.

I made a mental note to bring this up with Agent Liam later.

"A prayer vigil will be held tomorrow at 7:00 p.m. at Cedar Hill High School to honor his memory," said the main news anchor. ANTE really had its talons inside public opinion. He would be hailed a hero and given a Medal of Honor.

You could have been as loved as them if you hadn't failed.

I slammed the power button, silencing Maria Santiago's praise of ANTE's latest sleeper agent.

JULY 15 – 2:24 P.M. PDT

Sylvester Whitlock's slow clap resounded through the sound stage. "Great work, everyone. I'll call you back to set when we're ready for the next scene." The frozen scene in front of us moved as the crew dispersed into various activities.

Rosemary stood at my side, and we started to walk out of the sound stage together. Curiously she didn't slow her pace to avoid being beside me today.

"I guess they haven't found anything new about the congressman's house," I said in a low voice. "We haven't had a team meeting since after our last mission."

A production assistant passed in front of us. Rosemary waited for him to move out of earshot before responding.

"I haven't heard anything," she said. "I'm starting to get worried."

"Me too." I nodded. "And we have no leads on the Sedator." He almost got away with Rosemary. Why did he want her? Not to mention he almost beat me, and not many people could. I'd been training my whole life, which meant this guy must have too.

He also had powers. Had my father given him powers and not told me? What was going on with him?

"Let's hope Cloaker found a useful hard drive," she said. "Though I'm sure Sam would have told us if he was working on something."

"He would have." I hadn't thought of that, which meant we probably got nothing. Maybe the FBI had already confiscated it. I gritted my teeth at the thought. If they had I could slip in and out with it. I could do it alone given a tranquilizer and time to work up an adequate disguise.

She turned her head, her brown eyes staring into my soul. "You're thinking." My breath caught as my gaze involuntarily drifted to her lips...

Stop it. She hates you and you don't deserve her.

I nodded. "Where did the Sedator come from? Was he part of my father's experiments? Why only show up now?"

"I don't know," she said. "But if he's connected to ANTE, we'll find out."

"He showed up there, clearly he's part of ANTE." She should know that.

"Why take out a sleeper agent though?"

That was the one snag in my theory. "The congressman tried to kill you while you were unconscious. I'm wondering the same thing, but I can't say I'm mad about that part."

"Thanks? I think?" she broke into a grin.

"It's a compliment." Which she was only pretending to laugh about, but she looked stunning while doing it. *Which I shouldn't be thinking about.*

"Uh-huh."

For just one moment, things were "normal" and it warmed every part of me even though it was beastly hot outside (especially in my suit, which apparently I hadn't designed well enough to cool me off). Yes, I was now the official costume designer of VIGIL & ANTE Studios. You're welcome, America.

"I'll be taking a nap in my trailer if Agent Liam calls a meeting."

"Smart," I laughed. She headed her own way, and I went into my trailer. A nap sounded wonderful, but all I could think about was the taste of her lips and how much I wanted to do it again—

I blinked.

I should have restrained myself the first time. I didn't deserve her kiss—I didn't deserve anything. I needed to get kissing out of my head.

Before I knew what I was doing, Sam was on the phone.

"How's my favorite movie star?" Sam answered.

"Sam, I need you to focus." It's a good thing his voice was the only thing on the phone because I was not in the mood for that much Sam.

"I'm never letting that go," he said. I could feel him grinning mischievously, and I hated that I knew that.

I cleared my throat. *The case. The case will distract me.* "Did Cloaker get anything from the congressman's house?"

"Nope," Sam said. "The FBI took anything that was there. Not that much was there. The explosives seemed extra charged, though I don't know if that's even a thing."

"Great," I huffed. That complicated matters.

"What's up?" Sam sounded too excited.

"Do you know if the FBI found anything useful?" A plan was already forming in my mind to get it. Shouldn't be hard to break into their evidence locker. I could probably pull it off myself... though Sam would be helpful to take out security cameras.

You are the only one you can trust. Shut up, "Dad."

I was part of a team now. We worked together. I could trust them, even if they didn't trust me.

"Nothing important, don't get excited. I did some digging in their files, and the ANTE stuff was all destroyed," Sam said.

"Though if they did, I volunteer to help you acquire it." I was glad Sam couldn't see the smile forming.

"Can you go through the hard drive once more? I want you to search for anything on the Sedator," I said. I needed to know more about my father's experiments.

"Already checked, there was nothing on the Nap King."

"There has to be something," I said. "How does he fit in?"

"You're just salty he beat you," Sam snorted.

"We could have an ANTE sleeper agent in custody if it weren't for them." I gritted my teeth. "We could have a link to ANTE's communications. Their files. Something more than what we have."

Did my father know about the Sedator?

"We'll get them," Sam said.

I blinked again. "What's this? You being nice?"

"It happens occasionally, don't act so surprised, Ironfall."

I didn't know what to say, so I just said, "Thanks for your help."

"Wow, a thank you!" Sam said. Nope, not going there.

What would Rosemary do? "Goodbye." I hung up. Yeah, that was probably fine. Couldn't let this "nice" stuff go to Sam's head.

I took out my computer and typed something in about the Sedator. Nothing came up. I typed in a description of him. All I got were peoples' OCs in fanfiction, which wasn't helpful. Though I did skim through some of them to see if they could have been based off the Sedator.

Nothing.

He didn't exist. We had no DNA. We had no description. Just the white fabric drowning his identity and his touch that worked like anesthesia.

We needed a new lead soon, or I would start to go mad.

I looked deeper on the Internet for anything about superhero experiments. The deepest forums on the dark web. Maybe the Sedator originated from there. Maybe my father sourced people on there for his experiments. I sifted through a few of the top posts, looking for any mention of the Sedator or someone matching his description. Nothing.

I used the search bar. Human experiments. Human enhancements. Human enhancement trials.

One post from four years ago stood out.

Projectsatchel: Searching for subjects ages 20–30 willing to undergo human enhancement experimentation. If successful, subjects will develop special abilities. DM for details.

This couldn't have been my father. I hadn't seen record of this particular username in any of his files. In addition, it was too direct, he'd never be so blatant, he was far too smart for that.

Still, I hit the message button. But it came up deleted. I guess whoever Projectsatchel was had already found his people and deleted his account. Was he the one responsible for enhancing the Sedator?

I sent off the information to Sam. Maybe he would be able to hack into this guy's account and give us a list of people who responded. Then I kept digging to see if there was anything else familiar I could find. Unfortunately, nothing. I just hoped something would come out from this.

I needed the Sedator found. And quick. Then Rosemary would be safe.

JULY 15 – 8:20 P.M. PDT

Rosemary's trailer creaked as Agent Liam shifted his weight. "I won't keep you long as I know we're all exhausted from another great day of filming."

The VIGIL team—Manda, Ver, Cloaker, Rosemary, and I—all crowded in Rosemary's trailer. Sam was on video on the TV. If he could take up a little less space, that would be great.

Her trailer was dark, lit only by a couple overhead lights.

"Please tell me your next order of business is giving me a role as a featured extra? Or even just a normal extra?" Sam pleaded.

Everyone ignored him.

"We weren't able to get anything from the explosion," Agent Liam said. "There was almost nothing left."

"And trust me, you didn't want to see the remains of the congressman," Cloaker said. "I'm going to have nightmares for weeks."

"He's exaggerating. He won't," Ver laughed. "Don't worry, Sam."

"I wasn't worried." Sam looked around for show. I rolled my eyes.

"So we're back at square one," Rosemary said. She looked beautiful with her hair up in a ponytail, stray waves falling around her face. I glanced at her lips, again. Then quickly looked away. Focus, Ironfall, you're here to catch ANTE and keep her safe, that's the only thing you should be thinking about.

"I'm afraid so," Agent Liam said.

"Sam, did you look into the thing I sent you?" I asked.

"What did you do?" Manda narrowed her eyes. If looks could kill (and I wasn't quite sure it was impossible for her), this one was full of arrowheads.

"I did some digging on the dark web. I used to frequent there to search for freelancers," I said. "And to keep tabs on the competition."

I could feel Rosemary shrinking away from me. Yeah, I deserved that after everything.

"Another dead end," Sam said. "The original poster proved to be a kid playing a prank."

"On the dark web?" Ver grinned. "What a legend."

"So he wasn't holding experiments?" I said.

"No." Sam shook his head. "He wasn't the one who created the Nap King."

"Why can't you call him by his real name?" Manda said. Exactly. We were supposed to be professionals here.

Sam giggled. "Because it's funny." Why else did he do anything?

"Sam, there's something else I'm assigning to you," Agent Liam said. "But we need to fly you out here to do it."

Sam's eyes grew wide as saucers. "I've never been to California! What do you need?" He was about to bust through the screen.

Agent Liam glanced around the room before turning back to the screen. "I need you to be an extra in *I Am Stardust.*"

The scream Sam let out could be heard around the world.

AGENT LIAM BLAKE, DIRECTOR OF VIGIL
SOME NAMES AND LOCATIONS REDACTED FOR SECURITY
INTERVIEW CONDUCTED ON JULY 23
LOCATION OF INTERVIEW: **[REDACTED]**
CASE #: **[REDACTED]**

PROPERTY OF THE FBI

SPECIAL AGENT LAUDE: So you got nothing from the congressman's house?

AGENT LIAM BLAKE: Bold words for someone who got as much as we did.

SPECIAL AGENT LAUDE: Your agents didn't take anything before leaving?

AGENT LIAM BLAKE: You say leaving, but what you should say is escaped. Their lives are much more important than information.

SPECIAL AGENT LAUDE: More important than eliminating a terrorist organization?

AGENT LIAM BLAKE: If they had taken a few extra moments to

grab a hard drive they would've been lost along with the information. Did you think of that?

SPECIAL AGENT LAUDE: Just doing my job.

AGENT LIAM BLAKE: Maybe you should look into why the FBI didn't get anything from the explosion instead of questioning my agents.

SPECIAL AGENT LAUDE: You are the ones under investigation.

AGENT LIAM BLAKE: And I'm saying we did the best we could with the limited information we had.

CHAPTER 10

ROSEMARY

JULY 16 – *5:52 P.M. PDT*

I'd already gotten fifteen texts from Sam in the last five minutes screaming about how excited he was to make his on-screen debut. He would only get worse when we picked him up from the airport.

Ver laughed. "Agent Liam has created a monster. You think we should induct him with a certain east-coast burger chain after we pick him up?"

My phone vibrated again. Let me guess? Sam. "He wants the full experience, so yes." I glanced down at my phone, scanning over the message. "He also just threatened to put a virus on my computer if we didn't take him." He'd do it too.

She brushed a blonde curl behind her ear. "That settles it then."

Brake lights lit the interstate ahead. Ver slowed and soon we were at a standstill. Was the traffic worse than New York? I didn't know, but it was just as annoying.

Ver tightened her grip on the wheel. "Might want to text him that we'll be late. Hopefully this clears up soon." I nodded, typing him another message while ignoring the constant barrage of messages from him. That boy didn't know when to quit.

The GPS said we'd now arrive in thirty minutes.

Ver turned on the radio, and we jammed out to her productivity playlist as we inched forward.

Inched wasn't an exaggeration. The brake lights were relentless.

A motorcycle zoomed between cars. I jumped, heart thumping. I really needed to learn how to be less jumpy.

"Okay then," Ver said. "That's one way to do it."

"Yeah, it is." It was probably something we'd do on a mission. We'd weave through traffic, chasing the enemy. Ironfall would take the lead. Just now, all I could think about was how unsafe it was. I sat in that for a while, staring at the surrounding concrete and commuters.

"Are you doing okay after filming the betrayal scene?" Ver finally asked.

"What? Oh, yeah." I shrank into my seat. I didn't want to think about that either.

"I'm glad," she said. "I'll make sure to tell you when to leave so you don't have to watch that part at the premiere." I hadn't even thought about that, but now...

Everyone would have to see it.

"Thanks, Ver."

"How are you doing with Ironfall?" she asked next, sounding a bit hesitant. "Sorry, got to be a big sister about this."

Another motorcycle, but this time I envied it. This was not what I wanted to talk about. "Right. Um, things are fine I think. He's fun to co-star with."

"How are *you* doing though?"

How was I doing? I was thrown around. I was broken. I was... "I'm making it. Sometimes I start to feel like I could trust him, and I hate that I even think that. He can't be trusted." Had I really said all of that out loud?

"I know," she said. "It's hard to know who to trust."

"He's done so many horrible things. He's murdered people. He tried to overthrow the government. And somehow, I still want him to do the right thing. Do you think that's wrong?"

"No," Ver shook her head. "It's never wrong to want someone to do the right thing. Besides, if we don't care about our enemies, what are we really doing?"

I nodded, sitting back in my seat as traffic started to move again. We drove in silence until we neared the airport and I shot Sam a text. He said he was already through baggage claim and would head to the arrivals area for us to pick him up.

"Make a left here," I told Ver, as we followed the signs. Who designed airports to make them so confusing? It took us a couple times around the endless loop to finally make it to the pickup place. It was packed. Cars were lined up, some pulling into the right lane to stop and pick up loved ones, others driving through on the left to go around again.

"Look for Sam," Ver said. "I gotta try to not hit these idiots."

I searched through the crowd for Sam's iconic 2000s boy band hair. I know it hadn't been cool since before I was a teenager, but that didn't seem to stop him. I saw lots of people dressed a variety of ways, but no Sam yet.

"I think we need to go around again," I said.

"I swear if this is because he wanted to get Starbucks after getting off the plane…" Ver grumbled.

We reached the end of the line just as Sam texted.

Sam: I'm here lol

"Of course now he's out there," I laughed, shaking my head.

"I'd better not see a Starbucks cup in his hand."

I texted him back to tell him we'd be back through the loop in a few minutes. Somehow Ver and I made it through alive without getting cussed out. Amazing. We entered the loop in the left lane and I searched for him outside the first set of the doors. Not there. Second set. No one. He could have given more specific directions.

Something made my skin prick. My chest tightened. Someone was watching us.

"Ver, I think someone's watching us." I looked out the window again, not searching for Sam this time, but anyone staring at us.

There. Tall man, broad shoulders, black suit and tie. No sunglasses. But it was clear he was watching us. Was that an earpiece I saw in his ear?

"Him! That man is watching us!"

"Where?" She looked over, and I pointed the man out.

"And there's Sam." But we'd already gone way past him and were at the end of the loop again.

"Quick, go back around and see if we can catch that guy."

"He was looking pretty suspicious if you ask me," Ver said. "There's a baseball cap in the back. Get out when we stop and see if you can find him."

I texted Sam to not move and that we'd be back around, then I unbuckled my seatbelt and reached on the floor for the baseball cap, sliding it on my head. We went back around, and Ver pulled over where the man was.

But he was gone.

My gut told me he had something to do with...well...with everything. I didn't know who he was, who he worked for, or how he fit in, but someone was surveilling us there.

Ver pulled away and drove to where Sam was. She popped open the trunk.

Pulling the cap down over my face more and slipping on a pair of sunglasses to try to mask my identity, I got out. Sam immediately ran up to me, pulling his absurdly large suitcase (how was that thing allowed on an airplane?) behind him, and hugged me. No Starbucks cup. Ver would be relieved.

"Ahhh I'm so excited!" he exclaimed. The top of his head almost reached my ears now.

"Wait a second." I jerked away. "You grew. Like a lot."

He flashed a grin. "I did indeed, movie star." Had he also been working out?

I grabbed his suitcase from him and shoved it in the trunk. I glanced around for any sign of someone watching us. Nothing. Just people going about their own business.

"Hurry up!" a police officer called. Right.

Ugh.

Sam jumped in the front seat and shut the door before I could say a word. Thanks a lot, Sam. Not like I was just sitting there or anything. I scurried into the back seat, and Ver sped away as the police officer kept screaming at us.

Ah, good times. Gotta love airports.

"So, tell me everything I missed!"

"I just talked to you, Sam," Ver protested. "You know everything you missed."

"Yeah, but like the movie set stuff. The glamour. The lights. The camera. The action," Sam said. "See what I did there?"

Yep. Sam was here. And as annoying as he could be, it felt good to have him back. Almost like we were bringing the gang back together.

"Do you think I'll win an Oscar for this role?" Sam was almost jumping in his seat.

"You can't win an award for being an extra." I rolled my eyes. "Even I know that doesn't exist."

"Maybe I should make it a thing, then," he said. "I'll just give an award-winning performance."

"The job of an extra is to blend in and make the setting feel real," Ver said. "That means no funny faces."

"But those kinds of extras are the best!" he said. "They're the hidden Easter eggs in a movie."

"Hey, Sam, did you see anything suspicious outside the airport?" I asked.

"No…" he said. "Why?"

"There was someone watching us, I think, some guy in a dark suit. He was wearing an earpiece."

"Creepy," he said. "But I didn't see anyone."

"He was gone when we circled around again." Ver shrugged. "I'll be sure to tell Agent Liam either way when we drop Sam off."

"Yes! Sleepover at Liam's!" Sam exclaimed.

Poor Agent Liam. I laughed to myself.

It was cold. I shivered as water turned to ice which turned into patches of fire as more rain came down. It was day. Night. I couldn't tell with the way the stars were moving in coordination and separation from the moon.

I ran.

Ran across the sloshy field putting out the fires. Someone was out here. I wasn't alone. The back of my neck prickled as another keen sense to run overtook my body.

I ran again, and again, but I couldn't run fast enough. Whatever was relentlessly chasing us was too fast, and I was too slow. I couldn't make it.

To where was I running?

I didn't know. I didn't know.

I looked back.

White cloth. A mask covering his face. A loud hiss like a snake ready to pounce.

The Sedator.

No! I ran harder but somehow my steps became slower. He was gaining on me. No. He couldn't catch me. Couldn't take me. Couldn't kill me.

My heart pounded.

My legs pumped faster but still I couldn't keep up. Slowing...slowing...slowing...

Still, the faceless villain said nothing, only kept chasing me down. He wanted me. Wanted me dead. I knew that.

Why did I know that?

Something growled from behind.

I needed to get out. I tried clawing as this world seemed to close in on me, even though I was in the middle of a fiery field running for my life. I needed out.

Suddenly a building appeared before me. A white skyscraper, reaching toward the stars. I raced inside only to be met with white walls on all sides.

No way out. I turned around but the door had disappeared. How had I gotten here?

The Sedator was here with me. I was trapped.

"No!" I screeched. "You can't get me!"

The faceless creature said nothing as he seemed to grow taller and taller until his head brushed against the ceiling. I was so small. I backed toward the wall.

Disappear. Come on, disappear.

"Rosemary." A voice boomed. It wasn't the Sedator's…it was…my father's? "I want revenge. You're going to pay."

"No, stop." My foot hit against the wall as I started to cry. My tears were acid, burning against my face. Stop.

As the walls started closing in, one wall exploded. Ironfall. Only a small sense of relief washed over me. He picked up the Sedator, throwing him out. He ran to me, flinging his arms around me. For just a moment, I felt secure, like nothing more could happen.

But then he backed away, and the Sedator was back.

"Watch out!" I tried to scream, but my throat closed over and I couldn't say a thing. The Sedator pierced a knife into Ironfall's back.

"NO!" Nothing came out. I was voiceless.

Ironfall collapsed, blood pouring from his mouth.

I couldn't do this. He was gone. No. I leaned down to his body and finally I screamed, and screamed, and scream—

HELP

JULY 17 – 2:03 A.M. PDT

"No!" I jolted up, shaking myself as I stared around my room. My body and bed were drenched in sweat. "Just a dream, only a dream," I whispered to myself.

I threw off the covers with shaky hands, but got up only to sink to the floor with a cry.

I couldn't see him die. I couldn't.

Sobs wracked my chest as I curled up on the cold floor.

The image of Ironfall collapsing, of blood pouring from him. It haunted me in the darkness of the night. I reached for my phone, pressing on his contact before I even knew what I was doing.

"Hello?" A hoarse whisper. The relief at hearing his voice washed a wave of calm over me. He was alive. He was okay. He was safe.

The Sedator hadn't gotten to him.

"J-just needed to hear your voice." Another sob wracked my chest, but I tried to suppress it. Make myself sound okay.

"Rosemary? Did something happen? Is something wrong? Are you okay?"

"N-nothing happened, I'm fine," I said, but my voice betrayed me. "Everything's okay."

"Bad dreams?" He said this as if he knew.

"Yes." My voice was barely a whisper. I wasn't even sure he heard it for a few moments.

"Why call me?" He sounded more awake now. "I wouldn't think I'd be your first choice." A few months ago, he'd be right. But now...

"You d-died." I couldn't believe I was able to say it out loud. "I just...it's okay now. Sorry to wake you." I held back more tears, biting at my bottom lip.

He's okay. He's safe.

"Do you want to talk about it?" His voice sounded calm and open. And beyond all reason, it made me feel better.

"The Sedator was chasing me, and no matter how fast I ran, it wasn't fast enough. Then my father was there talking about revenge, and you saved me. But the Sedator showed up again and…"

"He killed me," he whispered.

"I'm sorry, I shouldn't have bothered you." I shook my head again, longing to shrink into my bed.

"Rosemary, it's okay," he said in a soothing tone. "I—I have nightmares too."

"You do?" I wouldn't think…

"Yes," he said. "I've had a recurring one since I was a kid. My father trapped me in the basement, then decided I wasn't worthy enough. He slit my throat, just like he'd taught me."

I sucked in a breath. I knew his father was cruel, but to be the never-ending villain of Ironfall's nightmares meant he was even worse. "Ironfall, I'm so sorry. I didn't know."

"I've never told anyone before."

My breath caught. Had I heard him right? Why tell me of all people? Then again, why did I call him?

"He can't hurt you anymore. You're free from him."

"That's what I have to remind myself every day," he said. "And don't worry, I won't let the Sedator get me."

"Good," I said. Because I didn't know what I'd do if he did. Just weeks ago, I never even wanted to think about him again, but now…

Now I didn't know how to feel.

"I won't let him get you either," he said after a moment of hesitation.

I couldn't breathe at his words as any sort of response left my brain. I closed my eyes, readjusting the phone against my ear.

I won't let him get you either.

It was something a partner—a friend—would say. But it was

Ironfall saying it to *me*. And that made my brain hurt. I wanted to wrap my arms around him and feel his around me.

I wanted to feel safe, even though he was the opposite of safe. I had to stop thinking like this.

I needed to change the subject. "I think someone was watching us at the airport today." There. There wouldn't be any...weirdness...with that would there?

"What happened?" He sounded wide awake now, having snapped out of whatever just happened. "You saw someone?"

"We were looking for Sam when I saw this guy wearing a business suit. Pretty sure he had an earpiece too. He kept staring at us, which was strange because—"

"You had tinted windows," he finished.

"Yes," I said. "I was going to go investigate, but by the time we circled back around, he was gone."

"Describe him," he said. "If he has any connection to ANTE, we need to know. It could be our only lead." Why did he sound so desperate?

"He was tall. Probably around six foot. Male Caucasian, broad shoulders, built sort of like a football player. Tan skin, dark brown hair. But he was definitely surveilling us."

"He knows which car Ver drives."

"He must." I nodded. "Which means he either has someone on the inside or has somehow seen Ver get into her car."

"Did you see anyone while you were getting in her car at your apartment?" he asked.

"No, I didn't even feel like anyone was watching us. The parking garage was deserted."

"So we're back to square one."

"Sorry I couldn't get more," I said. "It was unsettling."

"They're watching us." Us as in VIGIL. He thought of himself as a VIGIL agent now. "It's what I would do, anyway. Know your enemies." Why did that feel like a jab at me? Maybe it was. Maybe it wasn't.

"If only we could *know* them," I said.

"Yeah." He fell silent.

The quiet sucked the air from my lungs until his name rested on my tongue. "Ironfall?"

"Yes?"

"Will the nightmares go away? After this is over?" My voice shook.

"I'll let you know when it happens," he said. "But I hope so, because I don't know how much longer I can take it." So they wouldn't, and we would have to suffer together.

"What do you want when it's all over?" I tried not to sound nosy, but I was curious all of a sudden.

"I…" He drifted off. "I haven't let myself think that far. As a kid I used to dream of going on Broadway. Or being an actor of some sort."

"I don't know anymore either," I said. "But I want all of it to be over. I just want to feel safe."

He went quiet for a long while this time. I almost thought he drifted off to sleep before he said, "I will do everything in my power to make your life right again."

I…I didn't know what to say to that. Honestly, I still didn't know why I'd called him in the first place.

"Are you really different?" I dared to ask.

"I hope so," he said. "Because I hate the person I was."

Tears pricked my eyes again. Was this an illusion? Was this true?

"Will you stay on the phone until I fall asleep?" My cheeks heated with this question.

"Always. As long as you need."

"Thank you," I whispered. Grabbing a blanket, I situated myself on top of all the covers, laying the phone down beside my head.

He was here, and in the delirium-haunted night, he was there. My pulse settled into a normal steady rhythm as I stared at the screen with his name on it.

Ironfall.

I could almost feel his arms wrapped around me again, the same way they had in the studio, when we were *pretending*. My eyelids drooped.

"Did you have nightmares when I—when we...?" He trailed off, but I knew what he meant. When I was a double agent and he was a villain.

"Yes," I said.

He said nothing for a little while. When he finally spoke again his voice was almost inaudible. "I'm sorry, again."

Now it was my turn to say nothing, because I didn't know what to say. Could he really be trusted now? Had he truly changed? Ver had said something about being here for our enemies; did she mean that people were redeemable? That even our worst enemies deserved a chance to repent? Well, he was here for now at least, and it was comforting.

Could Ironfall really have changed?

A dreamless sleep swept me away.

Federal Bureau Of Investigation
Transcript Of The Interview Proceedings With

IRONFALL
SOME NAMES AND LOCATIONS REDACTED FOR SECURITY
INTERVIEW CONDUCTED ON JULY 23
LOCATION OF INTERVIEW: **[REDACTED]**
CASE #: **[REDACTED]**

PROPERTY OF THE FBI

———

SPECIAL AGENT LAUDE: She called you in the middle of the night, is that correct?

IRONFALL: That's private. It has nothing to do with what happened.

SPECIAL AGENT LAUDE: You don't have the right to privacy right now. Tell me about it. And remember, you are under oath.

IRONFALL: It was around two in the morning when she called me. She just wanted to make sure I was okay.

SPECIAL AGENT LAUDE: Why? Was there a reason for you not to be?

IRONFALL: No.

SPECIAL AGENT LAUDE: Why did she call then?

IRONFALL: She had a nightmare.

SPECIAL AGENT LAUDE: About you?

IRONFALL: About everything. Her father, the Sedator, me.

SPECIAL AGENT LAUDE: Is this something that happens often?

IRONFALL: That was the first night.

SPECIAL AGENT LAUDE: So she was worried about you.

IRONFALL: It seems so.

SPECIAL AGENT LAUDE: And what did you tell her?

IRONFALL: She wasn't the only one who dealt with nightmares. We talked through it and then she told me about seeing someone suspicious in the airport. You can read my report.

SPECIAL AGENT LAUDE: Yes, I see that there were things going on beneath the surface of that.

IRONFALL: Why don't you go ahead and write a gossip column about it?

SPECIAL AGENT LAUDE: Very funny.

IRONFALL: ANTE was surveilling VIGIL. They knew Ver's car and where she was going. Somehow they had a way of looking in.

SPECIAL AGENT LAUDE: Yes, so I've heard.

IRONFALL: Why don't you ask me about that rather than my personal life?

CHAPTER 11

IRONFALL

JULY 17 – *6:20 A.M. PDT*

Usually I didn't mind early mornings—they were often required as a villain—but the lack of sleep was really starting to get to me. The dull pain behind my eyes was constant these days.

I grabbed a coffee from craft services and made my way over to one of the tents. Extras would start showing up soon. Today we filmed on a studio lot set that looked like a New York City street. Faux brick buildings lined a street. It was smaller than an actual street, but a bit of movie magic would make it appear to be the real thing.

Rosemary caught the corner of my eye as I approached—she was chatting with one of the production assistants.

When I reached her she said, "Good morning, Rhett." She looked about as awake as I felt, but the sight of her still sent heat radiating through my chest.

"Good morning." My brain was too foggy to conjure her stage name at the moment.

She stepped away from the PA and we made our way to

another tent, taking in the city sounds that once more surrounded us. It didn't smell like a real city though... Often, it smelled like fresh paint.

"I would give anything to go back to bed right now," I said before taking another large swig of coffee.

"Me too," she agreed. "I had to get here extra early this morning because makeup wanted to try something different for this scene."

"Of course they did," I laughed. "It looks nice though." Beautiful even. Her hair delicately curled around her perfect face. But I didn't dare tell her that.

"Thanks," she said. "But was it worth it?"

"Probably not." I shook my head. "Let's hope they have an extra supply of coffee."

"Yes." She sounded distracted now. "I'm supposed to talk to Manda about something. I'll probably see you in the tent."

I nodded, and she walked off. I watched her go.

"Rhett!" For a moment I forgot that was my own name (lack of sleep, not lack of skills at this undercover job, don't worry), then I turned around. Oh yay, Sam at seven in the morning after like four hours of sleep. What a joy. There he was, a girl beside him. I couldn't wait to see what this was about. Yes, that was sarcasm.

"Meet my new friend, Mia." Sam gestured at the girl next to him. She was small, shorter than Sam, if you can imagine that (though he'd finally grown some since I last saw him). She had long dark brown hair that curled down her back.

I nodded.

She giggled, stepping closer to Sam.

I plastered a smile on my face, remembering I was an actor. "Hi, Mia, I'm Rhett. It's nice to meet you."

"I'm friends with most of the actors," Sam said. "London and I go way back."

Mia giggled again. Oh no, was this what I thought it was?

"Hi, it's so amazing to meet you," she said. "Um...I don't

know if I'm supposed to do this, but could I take a picture with you?"

I nodded, wishing I could send Sam a death glare without her noticing.

She took out her phone and handed it to Sam. He too had the biggest grin on his face. Leave it to him to spend today trying to impress a girl.

And oh gosh, this poor girl.

Sam took our picture, and Mia thanked me profusely.

"Sam, don't annoy her too much," I said.

"I don't think he could ever," Mia assured me.

"Let's go find Xavier Jay next!" Sam said. "Don't worry, before today is over, you'll have an in with all the actors."

Remind me to warn the other VIGIL agents that Sam was falling for this girl.

I stepped into one of the tents, and soon Sam was in there with Mia annoying Rosemary and Ver at the same time.

Rosemary glanced at me as they were talking, probably begging for help. I went to her rescue.

"My dad introduced me to the movies when *Project Safeguard* first came out. From then on, it was our thing," Mia giggled nervously.

"That's so sweet," Rosemary said. "I bet you had so many great times! I was a huge fan of the movies before I got a role in them. Still am a huge fan actually."

"I'm sure. You're basically living every fangirl's dream!" She almost bounced.

"It's much harder than it seems, but thank you." Rosemary smiled, then glanced at me again as if we were talking in a secret language. She was living a fangirl's dream in way more ways than one, but no one else could know it.

"No one was more shocked than me, though," Sam said. "I literally worked with her at this burger place we have in New York, and then boom, she gets cast as the lead role in a VIGIL & ANTE movie. Like what?"

"Now you're an extra too!" Mia said. "It's so cool how all this works together!"

"We're so excited to have you on set today, Mia," Rosemary said. "If you need anything, just let me know, and I'll help you. I know it can be a bit overwhelming. I was there just a few weeks ago."

Rosemary was way nicer than me.

"Right, this is your first movie!" Mia said. "Thank you so much, I really appreciate it."

"Well, I'd love to hang out here, but let's see if we can find Xavier Jay for you to meet," Sam said. "Anyone know where he is?"

I shook my head. Hopefully he was busy finding something more about ANTE.

"He's probably going over things with Sylwhit," Ver said.

"*The* Sylwhit? Sylvester Whitlock?" Mia's eyes sparkled. "Oh my goodness, I can't believe he's the director."

I couldn't either. He wasn't fun to work with, but from what I'd studied of his work, he got the job done well. That I could admire, even if I didn't like his personality (or lack thereof).

"He is indeed."

"Are you friends with him too?" Mia asked.

"Uh...no." Sam's face fell.

The girl looked slightly disappointed, but no less interested in Sam.

"It's probably best not to disturb him while he's working anyway," Rosemary said. "He can be very...particular about things." She put it so nicely.

"Maybe Agent—" I shot Sam a dark look. "I mean Xavier will introduce you."

"Shouldn't you be with the other extras, Sam?" Ver raised a blonde brow.

"There's a lot of them, they won't miss us," Sam said. "And you can explain."

"Maybe we should go back," Mia urged. "I wouldn't want us to get in trouble."

"Don't worry about it." Sam shrugged.

Rosemary stood. "I'll take you back."

"Really?" Mia's eyes lit up. "You don't have to."

"It's really fine. I have nothing else to do right now." Rosemary shrugged and flashed her contagious warm smile. The way she could instantly make people belong always warmed my heart.

"This is so cool." Mia's eyes were filled with stars.

"It really is," Sam said.

Rosemary followed them out without so much as a silent cry for help. I guess she hadn't needed me after all.

"Are those two—" Ver's mouth hung open.

"Yup." I nodded, almost in as much shock as she was.

"That girl likes Sam."

"And he likes her."

Ver rubbed her hands together. "He's never going to live this down."

"Never." I grinned. "Finally we have some dirt on him." My mind was already racing with ways to tease him over this. After months of torment from him about Rosemary, he was about to get payback. Lots of payback.

"If Sylwhit doesn't kill him first," Ver laughed. "That boy is about to get a rude awakening."

"You'd think the fact that VIGIL was real…and the time I—uh—almost killed him…would've been a rude enough awakening."

"It seems to have only created a monster," Ver said.

JULY 17 – 12:15 P.M. PDT

The lunch tent was about to be filled with extras, and I wanted to be gone before the fangirls flocked. Rosemary sat beside me finishing the last few bites of her Greek salad.

"I wonder how Sam and Mia are doing," she mused.

"You mean has Sam asked her out yet?" I said.

"That too," she laughed.

"Not sure I want to be here when all the extras are free to roam around. Everyone probably wants to get close to the big stars," I said.

"And you consider yourself a big star?"

"This is about the people." I nudged her. "They'll be all over you too." I glanced at the edge of the lunch tent to see a ton of people walking up. "I give it twenty seconds."

It took five for Sam and his girlfriend to pounce.

"Oh. My. Gosh. Today was everything I thought it would be and more." Sam grinned. Mia stood way too close to him but had the exact same smile. It was almost like looking at the same person.

Great, there might be two of them.

"Save us seats," Sam said. "We'll be back with food in a minute."

Then he walked off, not giving us the chance to protest.

Rosemary just looked at me and laughed. "So much for heading out before the crowd of people. Now we're stuck."

The people swarmed now, but not around us, around the food, which I considered a much better choice. Sam and Mia came back a few minutes later with plates full of salad and falafel. Mia looked like she was about to explode with happiness. And whoa, I did not just see Sam pull out her chair.

"How are you enjoying being on set?" Rosemary asked.

"It's amazing!" Mia said. "I've met so many great people, and it was so cool to see how the crew and actors work. I'm kind of addicted."

"You're legally obligated to let me be an extra in every scene now," Sam said. "Because I'm never leaving." Mia just laughed and I fought the urge to roll my eyes at him. Yes, I did talk to him all the time, but that was about work. Yes, I put up with his annoying comments, but I needed to.

He most definitely hadn't grown on me over the last few months.

Not at all.

"I'm so glad," Rosemary said. "It really is a lot of fun."

"When it's not exhausting," I said.

"It's true," Rosemary's golden voice sang. "I have definitely taken naps in my trailer between scenes."

She looked up, and the smile fell from her face. What was wrong?

She turned to me, leaning in. "That's him." She looked back up where she was looking before.

"Who?"

"The guy from the airport."

"Which one?"

She discreetly pointed him out to me. He did stick out. He held a plate of food, and just stood there watching us.

"Would you like to share with the class?" Sam said.

"Sam!" Mia smacked his arm.

"I thought I saw someone I knew," Rosemary said. "It's nothing."

"I'll take care of it," I whispered to her. "I'd better go study my lines for the next scene." I said this as I got up, making sure to only look at the man out of the corner of my eye. Dumping my empty plate in a trashcan, I moved in the stalker's direction. He noticed me fast, averting his eyes as he turned to walk away. His gait was steady and swift, but not quick enough to draw attention.

I sped up, hoping to cut him off, dodging various crew with their plates while still keeping an eye on him. Today the man wore a white T-shirt and jeans instead of the suit Rosemary described; he also wore a lanyard against his neck. I couldn't see a weapon on him, but that didn't mean he hadn't smuggled one in.

I always kept mine on me, just in case. You never knew where an enemy lurked.

He swept through the tent's opening onto the rest of the set. I brushed by the entrance, following him through the crowd. But the moment he was through, he broke into a run. I pushed through the last few people.

"Hey!" someone shouted. I ignored the person, breaking into a run after him.

He knew I was chasing him now.

Adrenaline coursed through my veins as I raced around one of the crew's tents. Ducking around it, I watched the man run straight toward the street, off the set. I followed, leaping over caution tape. He took a right on the street.

"Stop!" I shouted. "I have something you want!" Again, the man kept running, and I kept chasing him. "I can give you information on Rosemary Collins!" Of course, I wouldn't give up anything, but he didn't know that. All I had to do was get him to stop. Then I'd overtake him and bring him in.

He hesitated, just for a moment, looking back at me.

Who was he? I memorized his features so Sam could draw them up later. I'd never seen him in my father's files before. Could he be the Sedator? No, he was slightly shorter.

I sprinted towards him.

The man turned and ran. Apparently information about Rosemary wasn't quite what he was looking for. Though he'd known exactly where she was, so if he was here for her, what had stopped him from trying to take her when no one was around? Maybe his job was simply to surveil everything and gather data.

He ducked into an alleyway, and I lost sight of him for just a moment. I bolted around the corner. The alley was empty.

Where had he gone?

JULY 17 – 12:43 P.M. PDT

I found Rosemary in her trailer as soon as I returned.

She pushed open her trailer door, eyes widening. "Did you find him?"

I shook my head. "He disappeared in an alley." If only I'd outsmarted him. I should have anticipated his moves.

Failure.

She pressed her lips together, forming a soft frown. "So we still have nothing." That only made my father's words resound more. Maybe my father was right. Maybe I *was* a failure.

"I'll give his description to security. Make sure he's not allowed back on set," I said. "I'm sorry I couldn't get him."

"How do these people keep slipping away?" She rubbed her temples. "They're always one step ahead of us." She looked pale and dark circles were visible under her eyes now. How much was this weighing on her?

I should have caught him. I needed to keep her safe and end this, all of it.

"At least we know who one of their spies is," I said. "Hopefully that will slow them down enough for them to slip up."

"How do I know you didn't let him go?" Why did she look like it saddened her to ask?

"I didn't," I said. "You can pull up CCTV footage. He wouldn't even stop when I offered to leak information about you."

"You did what?" Her tone turned dark.

"I wasn't going to say anything, I just needed him to get close enough to take him down," I sighed. It clearly wasn't the right move. I didn't know my enemy well enough. "The Sedator killed the congressman to stop him from killing you. You must mean something to ANTE. Simple act of deception." Which failed.

"Oh," she said. "I guess that was a good plan."

"I wouldn't betray you." I took a step closer to the open trailer door. "I promise."

"I want to believe you."

My breath caught. She did? "But you can't," I finished. "I understand." This was my cue to leave.

Her mouth opened, then closed.

I spared her. "I'll leave you to it. Get some rest if you can." I walked away.

JULY 17 – 1:02 P.M. PDT

"He was on set?" Agent Liam crossed his arms, looking around the tents to make sure no one was in earshot. "You and Rosemary search through the list and headshots of extras. I want his name, even if it's an alias."

I nodded. "Yes, sir." We had to find this guy.

"If anyone else looks suspicious, I want to hear about them too."

"Of course," I assured him. "I won't let you down." Like I did before.

I should have been better.

"You'd better not." Agent Liam straightened. *I know.* I knew it too well.

"They're watching us," I said. "I think they're especially watching Rosemary."

"Why do you think that?" Agent Liam asked.

"The Sedator killed off the congressman—a sleeper agent—to stop him from hurting Rosemary. Then, he tried taking her alive. When I was chasing our spy, he stopped after I tried to convince him I'd give him information on her."

"But he didn't take the bait?" Agent Liam rubbed at his chin.

I shook my head. "He thought about it, for a moment, but ended up getting away. I shouldn't have failed, I'm sorry."

"It's an interesting theory. I'll make sure she has extra security," he said. "You're dismissed."

I nodded, stepping towards the door.

"And Ironfall," he said.

I stopped. "Yes?"

"Be careful with her," he said. "Because if you hurt her again…"

"I know." I nodded. I'd never get another chance. I'd be dead. I'd be in jail. I'd get everything that should have come to me in the first place. "I won't."

JULY 17 – 3:39 P.M. PDT

Rosemary and I sat in my trailer swiping through the headshots and resumes of each extra.

"Anything?" I asked. Another picture, another normal person.

"Nope. You?" She swiped again.

"Knowing ANTE, he just jumped the perimeter and blended in with the crowd."

"I'm in the E's now," Rosemary sighed. "But you're right. We have to try though. They can't stay ahead of us forever."

"It's time we know what their next move is," I said. "No one gets ahead of me."

"Well then, let's keep looking."

We sat in silence scrolling for a few more minutes until we'd both met in the middle of the alphabet. The man was all but a ghost.

"Looks like he got in another way," Rosemary groaned,

setting down the tablet. "Do you think we could find him in the background of the footage?"

"You didn't see him while filming our scene. Chances are he wasn't on camera. He clearly knows what he's doing." Which led us to yet another dead end.

A knock sounded on the door. Rosemary jumped, quickly turning off her tablet, hiding everything VIGIL-related. I did the same just in case, then got up to open the trailer door.

Sam and Mia stood on the other side, a little too close to just be friends.

I forced a smile. "Hello."

"Mind if we hang out with you?" Sam said. Yes, but I was also curious.

"I'm sure you're busy though," Mia added. See, someone with a sense of decency.

"Nah, he doesn't mind." Sam shrugged, pushing his way inside. Mia stood just outside the door, hugging her arms.

"Actually, maybe you can help us." Rosemary stood. "Come on in." What was she doing? But when I met her gaze, I could sense the wheels of her mind were turning. She had a plan. A twinkle in her eye.

Mia stepped through the doorway and the two of them perched themselves on the couch. *My* couch, I might add. Again, sitting a little too close together. I stowed that away in my mental blackmail file.

"What do you need?" Sam glanced at Mia before quickly averting his gaze. "Unless it's something…uh…one of those private group project things." Could he be any more subtle?

"Do you need to talk in private?" Mia glanced from Sam to Rosemary and back again. "I totally get it if you do."

"No, actually, I think you can help as well," Rosemary said. How would she spin this? "I'm wondering if you know anything about an extra. I met him once a long time ago, but I can't remember his name again for the life of me. He was friends with my parents." I could have grinned at the brilliance of it. She was the best.

"What did he look like?" Mia asked. "I talked to a lot of extras today. Maybe I got his name?"

"He was really tall," Rosemary said. "Broad shoulders, probably around forty years old. Today he wore a white T-shirt and jeans. He had brown hair too."

"Hmm…" Mia tapped her chin like she was thinking.

"I don't think I saw anyone like that," Sam said. "Sorry."

"I think I did," Mia finally said.

My ears perked up as I straightened, though I tried to keep up the front that this wasn't the most exciting thing for me to be doing right now.

"I didn't talk to him ," Mia went on. "But I remember him because he stood off to the side in the extras tent just taking everything in."

Spying on things.

"I can ask around, though," Mia said. "I'll tell Sam what I find. We still have a while on set."

"Would you?" Rosemary lit up. "You're a lifesaver. Thank you so much!"

"It's no problem at all." Mia grinned, obviously still starstruck. "And if I see him, I'll ask his name for you."

"Perfect, thank you," Rosemary said.

That was much more productive than anything I'd thought of. Still, our hopes were dashed when Mia and Sam returned toward the end of the day with bad news: the man was nowhere to be found and no one got his name.

Of course, the spy wouldn't slip up.

JULY 17 – 7:36 P.M. PDT

I whacked Sam upside the head as his eyes closed and his chin drooped. He sat in his fancy rolling chair he stole from Ver the moment he got to the LA VIGIL base.

Sitting across the table, Ver rolled her eyes.

"What was that for? Not cool," Sam groaned before readjusting himself in the chair. "I need my beauty sleep."

"The meeting is about to start."

"Yeah and guess who wrote the notes for the meeting?" he murmered, eyes still closed.

"Not you." Rosemary stepped in, leaning against the desk. "Agent Liam will be here in a second. He's talking to Cloaker." Her hair was a vibrant red in the interior lights, falling in soft waves that framed her face. I had the sudden urge to reach out and touch her, but I kept my hands to myself.

"I don't know how you do this," Sam said. "I'm exhausted."

"Yeah, remember the time you sent us on a mission after a full day of filming? Think of that." I almost smacked his head again just for good measure. "And I was a main character." Sam always had something to gripe about.

"Stop complaining." Manda walked in, glaring at me first, as always. Nice to see her too with her long black braid and fierce face. She still hated me, that much was for sure. "I've done this a lot longer than either of you."

"Hey, a hacker's life is hard." Sam smirked.

"I'll see you tomorrow morning at 4:30 for my special training session. Then you'll know the real meaning of hard work." Manda's eyes narrowed. Brave woman to challenge Sam. Though, to be fair, that teenager really needed to be put in his place.

Ver stifled a laugh.

"On second thought, my life is easy," Sam said. "Forget I said anything."

I tucked this tactic away for future use. Sam did not like to wake up early. Or engage in physical exercise. I stole a glance at Rosemary. A sparkle caught her golden-brown eyes. Was she thinking the same thing? She nodded as if she read my mind, though of course she didn't have that power.

Right?

Sometimes it seemed like she did with how she could cut right through me.

Sam rested his head on the desk, closing his eyes again. It took every ounce of villain-suppression to not slam my hands on the desk just to see him fly out of his seat in terror.

"It's been a long day, so let's make this quick." Agent Liam finally stepped in, placing a cream-colored folder on the table. Top secret. Another midnight mission? "Here's Ironfall's report on the man who infiltrated our set. I want eyes and ears open."

Manda nodded, then looked straight at me. "Convenient he got away."

I fought the urge to step away from this little team called a family. One I still didn't quite belong in.

"He tried," Rosemary said, even-toned. She didn't sound like she was defending me, but she wasn't not defending me either. "We're still trying to identify him but haven't made any progress yet."

"That's where we're at in the investigation," Agent Liam said. "Now I will gladly pass the baton to you, Ver."

She grinned. "Tomorrow's the premiere for *Project Safeguard 3*. We paused filming so everyone can get ready. Image is important here. These premieres are where we really sell this thing to the audience. Let's make the world fall in love with our actor personas."

Federal Bureau Of Investigation
Transcript Of The Interview Proceedings With

AGENT ROSEMARY COLLINS
SOME NAMES AND LOCATIONS REDACTED FOR SECURITY
INTERVIEW CONDUCTED ON JULY 23
LOCATION OF INTERVIEW: **[REDACTED]**
CASE #: **[REDACTED]**

PROPERTY OF THE FBI

————

SPECIAL AGENT LAUDE: Ironfall let him get away.

AGENT ROSEMARY COLLINS: Are you accusing him of something?

SPECIAL AGENT LAUDE: You sound defensive.

AGENT ROSEMARY COLLINS: How would you feel if you were in this situation?

SPECIAL AGENT LAUDE: Tell me. Did Ironfall let him get away on purpose?

AGENT ROSEMARY COLLINS: It's Agent Ironfall, and you read his report.

SPECIAL AGENT LAUDE: We both know he wouldn't put a betrayal in the report.

AGENT ROSEMARY COLLINS: Then take my word for it. He stayed true to us.

SPECIAL AGENT LAUDE: Forgive me, but your word isn't doing yourself any favors.

SPECIAL AGENT LAUDE: Ironfall let him get away.

AGENT ROSEMARY COLLINS: Are you accusing him of something?

SPECIAL AGENT LAUDE: You sound defensive.

AGENT ROSEMARY COLLINS: How would you feel if you were in this situation?

SPECIAL AGENT LAUDE: Tell me. Did Ironfall let him get away on purpose?

AGENT ROSEMARY COLLINS: It's Agent Ironfall, and you read his report.

SPECIAL AGENT LAUDE: We both know he wouldn't put a betrayal in the report.

AGENT ROSEMARY COLLINS: Then take my word for it. He stayed true to us.

SPECIAL AGENT LAUDE: Forgive me, but your word isn't doing yourself any favors.

CHAPTER *12*

ROSEMARY

JULY 18 – *12:57 P.M. PDT*

My movie makeover montage scene was about to begin.

"You're going to love this," Ver giggled, surveying the large hotel suite we'd spent the night in. It was mostly white with ornate crown molding and the softest beds I'd ever slept on. And now it would become a movie premiere beauty zone. I'd missed senior prom, but I had a feeling that this would more than make up for it. Me, an A-list actress who accidentally made it big... it still didn't feel real.

Manda rolled her eyes, sitting down on her plush bed. "I hope you like wearing makeup, because they're about to cake it on you."

"Oh hush," Ver snuggled deeper in her robe. "You're about to get the movie star treatment."

A soft knock sounded on the door.

Ver leapt to her feet. "That's them! London Peters, get ready to meet your new glam squad. I've always wanted to say that. I'm sorry, I'll calm down now."

Manda shook her head. "Sam is rubbing off on you."

"Maybe it's a hacker thing." Ver grinned. "Or the fact that he's everyone's little brother."

"Unfortunately," Manda said.

As they continued to bicker, I opened the door to a team larger than what was left of VIGIL. Did it take this many people to get us ready?

"Hi." I gave a little wave, then put my hand down quickly. That probably wasn't how they were used to being treated by a professional actress. Not that I was a professional. Though I guess technically I was now?

"…make you wear stilettos." Ver and Manda were still arguing, and Manda looked less than thrilled as three complete glam squads swarmed. Stylists, makeup artists, and hair stylists. Not to mention the racks of floor-length gowns that looked straight off a Broadway stage. Or a red carpet. I guess the latter was more appropriate.

Red gowns and pink gowns and blue gowns. Some puffy, some form-fitting, some embroidered, some satin.

Forget A-list actress, I was going to feel like a princess.

Manda no longer looked like the annoyed fighter who refused to wear anything but black pants and a black T-shirt. She was Jana Anthony, but when she thought no one was looking, she shot Ver a glare.

Ver only smiled her overly sweet smile. Manda was right. She was spending too much time with Sam.

A tall woman with brightly colored hair strutted over. Yes, she strutted. Did her six-inch heels force her to walk that way or was that the high-fashion oozing off her? Either way, I trusted her with whatever she had in mind for me. "It's so nice to meet you. My name is Tiffany, and I will be your stylist today. Are you ready to pick out a dress?"

I nodded, a giggle slipping out. I put a hand over my mouth to stifle the outburst as I followed Tiffany to one of the dress trains.

Then suddenly it was a few months ago and I was in Ironfall's apartment. Racks of clothes and costumes he'd designed and made. We'd laughed and tried on clothes. I'd found my white suit.

Why was I now sad he hadn't made what I was going to wear tonight? I shook off the feeling and ran a finger over a dark tulle skirt, the soft fabric rippling over my skin.

My stylist swatted my hand away. "Not that one."

"Oh, sorry," I murmured.

She acted like she hadn't heard me. "I was shown some of the costumes you wear in your movie, and I was thinking we could create a look inspired by that, but with your own personality to separate you from the character."

She gestured toward the rack of pastel gowns on her left. "You wear a lot of white and gold in your movie, and I was thinking we could do something inspired by that. And it makes your hair pop."

I couldn't help but grin. She was right.

Suddenly I was swept in and out of gowns, and I felt so beautiful in each one that I wasn't sure I would be able to choose. In the end, I picked a white gown with straps and a long satin skirt. A layer of tulle covered in gold and silver stars floated over the top and draped behind me like a cape. Yes, this was something my "character" would approve of.

I walked out and saw Manda and Ver also wearing dresses, but they weren't quite as long as mine. Manda's was a navy-blue velvet that draped just below her shoulders before tightening into a short dress. A long piece of velvet covered the back in a train that dragged behind her. I never thought I'd ever see her in something like that, and if the pained smile on her face was any indication, neither did she. She was bearing it better than me though; if I had to wear heels like that, I'd probably be crying.

Ver wore a simpler slim dress that hit her mid-calf. The only glamour was the large dark silver sequins that swayed as she moved.

Mine was a complete ballgown compared to theirs, but on

the red carpet anything goes...right? Not that I had any experience.

"You guys look amazing!" I said.

"I will stab someone with these stilettos if I have to wear them all night," Manda said, the mask falling from her face. "Miss Atkins"—she smiled through gritted teeth—"if you bribed someone to make me wear these..."

Tiffany whipped out a pair of white flats, grinning. "For the after-party. I know you too well."

Manda nodded.

Tiffany didn't really know anything considering the movies were just a cover for VIGIL, but she did know Manda hated heels. So, I guess that was something.

"Your dress is incredible," Ver said. "You look like a queen. A fierce Stardust queen."

"I sure feel like it." I grinned. "Do you think it's too much?"

"I think *Rhett* will see you in it and drop dead." Ver covered her mouth just as quickly as she said the word, eyes going wide. Heat rushed to my cheeks. "Oops, forget I said that."

Why did my heart keep doing that jumpy thing? "Ma—I mean Jana's right. Sam is rubbing off on you," I laughed nervously. Was I worried about what Ironfall would think?

"All right, ladies, time for hair and makeup." Tiffany clapped her hands. "Change back into something more comfortable for now."

Was it from what Ver said?

I didn't care what Ironfall thought...did I?

JULY 18 – 5:15 P.M. PDT

As I slid out of the limousine, the crowd pressed against the barricade that kept them off the red carpet. Cameras flashed, blinding me as they reflected off everything.

It was like a dream.

"London Peters!" I didn't know where to look as my name echoed and contorted in a wave across the crowds.

"London!" People were in cosplay as Commander Vigil, Cloaker, Illuman, and all the Safeguarders. Was that an Ironfall cosplayer hanging over the railing? A security guard ran over to him, but something else caught my eye.

Red hair and a white outfit. Was someone dressed as *me*? Another flash blinded me, and I blinked away the dots burned into my eyes, stepping farther away from the limousine.

Suddenly I felt so exposed, like everyone was watching me. Probably because they were.

"London! London! London!"

I touched the gold starred headpiece Tiffany insisted would be the perfect finishing touch. It glittered even more than the stars cascading across my snow-white gown, but if she thought I looked perfect, I must. I took a deep breath to calm my shuddering pulse and surveyed the carpet once more. What I would have given just a few months ago to be inside that crowd.

And now I was an actress on the red carpet. Time to play the part.

I smiled, not sure what to do with my hands and arms while everyone stared at me standing in this ridiculously beautiful gown. Finally I waved to both sides like I was in a parade.

The security guy who'd opened the car door leaned in. "Go ahead and say hi to some fans. You have time."

I nodded, thanking him before scanning the railing once more. My eye snagged on Agent Liam a little further up. I wasn't quite standing here alone. There were also a few other stars from various movie franchises as well. This was step one of the red carpet walk. The fans, then we would move to a smaller portion near the building for press interviews and all that terrifying stuff. My hands started to sweat at the thought.

I stepped to my left towards a group of fans all cosplaying as Commander Vigil. They grinned, phones out to film me.

"Oh my goodness, London!" one of them exclaimed. "Can we get a picture?" I leaned in, barely knowing what I was doing. I smiled as they snapped a picture. Then there were posters and fanart and who knew what else to sign. I gripped the marker in my hand, signing so many things I couldn't even look up at everyone.

They knew who I was. They were excited to see me. Hopefully I lived up to their expectations.

I took a few steps forward again, waving and shaking hands.

One girl caught my eye. She was probably twelve and dressed up as Ver. Her face beamed as I leaned down.

"Hi, what's your name?" I asked.

"Ava," she squealed. "I'm so excited for your movie!"

"Well thank you, Ava." I grinned. She was adorable. "I hope you love it!" I took a picture with her and moved on. If I made one person's night, I hoped it'd be her. A little while later, someone tapped my shoulder from behind and I whipped around to see Ver. Her short hair sat in soft waves above her shoulders.

She gave me a hug. "You look amazing!"

"You do too." I grinned. Whew, someone beside me who knew what she was doing.

More pictures, more slow walking, more autographs. My hands were starting to cramp up.

"I think if I sign anything else my hands will fall off." I giggled from the pure adrenaline rushing through my veins.

She shook her head, laughing.

I glanced back, spotting Ironfall for the first time. He was taking a picture with an Ironfall cosplayer (not the one who almost got arrested climbing the railing). His hair was perfect, shoulders accented through a tailored tux as crisp as his jawline. Wow, he cleaned up quite nicely. I blinked, staring.

The entire VIGIL gang cleaned up nicely.

Wait, did I just consider Ironfall part of the VIGIL team?

His eyes met mine, and he waved, his boyish grin never leaving his face. My breath hitched, and I looked away. Did he think I'd been drooling over him like the fangirls now hounding him?

No, of course he wouldn't. That was dumb.

"London!"

"Noelle!"

"You're my favorite actor!"

Finally, we reached the end of the fans. Though tiring, I was grateful for the experience. Goodness, the one girl, Ava, probably grew up on these movies. And I got to be a part of that for her, just like the movies were for me as a child. Of course, she had no idea it was all real—that this premiere was just smoke and mirrors and movie magic to protect us. Still, I let the fantasy once again sweep me away as we reached the backdrop with *Project Safeguard 3*'s logo printed across it.

Even brighter flashes blinded me as reporters captured more photos. I was nowhere near a model, but I attempted to strike a pose. After that security propelled me forward to a line of reporters waiting to drill me with questions.

"Hey, I'm Dana Hanes from CA Newsfest," said a woman with a microphone. "How excited are you to join the VIGIL & ANTE Studios universe?"

"Hi, it's nice to meet you!" I said. Oh gosh, my first interview, ever. Ver had given me a few pointers, but her advice seemed to drop out of my mind.

"Anything you can tell us about the new movie?"

Aside from the characters being real? My chest tightened. "I haven't seen it yet."

"So we can't expect a Stardust cameo, is that what I'm hearing?" I couldn't make out her facial expressions through the bright video light.

"Sorry to disappoint." I tried to laugh naturally. "You'll have to wait for *I Am Stardust* to come out for that one."

"And we are so excited for it," Dana said.

"I'm just thankful they invited me," I said. "I've been a long-time fan myself."

"So maybe there's hope for the fans who've dreamed of acting?"

"Maybe." I smiled, ignoring the wild situation that got me a movie part in the first place. I was nudged on by someone to the next interviewer.

Ver failed to mention how fast-paced this would move.

Between the flashing of cameras and video lights, it was hard to take in much of anything.

"Harry Townsend with Comic Cast. Can you tell us what you're excited about for the future of VIGIL & ANTE Studios movies?"

"You know—" I paused. What was I supposed to say? I'm a crazy fan myself? "I just want to keep bringing people joy and hope, and continue to encourage people to always do the right thing, even in the toughest circumstances." Wow, that came out surprisingly put together.

"Thank you, London."

"London Peters?" Oh my goodness, I'd know that voice anywhere. Ruth Saxon, a.k.a. Commander Vigil.

I turned. Seeing her in person was…wow, so cool. Her brown hair was straight, brushing her shoulders. She wore a long, bright green silk dress. "Oh my goodness, Ruth Saxon!" There she was, right before my eyes.

Sam would be so jealous right now. He would have loved this.

She smiled, giving me a hug as if this wasn't the first time we'd met. Oh my gosh, *the* Ruth Saxon just gave me a hug. "I've been looking forward to meeting you!"

"You? Look forward to meeting me?" Yup, I was starstruck. "I've been excited to meet you!"

"Oh, nonsense," she laughed. "Welcome to the VIGIL & ANTE Studios family."

My heart leapt. "Thank you! Wait, can I get a quick picture with you?"

"Of course," she said, wrapping an arm around my waist. I reached into my pocket (yes, that gorgeous dress had pockets!), fumbled with my phone, and turned the camera to selfie mode. Forget comic con. Forget that everything was real. This was the stuff fangirl dreams were made of. I checked the phone, and oh my gosh, was that Mason East (Illuman!) throwing up a peace sign in the background? Photobombed by *the* Illuman.

Sam would have died. I quickly texted him the picture before turning around. I wished he was here.

Mason wore a black tieless tux, a pattern of yellow beads floating down his shoulders onto his arms.

"Mason, hi, I'm R-London." I grinned, sticking my hand out. Good catch. Was that how one was supposed to greet someone on the red carpet? Who cares, I was already doing it.

He took my hand, shaking it vigorously. "I know exactly who you are. Welcome to VIGIL." VIGIL…oh, he meant *VIGIL*.

"Thank you," I said. "I still can't believe I'm here."

"You don't really get used to it." He grinned.

"Really? Because I'm totally fangirling right now." It was like someone injected fangirl directly into my veins at that moment.

"That part doesn't go away either," he said. "Will I ever get used to meeting Chris Evangelista in person? Nope."

"I don't think I will either." I still wasn't used to being Agent Ver Larsen's roommate.

I turned to my left and oh my gosh it was Alison Zhao (a.k.a. Degree Surge). Like literally a foot away from me.

"…you're going to love it," she told the reporter, smiling.

I just stood there in stunned silence. Was I a crazy fan? Well, I didn't fall into Sam territory, so that was something.

Alison turned toward me, gasping. She brought a hand to her chest. "Oh my goodness, you scared me."

"I'm so sorry." I covered my face. "This carpet is small." Okay, wow, way to make a good first impression, Rosemary.

"Don't I know it. It's so nice to meet you, I'm Alison." She said that as if the whole world didn't know who she was.

"Yes, I know, I mean…it's so nice to meet you! I'm London Peters." And the weirdest celebrity encounter award goes to —me.

"I know," she laughed. "See you inside?"

I nodded. "Of course." She moved on to the next interviewer. *Oh my gosh. She knew who I was.* I mean, of course she did, but wow.

"London Peters? Come on over here." An interviewer beckoned me over.

"I'm Jamie Peters with Nerd Info." The teen boy held out a microphone that was literally wrapped in VIGIL's logo. A blue halo surrounded the top ball. Where did he find something like that?

"Hi, I'm London Peters."

"Yes, I know!"

"That is such a cool mic!"

"Thank you! I decorate it for every premiere."

I leaned closer to inspect it further. "You did this yourself?"

"I sure did," he said.

I glanced up. He couldn't have been older than Sam. No doubt they'd have been fast friends. "You're so talented."

"Would you like to hold it?" His eyes gleamed.

"Yes, of course," I said. He handed me the mic. "This is awesome. I feel like I should be interviewing you now." I held the mic to his mouth.

"Interviewed by London Peters. Now that is an honor."

I held the mic to my own lips. "Now, how did you end up covering a premiere?"

I shifted the mic toward him. "I sort of got the gig by accident." He laughed. "I made too much fanart. Customizing mics is my thing, and then Nerd Info invited me to cover the premiere for them."

"They need to hire you full time, because this is the coolest thing I've ever seen." I grinned. "Thank you for letting me interview you. It's been an honor."

"Thank you!" I handed the mic back to him, and he was beaming as if I'd just given him every star in the sky.

Cloaker's voice sounded behind me. "London Peters."

"David Reyes." I giggled from the giddiness of the entire situation, hugging him. "You look great!"

"So do you," he said. "Are you excited?"

"This is the coolest thing I've ever done." Okay, to be fair, I could say that about so many things that had happened to me now. But at this exact moment, this was the coolest.

We moved on. Between the blinding lights and excited paparazzi, something in the crowd in front of me caught my eye. Tall. Broad-shouldered. Graying hair. His back was to me, but—

"London Peters!" Next interview. I glanced at the reporter. "What was your favorite part of filming?"

I looked over her. "Um…" I searched the crowd. Something wasn't right. There he was. "I enjoyed…" My voice trailed off as I saw the tall man again. He turned around.

Dad.

My stomach lurched. Dad was here.

"I'm sorry," I murmured, not looking away from my father. "I have to…" His eyes met mine, his steel, hardened eyes.

What was he doing here? So exposed, so open. I moved down the red carpet, or as much as I could without stumbling over someone. I pushed through, but as I slid behind Manda giving an interview, my father was lost to the crowd. I looked around, scanning the faces amidst the dots floating through my vision from the never-ending camera flashes.

My father was here.

"London!"

"London!"

Dad.

My mind only registered that he was here. I moved to the end of the carpet, finding a place to slip behind the barricade.

I had to find him.

Ice chilled my spine. If he was here, he had to have something planned. And the way he looked at me…

I pushed through the crowd again, ignoring the odd stares and whispers and shrieks of my name rippling everywhere. But I looked over them all, head craning to try to find him. I made my way to the back, picking up my skirts as I went so no one would trip on them or rip them. And so the dirty LA street wouldn't soil them either.

I reached the back, breaking into the open, surveying the crowds again. It was like he had disappeared. My heart palpitated in my chest.

Was he really here? He had to be.

And so I stood in the middle of the blocked off street, alone, breathing hard, looking for any sign of my father. Had I imagined him being here? There was so much going on with the interviews and screaming fans and bright lights.

Dad.

I reached into my pocket, pulling out my phone. I dialed Sam's number. He was at the hotel watching the premiere.

It rang once, twice. Come on, Sam, pick up.

"Where did you go?" Sam asked. "I don't see you on camera anymore."

"I need you to review the footage."

"Why? You should be out there. What is going on?"

"It doesn't matter. I just…I thought I saw my dad in the crowd. I went looking for him."

"Wait, what? Why would he be there?" Sam sounded confused. "He's like in hiding or something."

"Just do it, okay?" I snapped. "Sorry. I'm just freaking out."

He didn't seem bothered. "Okay, I'll text you if I see anything."

"Thanks, Sam." Hanging up, I scanned over the crowd once more. My heart still hadn't slowed. My father was nowhere to be found.

Footsteps behind me.

I whipped around, balling my hands into fists.

Ironfall.

"Hey, it's okay, it's me," he said, reaching toward me as if it would calm me down. "What happened? You disappeared."

I looked back at the crowd. "My dad. He's here."

Ironfall's eyes went wide, his head whipping around. "Where?"

"He was in the crowd," I said, breathless. "But I don't see him anymore."

My phone vibrated.

Ironfall's arm brushed against mine as he looked over the people as well.

I looked down at my phone.

Sam: Nothing, sorry. He's not there.

I looked back up at the crowds, panic rising.

"Sam couldn't find him?" Ironfall said.

I shook my head. "No. It's like he was a ghost." *Must keep it together.* "I really thought I saw him." My throat constricted as I broke my gaze away from Ironfall, fighting tears. The street we were now on was empty, but the lights and sounds from the premiere on the other side still roared our way.

"I know," he said. "I believe you."

I still couldn't look at him. The tears threatened to fall fast. I dug my fingernails into my palms.

I didn't think seeing my father again would affect me this much.

"What is even going on?" I whispered. It wasn't really a question that needed answering, it was just…everything. Everything going on, the balancing act between fiction and reality and what the public could and could not know.

Suddenly strong arms wrapped around me. I stiffened, but the warmth of him…something about it made the tears flow. I melted.

"We're going to win," he whispered into my ear. "I promise."

The lump in my throat stopped me from saying anything, so I didn't.

After a moment, I stepped away from him, wiping away my tears. Oh no...they used waterproof mascara...right? The panic must have shown on my face, because Ironfall said, "Your makeup is intact, don't worry." He flashed a smile that was contagious.

"Thanks," I said.

"Anytime." He smirked. "But you'd still look great with mascara running down your cheeks."

I blinked. "Thanks?"

"I mean...you could have done it for an emo look. You never know." His arm brushed against mine, making me shiver.

I rolled my eyes. "In what world?"

"It was a compliment," he said. "Accept it."

"Oh wow, *the* Ironfall giving me a compliment," I laughed.

"Hush," he said, but his grin had already grown wider. "Maybe I'll have to take it back."

"Nope, the thing has been said."

Suddenly there was flashing and shouting.

"Rhett! Rhett!"

"Are the two of you dating?"

"Why did you leave the red carpet?"

"London, over here!"

More panic as I realized I was totally not where I was supposed to be and this whole situation was very suspicious. What kind of agent was I? I stared around, unsure of what to do as the crowd of paparazzi around us grew.

Ironfall flashed a smile around, looking at me as if he wanted me to do the same. I forced a smile. The tabloids would be all over this mess.

And apparently, they thought we were dating.

Great.

Without so much as a word, Ironfall started pushing through the crowd toward the red carpet. I followed and we slowly made our way back. The crowd that had given me the excited thrill just a few minutes earlier now seemed to choke me.

We needed their support. We couldn't do anything suspicious.

This was all a show, but one I was no longer swept up in. I swallowed, keeping the fake smile plastered across my face as we were ushered back through the barricade and onto the red carpet.

"Just keep going," Ironfall whispered into my ear. I nodded, then moved away from him.

I went up to the next interviewer, and a hush fell over the crowd. It was strange. Silent. Too silent. Wide eyes. Something was going on. I stared at the interviewer as he looked up from his phone, his eyebrows scrunched together. Somehow I managed to keep the smile. It had to look fake. I resisted the urge to ask what was going on.

People seemed to be holding their breath. Waiting.

"What do you have to say about the article that just dropped?"

My stomach sank even though I had no idea what was going on. "What article?"

"This one." He thrust the phone into my face. "The one that proves VIGIL and its superheroes are real and part of a government cover-up."

The breath was knocked from my lungs as I stared at the small screen.

It was real.

They knew.

The world knew.

Chaos erupted as if his words broke through the ice. Shouting. A surge of people rushing forward.

"Do you have a comment!"

"Tell us what's going on!"

"Is the article a fake?"

Comments assaulted me. A guard came up, shoving me back

towards the theater as more security swarmed the barricades. The celebrities on the red carpet were herded through the gates, but it was all a blur.

Our secret…was out?

I looked around, trying to find the VIGIL team, but the crowd was too thick and people were already staring at me. Famous people I'd seen in a whole bunch of movies, so that was weird.

My phone vibrated in my pocket, but I ignored that too.

"What's going on?"

"Is what they're saying true?"

"I'm literally so confused."

Whispers and people starting to get angry.

Then I saw Agent Liam climb on top of the concession stand counter. "If I could have everyone's attention! We will get this sorted out as soon as possible, but for now, I'd like for you to quietly make your way into the theater and take your seats. I can assure you that you aren't in any danger. The movie premiere will continue as scheduled. So sit back, relax, and enjoy!" How could he sound so calm?

The crowd started to move like a slow, rippling creek, but I stayed back, pulse racing.

Soon it was only the VIGIL agents—and the Safeguarders—left in the lobby.

"What just happened?" Commander Vigil put her hands on her hips.

"Ver's already on it, and we're working on damage control," Agent Liam said. "For now, I need all of you to go in there and pretend like nothing happened."

"But—" I said.

"I know," Agent Liam said. "We're working on it. Everything will be okay."

I nodded, glancing at Ironfall who was by my side again.

Did my father have something to do with this? I thought I saw him…was it only a distraction?

"All right, let's head inside," Commander Vigil said, taking up leadership.

BESTVIGILMEMES.BLOGGINGLIFE.COM
FEATURING THE BEST VIGIL & ANTE STUDIOS POSTS
(DON'T @ ME)
– UNAVERAGEVIGILFAN2002

alwayswatching:
RHETT AND LONDON THOUGH

———

Level7andup:
London Peters's interview with Jamie Peters was so wholesome I can't even
USERNAME: Yesssssss she's literally all of us

———

Incorrectvigil:
ARE WE NOT GOING TO TALK ABOUT HOW LONDON AND RHETT WICKFORD JUST SNUCK OFF
USERNAME: You can't tell me they aren't dating
USERNAME: My new otp
USERNAME: Someone write a fanfic asap

———

cheeseluver47:
  DID YOU SEE THE ARTICLE?????

———

USERNAME:
  UMM GUYS

———

IAMSTARFALL:
  IT'S REAL?!?!?!?!?!?!

———

Degreesurgeeeeeeeeeee:
  ARE YOU FREAKING KIDDING ME SUPERHEROES ARE
  REAL????????

———

Iwasherefirst:
  BRB APPLYING TO BE A VIGIL AGENT

———

thatonefanficwriter:
  THEY WERE REALLY GATEKEEPING THE FACT THAT MY
  COMFORT CHARACTERS ARE REAL?!?!?!

Federal Bureau Of Investigation
Transcript Of The Interview Proceedings With

IRONFALL
SOME NAMES AND LOCATIONS REDACTED FOR SECURITY
INTERVIEW CONDUCTED ON JULY 23
LOCATION OF INTERVIEW: **[REDACTED]**
CASE #: **[REDACTED]**

PROPERTY OF THE FBI

———

SPECIAL AGENT LAUDE: Did you see James Collins?
IRONFALL: No.
SPECIAL AGENT LAUDE: So Agent Collins was the only one?
IRONFALL: That's correct.
SPECIAL AGENT LAUDE: What happened next?
IRONFALL: I saw her pushing through the crowd. I followed her.
SPECIAL AGENT LAUDE: Why?
IRONFALL: Well, for starters talent was supposed to be on the red carpet. I followed her to see what was going on.
SPECIAL AGENT LAUDE: What happened?
IRONFALL: She told me what she saw.

SPECIAL AGENT LAUDE: Did you believe her?

IRONFALL: Yes.

SPECIAL AGENT LAUDE: Yet no one else saw her father.

IRONFALL: If she said she saw him, she did.

SPECIAL AGENT LAUDE: And then the article dropped.

IRONFALL: Yes.

SPECIAL AGENT LAUDE: And now you're part of this mess.

IRONFALL: Are you saying I did this?

SPECIAL AGENT LAUDE: You're the one who said it.

CHAPTER 13

IRONFALL

JULY 18 – *6:45 P.M. PDT*

"Thank you so much for joining us for the world premiere of *Project Safeguard 3*," Agent Liam said from the front of the room. I'd seen him take on the role of Xavier Jay before, but I was impressed with how easily he did it in front of a large group of people, especially now that the truth may be out. "I'm Xavier Jay, the director of *Project Safeguard 3*."

"Aren't you really Agent Liam Blake?" someone shouted.

Murmurs rippled across the room.

Agent Liam only cleared his throat. "Welcome to the premiere of *Project Safeguard 3*."

"Tell us what's going on!"

Agent Liam's expression didn't change, and without missing a beat, he continued. "On behalf of the cast and crew, let me just say we are thrilled to have you here. You know what? Can I get the cast to come up here real quick?"

There was no applause.

I glanced over at Rosemary a few seats away. Her eyes were wide, hands gripping the seat rests.

The Safeguarders made their way up to the front. I'd met a few of them on the red carpet, but they weren't excited to see me. Guess I deserved that after battling, well—all of them. Of course, their jabs were so subtle that no one from the outside would be able to tell. They had an image to uphold after all. Not that I blamed them. I would have done the same thing. I'd hated them a few months ago anyway, though I had to admit, the movies were fun to watch.

"Do you really have superpowers?" Another rude shout.

Agent Liam raised the mic once more.

That was when everything went black.

Nothing, not even dim lights to prevent people from tumbling down the stairs. Pitch black.

This was planned. Cause chaos, get everyone on edge, then attack. It was something I would do, which meant it had ANTE's fingerprints all over it. I stood, reaching for the daggers I'd smuggled in. I know, I know, I wasn't supposed to have them. But they did come in handy, and I'd like that on the record.

Did Rosemary sense the same thing as me? She probably did. She was good like that.

The room was quiet. Still, like everyone was holding their breaths, thinking, "Is this normal?" No, in fact, it wasn't normal.

A loud thunk resounded, breaking the silence. Then another. Then another.

A snake-like hiss.

The Sedator. He was here.

I slipped out my daggers, readying myself.

Rosemary. I glanced over to where I knew she sat, but it was too dark to see her.

Seven blue clocks floated in the front of the room. That meant the Safeguarders were down for the count. Illuman wasn't even awake to make some light.

Suspicious whispers now rippled across the room.

"What's going on?"

"What are those things?"

"Is this a supervillain?"

"Is VIGIL actually real?"

"Is this an elaborate plot to…I don't even know?"

"Is this part of the movie?"

"I'm kinda freaked out." More whispers and rumors. Was it all real? What was going on? Could it be another publicity stunt?

No, an attack.

Pools of light formed from people's phones as they realized this was not, in fact, part of the movie magic.

I gripped my daggers tighter. Light. I knelt below the seats and got out my own phone, turning on the flashlight. Then, I rose, flashing the light around.

The whispers died down, and my light landed on the Sedator, who stepped back. His identity still wrapped in white cloth that almost seemed to mummify him. But his bare hands stuck out. Bare so he could sedate the audience. Heh. Sedate. I'd been spending too much time around Sam.

A gasp, then clapping. Applause rippled across the audience who was still awake. Cheering for who they thought was the new villain making a surprise entrance at a premiere.

The Sedator looked straight at me, but I doubted he could tell who I was from the distance, especially with my phone light pointed his way. He stalked toward the first row, thrusting his hand against a man's throat. Before the victim made any choking noises, his body collapsed on the ground.

People stumbled away from the collapsed man.

Once again, the room fell silent.

The Sedator drew back an arm and punched the man next to him, letting out a low growl. He collapsed too, a clock floating above his head.

The theater was still silent.

Where was security? Not that they would do much good against a supervillain.

"Flashlights on!" I shouted. The suspension of disbelief vanished from the room. Screams. A rush of skirts. Panic set in.

Now they really knew this was real. Within a few moments, dots of light filled the theater, sending sharp shadows spiraling in all directions.

The main lights flickered on.

I glanced at Rosemary. She stood, fists balled at her sides.

Adrenaline pumped through my veins, and I shoved my phone in my pocket, leaping across the top of the seats down toward the bottom.

People fell left and right as the Sedator made his way through the crowd.

Screaming. Crying.

Still no security. It was as if the world was oblivious to what was happening behind the theater doors.

People rushing from the theater, stumbling up the stairs to the back, climbing over seats.

Pure chaos.

But the Sedator continued, silently (and violently) making people unconscious.

I rushed onward, diving for him. He sidestepped and I stumbled into the chairs. Whipping around, I sliced a dagger toward him. He batted my hand away.

Then Rosemary was there, swinging a fist at his head. The Sedator reeled away from her and I kicked him back before batting away his hand and moving forward into offense.

"Everyone get out!" Rosemary shouted, taking her eyes off the quickly recovering supervillain for only a moment. He grabbed Rosemary's bare arms. She collapsed.

"No!" I rushed him, trying to kick his legs out from under him. He was fast, too fast. He snagged me, yanking me with him, twisting us over rows of seats, trampling me until he was on top.

A single touch.

Dazed.

There was…darkness coming…what was going on? Was Rosemary okay?

WE WILL BE HEROES

Someone grunted, a blurry form grabbing the Sedator from behind.

Warmth radiated. The fuzziness began to fade. Slowly, too slow.

Lights. What was happening?

The Sedator jerked back as his attacker tightened his grip around the shrouded man's neck. I couldn't see his face, but I could tell he was strong yet an inexperienced fighter. Probably another Hollywood heartthrob.

He wouldn't last long, and I had to get Rosemary out of the way. I rolled over. Rosemary. She was only a few feet away in the aisle. I crawled for her.

Staying low, I dragged her out of the aisle, a few rows back, onto the floor between the seats. She looked so peaceful, so free from the stress her eyebrows always carried, but the ominous clock still loomed over her.

More chokes and thumps, and then silence.

The Sedator won. Probably.

Movement a few rows over.

I ducked, gaze fixed between the seats. I could see the Sedator; he seemed to be looking for something. It was near where I'd found Rosemary.

My teeth clenched.

Was he trying to get her, just like he had back at the congressman's basement?

I had to get her out of here.

Everyone else in the theater was asleep.

I laid a hand on the side of her face, warmth traveling up my arm and into her.

"Iron—" I covered her mouth, placing a single finger to my lips.

"Shhh," I whispered, leaning closer.

I moved my hand away.

"The Sedator," she whispered. It seemed so loud in the eerie silence of the theater. Had our enemy heard?

I only nodded. "He's here. I think he's looking for you."

"Has he hurt anyone?"

I shook my head. "I hope not."

Her eyes widened as she slowly started to sit up. I pressed a hand against her shoulder to keep her down. "This is a public attack." I looked over the rows.

The Sedator paced through the rows.

"I know," I whispered, placing a knife in her hands. "He's looking for you. We have to get out of here."

Rosemary stared at the knife. "How did you get this in here?"

I smirked. "Oh, you know me."

Fabric rustled. The Sedator was closer.

Rosemary gathered up her skirt and we crawled between the seats to the right aisle. She stopped at the end, peering around, then turned and nodded. We crawled through the aisle, stopping every few moments.

When we reached the front of the theater, I slipped behind the front row of seats, catching a glimpse of the Sedator with his back turned. I whipped around, making sure the seats hid me once more. Rosemary's golden-brown eyes met mine knowingly before I turned my attention to the Safeguarders slumped in front of us, just out of reach. I'd be in the open if I dared move to wake them.

Holographic clocks hovered over each one, counting down. Thirty more minutes. We needed a distraction to either wake them up or get out. But waking them up would strengthen our chances of winning. Of keeping Rosemary safe.

I stole a peek back around the aisle.

The Sedator turned. Looked like he was going to come down the aisle. Maybe he thought Rosemary left the theater room and entered the lobby.

I pointed to the other side. Rosemary nodded, and we scrambled as quietly as possible to the other aisle. We hid, each taking a row of seats. I peeked again, and the Sedator walked out.

Breath released from my lungs.

"He's gone," I breathed.

"Wake them up," Rosemary said. "Then we go after him."

"You need to stay safe. He's after you," I said.

"The safest place is with like six superheroes." She looked away. "...And one reformed supervillain." *Reformed.* Did she... did she trust me?

"Yeah." I looked away, then rose to my feet, jogging over to where the Safeguarders and VIGIL agents slept "peacefully." Warmth rippled through my hands and into each one of them. I stepped back as they stirred.

Something told me the beautifully attired Safeguarders would not appreciate waking up to my face.

Agent Liam sat up first. "What happened?" He looked around, sighing as he saw his team waking up.

"The Sedator, sir, he's here." Rosemary's eyes were wide. "Ironfall thinks he's after me."

Commander Vigil leapt to her feet, brushing off her green skirt. "Who's the Sedator?" Her shrewd eyes scanned her surroundings, landing on me.

All eyes were now on me. I gulped, unusually nervous. Not that anyone enjoys being in the presence of those who were once sworn enemies. "ANTE's newest pet villain. He can put you to sleep with just a touch." I raised a hand, touching my other bare hand to demonstrate.

"Well that's embarrassing for us," Illuman chimed in as the rest of the superheroes and agents rose to their feet. "Wait a second...what's Ironfall doing here?"

"Long story short, he works for us now," Manda said. "Lucky us."

Commander Vigil narrowed her eyes. Still ticked I stabbed her once, no doubt. Not that I blamed her. I'd hold a grudge if someone stabbed me too.

"He's fine now," Ver said. "I'd say he's reformed." Rosemary remained silent.

Agent Liam looked around at the quiet theater. "Where is the Sedator now?"

"Probably looking for me." Rosemary stood straighter now, as if she was ready to take on the world.

Degree Surge scrunched her eyebrows in concern. "Why does he want you?"

"It's a whole thing." Ver brushed a curl out of her face. "We'll fill you in later."

"Where is everyone else?" Agent Liam stepped back, once more surveying the area. "Is anyone hurt?"

I shook my head. "Asleep or hiding. Not sure of injuries." Rosemary and her Safeguarders were kind of my top priority at the moment.

"You sure he didn't cause this?" Commander Vigil stared at me.

"This isn't him." Rosemary shook her head. "Whether he's changed or not, I think he's on our side."

Commander Vigil looked like she was ready to take charge and kick me out, but Agent Liam raised a hand. "Enough. Canvass the area. If you find anyone unconscious, leave them. The less people see, the better. Find the Sedator and take him alive if you can. He has information on ANTE that we need."

I nodded. Time to prove I was really on their side. Again.

"Degree Surge, up the heat, make him sweat," Agent Liam said. "Cloaker, blend in. See if you can surprise him. Ver, get into the security system, get what you can. Everyone else, split into teams. Rosemary, stay close to Ironfall. If all else fails he can combat the Sedator's sleep touch. I'll call in reinforcements."

"Did I miss a few chapters? Why can Ironfall combat his touch?" Degree Surge asked.

"His real power is healing," Ver said. "Yeah, I was shocked too." I didn't know how to feel about my secret now being broadcast to the Safeguarders.

"Hmm, ironic power," Illuman chuckled. "But handy."

"Stay on topic," Agent Liam directed. "I know you aren't

thrilled about Ironfall, but he's here to help, and we're here to protect Agent Rosemary Collins from our current threat."

"I'll protect her, sir," I assured him. Rosemary still gripped my knife.

Before anyone could do anything, Manda had a blade out and was sawing off the train of her skirt. Smart move, but it did make me cringe a bit. What can I say? I knew exactly how much work went into the gown.

Degree Surge looked shocked. "You know that's designer, right?"

Manda didn't even look up from her work. "I'd rather be alive in a ruined outfit than dead in a designer dress." She tore off the last piece, with a loud rip, tossing the fabric into a heap.

"Words to live by," Illuman said.

"It's smart." I shrugged. "I'll make a duplicate. No one will ever know."

"Except everyone knows everything now." Rosemary's voice was almost inaudible.

"Is that how you faked your power? With wizard costuming skills?" Illuman grinned. "Respect, dude." He held a hand out to shake mine. I stared at it a moment. Did he really want to shake my hand after everything I'd done?

I took it. "Yes." He let go and turned away as if the gesture was nothing.

"Hey, give me your knife when you're done, Manda," Ver said.

Rosemary too started cutting off the skirt of her dress with the blade I gave her. Soon, there was a heap of fabric on the floor from all the ladies and a lot of sewing work I wasn't expecting to do. But life over fashion.

Everyone moved out on their orders as Rosemary and I made our way to the door. I peeked around the side into the hallways. They was deserted, no one to be seen anywhere. I motioned for her to follow. Keeping low, slowly moving out to the left.

"We can do this," I heard Rosemary whisper under her

breath. I said nothing, pretending I hadn't heard. A corner came up, and as if in sync, we pressed against the wall.

Nothing around the corner.

"Do you think my father's here?" Rosemary whispered.

I looked back at her. "I don't know."

"He was outside, I know he was." Fear shone in her eyes. I wanted to kiss her until it was gone.

Focus.

"We'll get him," I assured her. "The coast is clear."

Up ahead was a sign for restrooms. I pointed.

"You take the men's, I'll take the women's."

I shook my head. "We don't split up."

"Right," she said, unblinking. "Together." *Side by side.* Knife in hand, I kicked open the women's bathroom door. Harsh breathing. A shuffling back of feet.

"We're not here to hurt you. Come out with your hands up," I said, the words foreign on my lips.

A moment later, a stall unlocked, out tumbling a tear-streaked woman. Wait a second, wasn't this the star of last year's Oscar-winning film?

"What's going on?" she said in a shaky voice. She was against the wall, sliding to the floor as if her legs couldn't take anything. "He was punching people and they were unconscious and floating clocks...Is it all real?"

"Yes. We were attacked, but we're going to be fine. Stay here. Someone will come get you," Rosemary said. "Don't come out until it's safe."

"I thought it was all some huge publicity stunt...that maybe superheroes and supervillains aren't actually real—"

"But they are." Rosemary nodded, placing a hand on her shoulder. "I know. It's going to be okay."

I glanced back at the door. "We'd better move. He's not here."

Rosemary nodded again, rising from the marble floor. "Hide. Help is on the way."

The traumatized movie star nodded vigorously as more tears

streaked down her cheeks. I'd once caused this kind of fear in people. Worse, even. I turned away, unable to look at the mirror she held to my dark soul. It was a harsh contrast to Rosemary's compassion.

I took a deep breath, a spark igniting in my chest, small and foreign, but it was enough. We had to save these people. When I stole another glance at Rosemary—still beautiful in her torn dress and half-ruined makeup—it only grew.

Without another word, we snuck out of the bathroom.

My phone vibrated in my pocket. I took it out. Miraculously it had survived the fight with the Sedator.

Agent Ver: He's back in the theater. Hostages.

I stuffed it away. "He's in the theater. There are hostages."

Rosemary's brows knitted. "We have to get there."

We ran. My dress shoes clacked along the marble floor, but Rosemary made no sound as she'd long since deserted her heels. We made it back to the theater just as the Safeguarders arrived.

"Agent Liam is outside coordinating with SWAT, so here's the plan. Cloaker, pretend to be a hiding victim," Commander Vigil said. "You go in first and protect civilians as a hostage. Illuman, Ironfall, you're inside with me. We bring him down three against one. The rest of you, block the exits. We can't let him get out."

"If he's threatening innocent people, let him have me." Rosemary stepped forward. "Or at least let him think you'll give me to him."

I wanted to protest, but Commander Vigil nodded and gave her command before I could say a word. "Okay, everyone in position."

Cloaker reached into his pocket, then, right before my eyes, he shifted into a completely different person. Hair morphed. Skin morphed. Face shape warped. Height warped.

"See you on the other side," he said, sending a fake salute Illuman's way. He went inside.

I turned to Rosemary. "You're not going anywhere near the Sedator. Don't try anything heroic."

"Commander Vigil gave her orders," Rosemary said.

I breathed a sigh of relief. She'd be out here away from immediate danger.

Turn her over and get out alive, my father's voice taunted. I balled my fists, shoving the thought out of my mind.

So we waited. And waited.

But waiting was good. Let the man sweat in the heat Degree Surge was creating. Let him think he was winning.

And then crush him.

"All right," Commander Vigil said. "Let's go."

The three of us rushed in, Rosemary staying put.

"Freeze, Sedator!"

The hooded white figure turned, but said nothing.

"Nothing to say for your actions?" I glanced over at the seats. Still people asleep. Still clocks.

Cloaker (in disguise) sat at the top, hands above his head. Guess he didn't have to do much since everyone else was unconscious. Why hadn't the Sedator put him to sleep too?

"Bring me Rosemary Collins, or they die." The garbled voice boomed through the theater. Even I had chills running down my spine.

"He does speak." Illuman laughed as if this wasn't a serious situation. I could get behind that. "But we can't do that."

"You have five minutes to decide." The Sedator's tone was threatening, made harsher by some voice modulator built into his suit. Handy if one wanted to conceal his identity.

Commander Vigil launched her powerful fist, but the Sedator side-stepped, swiping toward her stomach. She crumpled, no clock floating above her.

I rushed toward the Sedator, slicing my knife at him. Hit, dodge, hit, dodge. I kept his hands away from me. "You'll never get her," I hissed, sweat dripping down my brow.

The Sedator said nothing. My arm shook under his weight.

"What's going on?"

"Wait, is Ironfall real too?"

"I must have fallen asleep?"

People were starting to wake up. Whispers swept through the room. Grunts and groans. The Sedator looked away for just a second.

I sank my knife into his gut.

He grunted when I yanked the knife out, but as I pulled back, hoping he'd crumple, he jumped away, running, disappearing into a small section in the nearby wall. Into the duct? A trail of blood was left behind on the already red carpet.

Blood dripped off the tip of my knife.

"He's in the vents!" I didn't follow though, instead I ran to Commander Vigil to heal her from the Sedator's wound. He hadn't put her to sleep. Why?

"Thanks," she said, but it didn't sound like she loved it.

Rosemary and the others guarding the exits rushed in.

"He's in the vents!" I called again. "Tell SWAT to keep an eye on those exit points."

Manda nodded, running out of the room.

I turned around, surveying the scene that the public had just witnessed. VIGIL was out of the shadows. Everyone knew it was real now. They knew about us. They knew about me. *That I was a villain.*

SPECIAL AGENT LAUDE: The Sedator magically got away after such a public attack?

AGENT LIAM BLAKE: Not magically, but yes, he did. We're still investigating.

SPECIAL AGENT LAUDE: Did he have someone on the inside?

AGENT LIAM BLAKE: If you're referring to Ironfall, he's clean. Commander Vigil witnessed the whole thing. He even saved her life.

SPECIAL AGENT LAUDE: He does have a history.

AGENT LIAM BLAKE: He does.

SPECIAL AGENT LAUDE: Were you worried about state secrets

leaking to the public? There were multiple witnesses. High profile witnesses.

AGENT LIAM BLAKE: Our existence had already been leaked, so my top priority was keeping them safe, not in the dark.

SPECIAL AGENT LAUDE: So you would put national security risks below people's lives?

AGENT LIAM BLAKE: Without question. Is that a problem?

SPECIAL AGENT LAUDE: Who do you think was responsible for the leak? Someone on your team?

AGENT LIAM BLAKE: Why do I get the feeling you have a personal score to settle? Seems pretty messy for an investigation.

SPECIAL AGENT LAUDE: It was Ironfall, wasn't it?

AGENT LIAM BLAKE: It was ANTE.

CHAPTER

14

DREAM SEQUENCE – ROSEMARY COLLINS

A ROOM FILLED *with beds flitted in and out of focus. Glowing liquid squelching through bags and tubes. Flickering lights.*

Dizzy. Everything was turning, turning, turning into nothing but a blurry circle of light and glow.

The image stabilized onto a domed ceiling, at least it appeared to be a ceiling. A dome of concrete, fitted with lights and shapes. Things were going fuzzy again. White and black and colorful swirls.

The image moved, shifted, like a camera moving. The bed came closer, along with a table and...an IV bag? Glowing green sludge. Tubes. Wires.

Blurriness.

Looking down, hands worked with an IV. Arms wrapped in white fabric, wound round and round about a large arm. Large hands handled the IV bag with such care, pushing and massaging the green liquid.

The dexterous fingers reached up, hanging the glowing bag on a metal stand.

"It's done." A dark voice, distorted, unrecognizable.

Man? Woman? Who could tell?

Vision was going dark again, then white, then bright green, then a psychedelic mishmash of all three in a kaleidoscopic dance.

"Ready for—" Another indistinguishable voice, someone else, but no one identifiable.

"...can't show our hand before..."

Vision became clearer but the voices remained indistinguishable.

"They have to pay for what they've done." Raised voices. Anger.

"Don't be irrational."

"You work for me," said the first voice. "And what I say goes."

"Maybe I should be in charge," said the second. This one sounded closer.

"You're nothing more than muscle..." Now everything went wobbly once more. Voices came and went.

"...premiere on July 18."

"...go in through the vents..."

"...witnesses..."

"...attack goes forward..."

"...don't question my leadership..."

"They'll never see—"

Federal Bureau Of Investigation
Transcript Of The Interview Proceedings With

AGENT ROSEMARY COLLINS
SOME NAMES AND LOCATIONS REDACTED FOR SECURITY
INTERVIEW CONDUCTED ON JULY 23
LOCATION OF INTERVIEW: **[REDACTED]**
CASE #: **[REDACTED]**

PROPERTY OF THE FBI

———

AGENT ROSEMARY COLLINS: I told you before, I didn't see my father inside the theater. Only the outside.
SPECIAL AGENT LAUDE: Why didn't you report to your superiors as soon as you saw him?
AGENT ROSEMARY COLLINS: I asked Sam to look into it. Listen, it was the middle of a blockbuster movie premiere. What was I supposed to do? Interrupt Liam Blake on the red carpet and broadcast that I'd seen a wanted fugitive, leader of an organization that's supposed to be fictional? I wasn't even sure what I'd seen.
SPECIAL AGENT LAUDE: But then there was a leak and ANTE attacked.

AGENT ROSEMARY COLLINS: They did.

SPECIAL AGENT LAUDE: Do you think reporting it would have stopped it?

AGENT ROSEMARY COLLINS: I—I don't know.

SPECIAL AGENT LAUDE: You realize how bad this is, don't you?

AGENT ROSEMARY COLLINS: The nation's biggest secret was leaked. Yes, I'm aware.

CHAPTER 15

ROSEMARY

JULY 18 – *7:53 P.M. PDT*

Sirens pierced through the walls of the movie theater. FBI were everywhere. There were celebrities in ballgowns wrapped in foil blankets, sitting on the floor with blank faces as they waited to be transported to the hospital. Some were crying, others rocking. It was a disaster.

Ironfall rushed up to one woman, touched her, then moved on to the next person. I noticed how they shrank away from him.

Right, because they knew who he was now.

Did they not see how he saved them?

No, they only saw his persona from *Project Safeguard*, and not even in the new movie.

Agent Liam stood in the front of the room, speaking with agents wearing FBI bomber jackets.

I was frozen, trying to process what had just happened.

Ironfall stepped over to me. "That's everyone. I made sure they're all healthy from the Sedator."

I nodded. "Good." It was all I could manage.

"You okay?" he asked.

I didn't tell him my limbs ached and I wanted to curl into a ball, but his arm still brushed against me and a warmth passed through my bones. His healing power washed over me. Suddenly my mind was the only thing that ached.

"Thanks." I wasn't sure what else to say. "Um...you know..." I started, gulping.

Three FBI agents came up behind us.

"Ironfall," one said in a stern voice.

Oh no. A sinking feeling lodged itself in my stomach.

"We're placing you under arrest."

Ironfall stepped back, lips quirking up into a smile. "Figured as much."

"He's been helping us. VIGIL, I mean." Why was I defending him? Finally he would get what he deserved. Why did my heart sink at the thought of it?

"The FBI is in charge now," said another agent.

"It's okay." Ironfall met my gaze. "I can handle it." Was he planning an escape? That wouldn't do anything to make him look innocent. They'd probably blame him for the entire attack if that happened.

The FBI agent stiffened, producing a set of handcuffs.

"That's not enough." Manda came up behind them. "But I guess some people have to learn."

Ironfall laughed. How could he be laughing on the brink of arrest? The FBI agents looked dumbfounded, then looked at each other before pulling out another pair of shiny silver handcuffs.

"Turn around with your hands on your head," they told Ironfall.

He shrugged, then did as he was told.

The agents handcuffed him twice as stars danced at the edge of my vision, my heart plummeting to my stomach. How would everything ever be the same again? It wouldn't.

"You have the right to remain silent."

My legs went weak.

"Everything you say can and will be used against you in the court of law."

I bit back tears.

No.

Ironfall left with them while I stood frozen, unable to say anything.

"Would someone like to explain what the heck is going on?" A voice came up behind the VIGIL agents. Wait, I knew that voice.

Sylvester Whitlock.

We turned.

"Why was I not told that my movie was nonfiction?" he asked, adjusting his large glasses.

Agent Liam nodded. "You didn't have the clearance level."

"I'm Sylvester Whitlock. I win awards. That should be enough," said the director who deserved a throat punch. Manda, who would probably never again don her Jana Anthony persona, also shot him a dark look.

I jumped when my phone rang. Sam.

"Oh my gosh, what is happening?" Sam said. "Everyone knows! My meme page is blowing up."

"They know, Sam." I tried to keep my voice from quivering. "And the Sedator…" I trailed off. "The FBI took Ironfall, and…" I bit back a sob.

Now was not the time to lose it.

"The Sedator was there? I knew there was some kind of attack," he said.

"Yes. But they arrested Ironfall."

"That's not fair! He's changed!"

"I don't know, Sam, but he just went with them." And I didn't know how I felt about it.

"Wait, Mia is calling me," Sam said. "Probably to ask if I knew VIGIL was real, so yeah."

"Don't tell her anything," I said. Yes, change the subject, please.

"But I really like her," Sam whined.

"Sam." If he only took one thing seriously, let it be this.

"Ugh, fine, my lips are sealed." Good. He wasn't the best at keeping secrets, but hopefully he grasped the severity of the situation.

"We can't let this get any worse."

"Excuse me, I am about to push away the love of my life."

Now was not the time for his shenanigans. "You've known her for two days."

"Future love of my life. Fine."

"Sam!" I snapped, ready to hang up on him.

"I won't tell her anything classified."

The knot in my stomach didn't release because I didn't know what would happen from here.

JULY 18 – 10:59 P.M. PDT

"...we are still waiting for an official statement, but sources say many of Hollywood's biggest stars have been taken to the hospital after the attack. Authorities are labeling it as a terrorist attack, but they have not released any suspects. No one is in custody at this time. The attack took place soon after the start of the premiere for hit blockbuster *Project Safeguard 3* from VIGIL & ANTE Studios. The film studio is known for its elaborate publicity stunts including live action staged fights across New York City. Authorities have confirmed that this was a legitimate attack..." said the news reporter on the screen.

I couldn't take my eyes off the TV as the story continued. "This comes just after user 'VIGILISREAL' leaked documents addressing the president's order for a secret superhero division following the discovery of people with powers."

I bit my lip, glancing around at the Safeguarders piled into our hotel room.

It wasn't safe to go back to the VIGIL base right now.

Agent Liam was in the next room over, meeting with the FBI.

We had the best superheroes with us, and still, we failed.

"'Making an entire saga of movies to make everyone think superpowers don't exist? That shows they have even more to hide,' says one social media user," the news anchor droned on.

Illuman stood, crossing his arms as he turned away from the TV. "There goes my acting career."

"That's what you're worried about?" Commander Vigil frowned.

Illuman shot her a glare. "Just trying to lighten the mood."

"Not sure if this helps, but there are some people who don't think this is legit," Ver said. "Though according to three viral social media polls, most people believe it, so that's not great."

My phone buzzed just then, not that it had stopped doing that. Seriously, random people from middle school group projects were texting me about this. I'd blocked everyone but Sam.

Sam: I'M ALMOST THERE DON'T WORRY

I looked up. "Sam's coming to help figure this out."

"Oh great," Manda said. "More drama. Just what we need."

"Sam," Cloaker mused. "Interesting fellow."

"Prepare yourself. He's a lot," Ver said.

"That's an understatement," Manda groaned.

"Yeah, yeah, I know you're talking about me." Sam stepped into the room. His jaw dropped. "Oh. My. Gosh." The poor boy was starstruck.

"So you're the famous Sam," Illuman said, motioning for Sam to sit down in an empty seat. I think Sam just went weak in the knees. Or his eyes were about to pop out of their sockets. Probably both. "I'm famous?" he said. "You know who I am?"

"Rosemary told us you texted." Manda rolled her eyes. "Don't let it go to your head."

"ILLUMAN KNOWS MY NAME!" Sam shouted, nearly dropping his laptop in the process. He scanned the room. "And Commander Vigil and *Degree Surge*. Cloaker, I already met you, but OH MY GOSH."

Commander Vigil rolled her eyes. Even though the movies weren't totally accurate to real life, I'd seen enough of her to know she wasn't having this.

"Hi, Sam," Degree Surge said.

He turned, stepping closer to the group. "Degree Surge, hi. I love you. I mean not that I love you love you but I love you and you're my favorite except Illuman is my most favorite and—" He waved awkwardly. "I love you all and you're amazing."

That was the exact moment it hit me. Sam Hunt's celebrity crush was Degree Surge.

I looked instinctively for Ironfall, but he wasn't there. A pang hit my stomach. The room felt empty without him, like the VIGIL team was incomplete. I could almost see the sliver of blue in his eye flash as he mouthed, "Blackmail." He'd never let Sam live this down.

But he was in jail, and the entire world knew VIGIL and its superheroes (and villains) were real. Nothing would ever be the same again.

"That was painful," Manda sighed.

Sam raised his chin as if shrugging off the awkwardness of his introduction. He'd never lacked confidence, that was for sure. "I know my reputation precedes me, but I'm Sam, the best hacker in the world and almost a VIGIL agent. Probably. I haven't actually asked Agent Liam about it, but now is the perfect time. Illuman, will you please be my supervising officer?"

"So...I'm not an active agent?" Illuman said, his hand starting to illuminate the darkened room. "Not to mention Agent Liam's meeting with the FBI about our fate."

"Your powers! Oh my gosh, your powers! This is not a drill!" Sam shrieked.

Illuman shook his hand, and the light went out.

"This is the coolest thing I've ever been a part of," Sam whisper shrieked. And now it was all about to burst into a fiery flame.

Just then Agent Liam came in with a man wearing a suit that seemed too small for his lean frame. He had bright blond hair that looked bleached nearly into oblivion. And the scowl on his face told me that whatever he was about to say would be bad news.

"VIGIL is under investigation," Agent Liam said.

"Which means you're shut down," said the blond agent.

"Yes, thank you for that clarification, Agent Laude," Agent Liam said. I could tell he was annoyed. His hand rested where a weapon should be.

"We'll need to talk to each of you individually, of course," said Agent Laude, ignoring Agent Liam's jab. "You still aren't allowed to go around using your powers in public." Why was he looking directly at Illuman as he said that?

"What about Ironfall?" I cut in. Why was I saying that? He saved our lives.

"Whatever arrangement VIGIL had with him doesn't exist as long as VIGIL doesn't exist." He shrugged. "He'll remain in our custody and will go to trial. But we need him to talk."

"Why?" Sam asked. "Didn't you read the VIGIL reports?"

"Forgive me, but I'm not sure how thorough they were," Agent Laude sniffed.

"Let me guess, his lips are sealed," Sam said. "And he'll only talk to someone in particular." Why was he looking at me and why did he have that stupid grin on his face?

"Yes, actually," said the FBI agent. "He will only talk to Agent Rosemary Collins." My heart panged at my name. Once again, it was a smart move on Ironfall's part though.

"I thought you shut us down." Manda raised an eyebrow. "Now you want us to work again?" She was playing him.

"We'll see." Agent Laude shrugged again. "We might not need her after all."

"Trust me, that man is stubborn. When he makes up his mind, nothing will change it." Ver smoothed a curl. "Last time he also refused to speak to anyone but her."

"And why is that?"

"Because—" Sam started, but clamped his mouth shut when Agent Liam gave him a stern look. "Because no one knows his reasons. Yes, that's definitely what I was going to say."

"Agent Collins, I'm going to need you to come with me." Agent Laude motioned me toward him. "And you're going to make him talk."

BESTVIGILMEMES.BLOGGINGLIFE.COM
FEATURING THE BEST VIGIL & ANTE STUDIOS POSTS
(DON'T @ ME)
– UNAVERAGEVIGILFAN2002

———

WEBSITE DOWN

JULY 19 – 12:26 A.M. PDT

"Hey, you're that girl from—"

The VIGIL movies. "I know," I said, staring at the floor of the prison. "Can I just see him, please?" My voice cracked.

"He's not allowed to—" said the guard.

Agent Laude stepped forward, gripping my arm. "She's with me. Guess this is a little bit above your pay grade." I tried to pull away, but his grip was firm. Who was the prisoner here, Ironfall or me?

The guard nodded. "Right, sir." He motioned us through the fenced doorway.

As Agent Laude dragged me through the concrete hallway, he spoke. "He says he won't talk unless it's to you, so your job is—"

"To question him. I know." I nodded. "Look, I think you're making a mistake. He could help us take down ANTE." I winced as his fingers choked my arm.

"There is no 'us' here. It's the FBI's case now. In case you forgot, VIGIL isn't a secret anymore. You blew your cover." Wow. So much for sympathy.

"ANTE blew our cover," I said, finally pulling free. I massaged my bruising arm.

"Well, there's nothing Ironfall can do out there that he can't do in here, where he belongs. You do know everything he did, right?" Agent Laude raised a single brow.

"All too well." I pressed my lips together. Why was I defending him? "What do you need to know?"

"How to beat ANTE. We know he has a relationship with them."

"Not anymore." I shook my head. "He's helping us fight them."

"You're here to ask him the questions, not make judgments."

And I hated it.

The rest of the walk was a blur of security checkpoints and constant jabs about how much we messed up, and how terrible Ironfall was. Did he miss the part about how Ironfall saved everyone at the premiere? Was that only a few hours ago? Gosh, I needed sleep.

"Here we are."

It was a gray door with one tiny, fenced window that

matched each door for as far as I could see. In a way, it reminded me of the corridors in the ANTE bunker where my parents had held me captive. Sterile lighting flickered overhead.

The guard shouted inside for Ironfall to get away from the door. I couldn't see inside, but a few moments later, the door opened and Agent Laude motioned me in. The walls felt like they were closing in around me as I shuffled into the cage, eyes on the ground. The door hissed shut behind me.

Look up, Rosemary. It's okay. I took a deep breath.

Bright orange scrubs did not look good on Ironfall, at all. I swallowed, eyes dragged down so as not to look at him any more than I had to.

This couldn't be happening.

"Hey," he said.

"Hi," I replied, because if I said anything else my calm facade would slip. Funny, I'd masked my true feelings and allegiance from him for months, but now another word and it would all come crashing down. It already felt like everything was disintegrating around me.

"I'm not talking with him here." Ironfall pointed at Agent Laude.

He was still here. My breath hitched, as I steeled my nerves and straightened. "Leave us, please."

Agent Laude lifted his chin, then said, "I'll be right outside."

I said nothing, not looking up at Ironfall until the door crashed shut once more, locking me in. I didn't feel afraid… just…I didn't even know. My chest was caving in and my muscles tensed.

Ironfall sat on the bed, if it could be called that, a chain linking him to the wall. Dark circles I never thought I'd see ringed around his eyes, making him look so much different than the Rhett Wickford of the movie premiere just a few hours before. The premiere where he saved me. Where he saved all of us.

"How are you holding up?" His voice was soft, calm, as if I was the one chained to the wall.

I only nodded. *Don't cry.*

"Forgive me, but I'm not convinced." No, he probably wasn't.

"You're the one in a cell. I should be asking you." I sucked in a fast breath of air. "Don't worry about me."

"Okay." He lowered his voice. "They want you to interrogate me."

Again, I nodded. "They want me to, but I'm not here for that. They shut us down. Everything's done."

"I figured as much," he said, pressing his lips into a thin line.

I stepped closer, everything threatening to spill out. "They said that's why they broke our agreement with you. We didn't…"

"I know."

I froze, meeting his eyes. "You believe me?" I'd done nothing to gain his trust. I hadn't even wanted to. I'd threatened him. Made him join us. Kept him as an outcast.

"Yes."

I blinked. "I didn't think…"

"I do."

It was an unspoken moment of understanding. I stepped closer, then took up the spot next to him on what was supposed to be a cot. There wasn't even a pillow for him to rest his head on. My fingers joined together, trying to calm my churning stomach.

"Thank you," I said.

He turned. His eyes were soft; I could hardly stand to look at them. "For what?"

"For saving everyone," I said. "You could have let the Sedator take me. You could have left the Safeguarders. You could have saved your own skin from being arrested." The reality of that hit home now. The news broke before the attack, which meant Ironfall had to know he was first on the FBI's hit list. The list of his crimes…they were so many. Of course, the FBI wouldn't see the… good…he'd done since then. That maybe…that he had changed.

"No thanks necessary," he said. "It's okay." He nodded, turning back to stare at the door and the back of the prison guard's head through that tiny, fenced window. "I deserve to be here." The weight of his words crushed my chest, burning inside my heart.

"Ironfall."

He stiffened.

"I never thought…I didn't believe…"

He said nothing.

I bit my lip. "You really have changed, is what I mean."

His eyes met mine. He remained silent, waiting.

"And I trust you," I breathed. The pressure released. I trusted Ironfall. He saved us. He saved me. He let himself be arrested. He was willing to face the consequences. "You have my back, and I have yours. Simple as that." And I believed it now.

He had changed.

"Not sure how I can have anyone's back from in here, but side by side?" His eyes, pleading, nothing like those cold brown and blue eyes I saw months ago. These were kind, filled with light, filled with hope, even inside of this cold cell. People could be redeemed.

The corners of my mouth tipped up. "Yeah." Breathless. "Ironfall." I felt free now. Light, as if I wasn't just attacked by terrorists, and the secret was out, and the man sitting next to me wasn't in prison.

"I think this is the part where I thank you," he said, still serious. "You're the one who showed me who I really was."

"But I lied to you. How can you—?"

"Stopping me saved me," he said. "You gave me a family… even though some of them are incredibly annoying." Sam, of course.

We both laughed as if on cue.

"Don't forget the times Manda beat you in training." I smirked. "Regretting your decision to join us?"

"If you tell anyone, I will kill you, but I don't think anything could make me regret it," he said, a soft glimmer of hope shining in his eyes.

"Thank you for the blackmail." I nudged him. It was cautious, but still there. The semblance of something new.

"Why does Sam rub off on everyone?" Ironfall rolled his eyes.

Suddenly, I grinned. "Speaking of blackmail, Sam 100% has a crush on Degree Surge. He met the Safeguarders in the hotel room we're holed up in."

"A crush you say?" Ironfall now shared my smile. "Yes, this bit of blackmail will do nicely."

"He's never going to live this down." I nodded.

"Nope." He paused, becoming serious again. "I guess all this is to say that I forgive you." Water filled the corners of his eyes, and that sent another pang through my chest.

"And I forgive you," I said. "I know you 'don't have friends,' but you think you can make an exception?"

"Just this once." He turned away, brushing a sleeve across his face. "And maybe for the rest of VIGIL as well, but they're on a probationary period." He laughed; it was light, not dark like I'd heard so many times before. He was alive, probably for the first time in his life.

"Right, of course," I chuckled. "But I'm a solid yes?"

"Always." His eyes met mine again and there was another strange look, unlike anything I'd ever seen there before. Something good. Something so free and alive.

Then he paused, lowering his voice to a whisper. "I know you said you didn't come to interrogate me, but there's one thing you do need to know."

"Okay," I said, eyes wide. What was it?

"I got him, the Sedator, with my knife." He leaned toward

my ear now. "The FBI has it, but the Sedator's blood is on it. They just don't know it's his."

"They'll probably run it—" I said just as quiet.

"But they don't know it's the Sedator's." He leaned closer, our noses inches apart. "And I need you to get it from them so VIGIL can run his DNA and figure out his real identity. Forgive me, but I don't exactly trust the FBI."

"I don't either." I glanced at the door.

"You think they're ANTE?"

"I don't know." I shook my head. "But they care more about optics than actually saving people, so they're not exactly with us."

He nodded. "I figured as much."

"Because they put you in jail?"

"No, that was very much thinking about the public." His shoulders sagged.

"You were helping," I said.

"Well, I doubt most people would think so. Can't blame them." He looked so defeated sitting there, staring holes into the ground of the cold jail cell.

I pressed my lips together. He was right. People wouldn't trust him.

But I did. I wanted to reach out to take his hand, but knew we were being watched, so I changed the subject instead.

"I haven't told anyone this yet, but both times the Sedator touched me, I had these weird dreams." The memory was still fuzzy.

He laughed, but it didn't reach his eyes. "Like…random things popping out of walls and stuff like that?"

I shook my head. "No, it was more normal, but everything is fuzzy, as if it was a memory I was desperately trying to hold on to. These voices, they were talking about ANTE, and these hands —my hands—they were doing something with an IV. Only they weren't my hands, they were someone else's. It was like I was in someone else's body or something. It's hard to describe."

"Were you a doctor?"

"I don't know." I rubbed my arm, trying to remember. "But the voices mentioned an attack on the premiere, which makes sense because it was during the attack I dreamed it. The dream was cut off when you woke me up with your healing power."

"So, the Sedator also gives people weird coma dreams," he chuckled. "Noted."

"I just remember two voices, and they were arguing. And they said something about coming through air vents. Escaping through them maybe?"

"Just like how the Sedator escaped." Ironfall nodded, eyebrows scrunching together like he was trying to figure something out. "But he hadn't gotten away yet."

"I've probably just seen too many movies where people sneak in and out of places through air ducts." I shrugged. But something still didn't sit right with me. The dream just wasn't normal.

Not that going unconscious with the touch of a finger was normal.

The door opened and the FBI agent strode in.

I stood.

"Nice chat," Ironfall said, narrowing his eyes.

"Thanks for giving me nothing relevant." I narrowed mine back. Was that amusement in his eyes?

"I thought you said you'd talk to her," Agent Laude spat.

"I did," Ironfall said. "But I didn't say I'd give her the details you were looking for."

The agent looked between us. "Something weird is going on here."

I put on my most innocent face. "Like what, agent?"

"Hmm," Agent Laude simply said.

Federal Bureau Of Investigation
Transcript Of The Interview Proceedings With

AGENT LIAM BLAKE, DIRECTOR OF VIGIL
SOME NAMES AND LOCATIONS REDACTED FOR SECURITY
INTERVIEW CONDUCTED ON JULY 23
LOCATION OF INTERVIEW: **[REDACTED]**
CASE #: **[REDACTED]**

PROPERTY OF THE FBI

———

SPECIAL AGENT LAUDE: You can confirm your entire team complied with our shutdown?

AGENT LIAM BLAKE: At the time you shut us down, yes.

SPECIAL AGENT LAUDE: Seems like you're trying very hard not to lie.

AGENT LIAM BLAKE: You gave the order, I passed it along.

SPECIAL AGENT LAUDE: You don't think the shutdown was a good idea?

AGENT LIAM BLAKE: Shutting down our superhero division won't get rid of a supervillain.

CHAPTER 16

IRONFALL

JULY 19 - TIME UNKNOWN

The cot, if it could even be considered one, was giving me a backache. If I had a few yards of fabric and a couple hours, I could do something to make it a little more comfortable. Maybe a few inches of memory foam as well. Yes, memory foam would be nice.

I turned, staring at the wall.

I didn't deserve an inch of fabric.

My actions had finally caught up to me.

They came in flashes, the memories. Starting with the first person I killed—I was only a child—all the way up to Rosemary's own mother. I'd suppressed them for so long and with each one, my insides burned. Time stilling before them.

Would Rosemary still have forgiven me if she knew just how much I'd done? I clenched my fists, suddenly too antsy to lay down and wallow. I sank to the floor doing push-ups, but the weight of my own body wasn't enough to banish the assaulting memories. One quick slice here. A clever ruse there. That was all it took to take a life.

Until there was nothing left of mine.

I was terrible.

A villain.

A *supervillain*.

I could have healed, but no, I'd killed. An assassin of my father's making. A failure destined for greatness who took a fall...a fall into good.

Why? Why me? Why couldn't I stop seeing my bloodstained hands?

138, 139, 140...

I rose faster, my arms burning, but I couldn't shake it away.

I deserved to be in here.

Would I ever be able to forgive myself? Was there a way to right my wrongs?

I didn't know, but I did know that I had to change. I was *going* to change.

Hours of void dragged on as my thoughts wandered.

Escape would be easy. Well, not easy, but I could do it. I already knew how to get past the door. I'd counted the number of guards on the way in, and they would be easy to take down. In a non-lethal way, for the record.

To pass the time, I continued planning an escape until dinner.

They brought food to me, or what they called food. It was beyond terrible, so I just picked at it, fiddling with the plate until it shifted on the tray. A small red slip of paper peeked out from beneath. I snatched it inconspicuously, turning my back to the door before I opened it. "The betrayer is now the betrayed. We have talons everywhere." A touch dramatic but I got the point.

Somehow ANTE had gotten this in here. They knew where I was.

And they had a vendetta against me too.

VIGIL needed me—Rosemary needed me—and this place wasn't exactly safe. I resumed my plans to escape. For real this time.

CHAPTER
17

ROSEMARY

JULY 19 – *5:45 A.M. PDT*

The apartment wasn't completely dark when we arrived. It was near dawn though, that time of day when the sky wasn't quite black. I yawned, but knew I wasn't even close to going to bed.

"I don't know about you, but I'm going to sleep for a few hours," Ver yawned into the void, heading off to her room. I watched her go before running into my own room to dial Sam's number.

"What the heck, Rosemary, who died?" Sam muttered.

"Are you alone right now?" I whispered, glancing at the door as if an FBI agent would bust through.

"Yeah. Why?" He sounded ready to kill me.

"I know, I'm tired too, but can you look into something for me?" I ran over the plan in my head once more. Get him to hack into the FBI, see what the status of the knife was, and go from there. Just like Ironfall asked.

"Is this an illegal something? I'm in."

Well, that was easy. Too easy. I narrowed my eyes, falling back on my bed. "What's the catch?"

"No catch! Honest!" Now he sounded more awake.

"Okay, whatever," I said. "Ironfall managed to stab the Sedator, and the FBI has his knife…"

"…which has the DNA on it," Sam finished. "That's genius. You want me to find the Sedator."

"Yes." I fidgeted. "The FBI doesn't know who they're dealing with."

"The OG trio working together again," he laughed. "Love it. Give me like five minutes. And time to grab an energy drink from the fridge." An energy drink didn't sound bad right now, even though it would spike my anxiety through the roof and make me sick all day. Was that better than potentially falling asleep? I wasn't so sure.

"Okay, I'm back," he said. "Now time to sneak into forensics. Virtually, of course."

"I'm too tired for a heist." I glanced at the clock and instantly regretted it.

"Good, because…" He paused. "You won't have to. Just give me a sec, which is where Ironfall would tease me that I've lost skills because I'm being too slow."

"Just keep working," I groaned.

"You're starting to sound like him," he said.

I was? "Just do it."

JULY 19 – 6:32 A.M. PDT

"I'm in!" Sam's voice blasted through the phone, startling me out of a daze that definitely would have ended in sleep.

I jerked to a sitting position. "You got it?"

"Almost. One sec, let me…" He trailed off. "Got it."

"What does it say? Who is the Sedator?" I rubbed the sleep from my eyes. This could be the first real breakthrough.

"The Sedator is…drumroll please…Dr. Callaghan Sutherland," Sam said. A name. We had a name. A spark of hope ignited. "He came up on a military database. It's a little obscure, but it looks like he had a private practice and also did work for the military. There isn't much of a digital trail here."

"But we know who he is. What does he look like?" All this time, and we finally had something.

Thank you, Ironfall. A small smile played at my lips. I never dreamed I'd be thanking him a few short months ago. In fact, had the thought crossed my mind back then, I'd have gone to a therapist. I probably should see a therapist anyway, but I digress.

"Just your average man who works out. Like a lot," Sam said. "A health nut who would knock this energy drink right out of my hands. Let me see if there's anything else the FBI has on here about the Sedator or the attack." Sam clacked at the keys. "Okay, there's a lot of reports and stuff. They're interviewing the premiere's attendees." He paused again. "Dang, there's last year's Oscar winner on here."

"Anything relevant?" I pushed. "Anything would be helpful."

"Wait, they're all reporting these dreams they had," Sam said. "Seems a little weird, but I'll download it and send it over to you."

"Just make sure no one knows we have this." My voice lowered instinctively. "We can't let Agent Laude shut this down."

"Come on, this is me we're talking about."

Federal Bureau Of Investigation
Movie Premiere Notes

Note to investigator: Conversation Pieced Together Through Interview

———

Location: Appears to be a small convenience store of some sort. One other person of an unknown identity (SHOPPER: young, adult male) is browsing the shelves while answering questions. The questions are allegedly being asked by the SEDATOR.

SEDATOR: Tell me about your time in the service.

SHOPPER: Marine for five years.

SEDATOR: But you were recently discharged.

SHOPPER: You could say that.

SEDATOR: Dishonorable?

[Pause]

SEDATOR: I'll take your silence as a yes. Manslaughter, right? You're avoiding prison too.

SHOPPER: No...

SEDATOR: Oh, I think so.

SHOPPER: [lowers voice] How did you find me? You some kind of bounty hunter?

SEDATOR: I'm here to offer you a job. Keep shopping.

SHOPPER: Not sure I'm in the market.

SEDATOR: You're running out of places to hide.

SHOPPER: Is that a threat?

SEDATOR: A friendly reminder. You need us, and we need your skills.

SHOPPER: What, are you with the mob or something?

SEDATOR: That's classified, but if we succeed, that dishonorable discharge will go away. Are you in?

———

Location: Office, no windows. Conversation between unknown middle-aged man (UNKNOWN) and who is assumed to be the SEDATOR.

UNKNOWN: Update me on the formula.

SEDATOR: The doctor says he's almost finished with animal trials. These things take time.

UNKNOWN: We don't have time.

SEDATOR: Patience. Jasper understood that.

UNKNOWN: Don't speak to me of what Jasper understood! You were nothing more than a foot soldier.

SEDATOR: A good one. I made it out. And I would like to do so again. Jasper was good at playing the long game.

UNKNOWN: And he lost. Maybe it's time to take a different approach.

SEDATOR: He lost, but look at the progress we've made. We only have two bases gone because of his patience in splintering our organization.

UNKNOWN: You're right.

SEDATOR: So, we're patient.

UNKNOWN: The serum already worked with you. I don't understand why we can't apply it to all our test subjects.

SEDATOR: The doctor wants to vary results, and adjusting the formula takes time.

UNKNOWN: [inaudible]

SEDATOR: Remember your place!

UNKNOWN: But I know my worth to you. You can't win without me.

JULY 19 – 7:41 A.M. PDT

"What are you doing?" Ver said.

I looked up from the documents strewn across my bed.

Oh no.

"Uhhh." I looked down. I didn't want to lie to her, but I also didn't want to get her in trouble. Yet what Sam and I had found was big.

"You're still on the case, aren't you?" she said, a gleam in her eye. She wanted to help.

I nodded. "Sam and I—"

"Have been working together," she said. "I know."

"How?" If Sam told her...

"Lucky guess," she laughed. "And I didn't think you could get into the FBI's database on your own."

"We found the Sedator's real identity," I said.

"You what?" She jumped on the bed like we were about to have a slumber party.

"Ironfall managed to nick him with his knife." I grinned with pride. "The FBI didn't know who exactly Ironfall stabbed."

"But he told you." She smiled back.

"And we found something else," I said. "The FBI interviewed everyone at the premiere. They all had these dreams."

"Dreams?" Her brows rose. "They had them too?"

I leaned closer. "You had dreams?"

"Yeah, but it felt different than a normal dream." She rubbed her forehead as if trying to remember.

"Mine was fuzzy, and I can't remember everything. It cut off when Ironfall woke me up," I offered.

"I was looking over blueprints in mine," Ver said. "I can't remember what they were of, but they were blueprints. The confusing thing is that the hands holding them weren't mine, but they looked like they were. They were a guy's hands. Definitely. It was strange, because wrapped around his arms was a white cloth, almost like strips of a bandage or something."

My stomach dropped. "Yes. That's what I saw too. Not the blueprints, but the weird bandage sleeves. A lot of the reports said something about that."

"We need to tell Agent Liam."

"He's going to be so mad." I bit my lip.

"Ehh, he's pretty mad at the FBI too." Ver smirked. "I think we'll be okay. And weird dreams...that's more of a VIGIL thing than an FBI thing. The weird stuff is our job."

I texted Sam to tell him we were going to tell Agent Liam.

JULY 19 – 7:48 A.M. PDT

The phone seemed to ring forever before a very groggy Agent Liam picked up. "Agent Liam."

"Hey, Liam," Ver said. "It's me and Rosemary."

"Is there a reason you called so early?"

"Yes," I said. "We have an identity on the Sedator."

"I thought I told you VIGIL was decommissioned," he snapped.

"Ironfall told me something, and I followed up." I cringed internally, but continued. "The FBI doesn't know they have his identity."

"There's more too, a side effect from the Sedator. The FBI took statements from everyone who attended the premiere, and they all had similar experiences. Dreams, that is," Ver said. "We think it could be important."

"Ironfall didn't trust the FBI with this information," I added.

"I wouldn't either." Agent Liam yawned like he was waking up. "They don't know who they're up against."

"Does that mean we're back on the case?" Ver smiled at me. "Because we kind of already are."

"Sam is rubbing off on both of you." I could almost hear Agent Liam shaking his head.

"Hey, I was always like this," Ver chided.

"I'll call a meeting." Agent Liam yawned again. "If we're

going to take down ANTE for good, we're making sure people we trust are on the case."

JULY 19 – 8:29 A.M. PDT

The VIGIL agents and Safeguarders were already gathered around the conference table in the LA base. The VIGIL logo glinted in the center of its glossy top, and I looked around the table at each of my heroes backlit by computer screens flashing picture after picture of the premiere.

Of our failure.

Of losing Ironfall.

"We could get into serious trouble for meddling in the FBI's case." Commander Vigil stood with her arms crossed.

Illuman raised a hand as he lounged his feet on the tabletop. "I'm in."

Sam shot to his feet. "You already know I'm in. Let's do this thing."

Agent Liam nodded, standing at the head. "We know things the FBI doesn't, and they're going up against a supervillain which is not something they're good at."

Manda leaned back in her chair. "That's an understatement." Though she was the hardest person in the room to read, I knew she was in too.

"We have one shot at taking ANTE down, and I'm not willing to allow the FBI to let them slink into the shadows for decades before they decide to enact one of their backup plans." Agent Liam rested his fists on the tabletop. "But seeing as we are technically shut down, is there anyone who wants out?" The only thing I could hear was the whir of machines. My heroes were all in.

"Rosemary? Want to explain the situation?"

"Oh, uh, sure," I said, palms sweating as I stood to my feet. "Have you read the reports on the takedown of Jasper Emmerling?"

"I read it just after it happened." Commander Vigil nodded. "I may not have been active at the time, but my security clearance keeps me up to date."

"I…uh…read Sam's summary," Illuman said.

"You read my summary?" Sam shrieked, falling back into his chair with a dramatic wheeze. "I can't believe it. Illuman has read my work!"

"Oh you would do that." Degree Surge rolled her eyes, addressing Illuman.

"You really want to tell me you read the whole thing?" Illuman said. "That thing was like a novel."

"Hey, reading is one of my favorite hobbies." Degree Surge shrugged.

"Me too!" Sam squeaked.

Ver glared at him. "It is not." He obviously just wanted to impress his celebrity crush.

"Back on topic, I believe everyone has enough context for now." Agent Liam nodded to me. "Rosemary, please continue."

"Right," I said. "Since the thing with Jasper Emmerling, we've been working to take down the rest of ANTE's web. That led us to Senator Norman Spencer, who we learned was an ANTE sleeper agent. And that's where we first encountered the Sedator."

"Also known as the bad guy from the movie premiere," Sam interrupted. "I came up with the name, by the way."

"Right." Agent Liam gave Sam a side-eye before continuing. "There are two ANTE bases left, and the Sedator is the best lead we have."

"He's very mysterious though. Very anonymous," Sam piped up again.

"Yes, thank you for the commentary, Sam." Agent Liam's jaw feathered.

"Ironfall got him with his knife, which the FBI has in custody," I said.

"But we broke in, and they'd already run the DNA," Sam interrupted again.

I groaned. "Yes. The FBI doesn't know the blood sample they have belongs to the Sedator because Ironfall refused to say who he stabbed. We're the only ones who know. The Sedator is a man named Dr. Callaghan Sutherland."

"I did more digging—because energy drinks—and get this!" Sam said. "He researched cell mutation. He could be the one who gave himself powers."

"That's possible," Agent Liam sighed. His patience was getting thin. "Get anything else, Sam? An address?"

Sam shook his head. "He went off grid three years ago. I got nothing else. Hate it when people don't have social media."

"You could look at records, you know," Ver said.

"Oh I did." Sam smirked. "Social media is just easier since most people overshare."

Ver tapped the table. "That's for sure."

"We also found something else," I said. "A side effect of the Sedator's powers. Everyone had dreams."

"Makes sense because he put you to sleep or whatever using his weird anesthesia thing. He controlled your dreams," Sam said.

"Everyone had similar dreams though," I said. "All first person. Did anyone else see these bandaged strips around a man's hands? It was like they were your hands, but not really—"

"Oh my gosh, wait, that sounds like the Sedator. Could it be the Sedator's hands?" Sam cut me off once again.

"I couldn't tell who was talking, but they definitely said something about escaping through the vents," I continued with my own sigh. "This was before the Sedator got away. There was a room filled with these hospital beds. He was hooking up some sort of IV bag. And there was arguing about who should be in charge."

"And there was a green substance in the IV bags, right?" Manda tugged her long braid over her shoulder. "I saw that, and the room. No one said anything in mine, though there was a medical chart."

I nodded. "Yes, it was glowing too. And the voices said something about the premiere."

My mind worked as if putting together pieces of a puzzle. "Guys. What if these aren't dreams? What if they're pieces of the Sedator's memory?"

"The blueprints, the vents, the premiere," Commander Vigil said. "It makes sense."

"I want reports on my desk of each of your dreams in an hour. Then I want reports on what everyone at that premiere dreamed," Agent Liam said. "The Sedator might not know what we have on him. Let's keep it that way."

JULY 19 – 2:45 P.M. PDT

It was time to reconvene. Illuman clutched a coffee so tightly in his hand the cup looked like it was on the verge of exploding.

"All right," Agent Liam said. "The interviews with premiere attendees gave us a lot of dream details. Ver was able to identify two people ANTE recruited."

"Roy Stinton and Timothy Baker. Both ex-military. The first was dishonorably discharged and running from a manslaughter charge. The other was honorably discharged for medical reasons. Since getting out, he's been struggling financially. It looks like he's been supporting a sister with a gambling addiction and his mother who's dying of cancer," Ver said. "He was a good soldier, but he's desperate for money."

"Both additions to a private terrorist military," Commander Vigil said. "They may not even know what they signed up for. Offer the first protection from the law and the other the cash he needs? They might not ask questions."

"We've put traces on their phones," Agent Liam said. "But we believe they are in this area of LA."

An on-screen map of a few streets was brought up on one of the monitors. "The base might be somewhere in here." Ver pointed. "Someone saw this map in a dream."

"Other dreams talked about a lab, and more rooms filled with hospital beds," Agent Liam said. "Only one other corroborated the story of the glowing liquid in IV bags."

And then the pieces started coming together. "Because of the doctor's history, I think they're creating super soldiers." My voice was so low I wasn't sure anyone heard me.

"Then we'd better find that base quick," Agent Liam said. "Ver and Sam, keep trying their phones. Use satellites to see if there's anything unusual in that mapped area. The rest of you, get a few hours of sleep. We need to be at our best. I'm going to bring the FBI in. We need more manpower if we're going to take out these bases. I'll also put out a BOLO on our Dr. Sutherland."

JULY 19 – 5:03 P.M. PDT

The door to the conference room slammed open.

In walked Agent Laude, face dark with anger. "Agent Liam, would you like to explain why you're continuing operations when you were ordered to stop?"

I dug my fingernails into my palm.

Both Illuman and Sam stood up, looking as if they were about to pop this guy's head off. Though honestly Sam looked more like he was just trying to copy Illuman.

"Do you want the locations of the remaining ANTE bases or information about how they're actively creating super soldiers, or would you like me to stop like you ordered?" Agent Liam said calmly. I glanced between them, Agent Liam as commanding as always.

The FBI agent groaned. "Go on."

Everything was explained, leaving out the base locations until the very end.

Agent Laude sighed. "So you figured all this out based on dreams?"

"Yes, they line up and gave us locations." Agent Liam stood with his legs apart, like he was ready to pounce if Laude decided to question anything.

He didn't. "Fine. Tell me where and I'll send in strike teams." I sighed with relief as Agent Laude said these words.

"Are your strike teams prepared to take down super soldiers at the first base?" I thought Agent Liam might roll his eyes in exasperation, but he somehow maintained his composure as he said, "We don't know whether or not they've already been created."

"My people are highly trained—"

Agent Liam strode closer to the other agent. "But do they have superpowers? Because last I checked we have a woman stronger than four of your men, a human glow stick, a woman who can control temperature, a man who can shapeshift, and someone in prison who can heal injuries."

Commander Vigil nodded. "I think it's best we go, Agent Laude."

"You're some of the most famous people on the planet right now," the FBI agent countered. "If things go south…"

"Pretty sure things will go much further south if we aren't there," Sam said. Yes, because Agent Laude would listen to a seventeen-year-old. He was barely listening to the director of VIGIL.

"I agree," Illuman said.

"Fine. Your team takes down the super soldier base. But I'm going with you, and Ironfall stays put." My heart clenched at his mention.

"Deal," Agent Liam said.

"This doesn't mean VIGIL is back." Laude waved a finger. No, it wasn't, but it was something. ANTE had to be defeated, and right now, that was our top priority.

IRONFALL
SOME NAMES AND LOCATIONS REDACTED FOR SECURITY
INTERVIEW CONDUCTED ON JULY 23
LOCATION OF INTERVIEW: **[REDACTED]**
CASE #: **[REDACTED]**

PROPERTY OF FBI

———

SPECIAL AGENT LAUDE: What did you and Agent Collins talk about? She talked to you for a long time.

IRONFALL: Well, I suppose she's already submitted her report so you'll hear about it there.

SPECIAL AGENT LAUDE: She told us at the time you refused to talk, but her report says something different entirely.

IRONFALL: I don't control her actions.

SPECIAL AGENT LAUDE: No. I want to hear you say what happened.

IRONFALL: We talked about what had happened. She said she trusted me.

SPECIAL AGENT LAUDE: Trusted you?

IRONFALL: Don't sound so shocked.

SPECIAL AGENT LAUDE: There are more trustworthy people.

IRONFALL: I know. But I like to think I've at least proven myself to her.

CHAPTER

18

IRONFALL

JULY 19 – *5:30 P.M. PDT*

The changing of the guard marked the beginning of my escape window.

The lock was mechanical and controlled from the outside of the steel door. Connected to a computer system as I saw during my one hour allowed outside. But I'd already figured a way past that earlier. A piece of fork that had "accidentally" broken off at breakfast this morning slipped into just the right place. A sliver of ripped fabric from the inside of my prison uniform's lining slipped into the door's tongue earlier. The small blanket and pillow I'd finally received in the middle of the night. Or was it during the day?

It was difficult to tell in here, but I did know one thing…

The guard changed in five, four, three, two, one.

Go.

I stripped down as much as I dared—wouldn't want anything too scandalous on the news should this go awry—and stuffed the uniform with part of the blanket and pillow. I stood back. From the tiny door window, it would pass for me sleeping.

The guards hardly even looked in here anyway; I had already made sure of that.

Intense staring usually did the trick.

They were already scared of me anyway.

All according to plan.

A quick glance and they'd see the prison orange. It should buy me a little time...hopefully, until they came to give me breakfast. That was optimistic. I just needed enough time to get out of the compound.

I dug my fingers into the metal door—a handle was too much to ask for apparently—and pulled. Good, it was unlocked. Had been for hours, I just needed the right time. The door opened, I pulled out my homemade gadgets, and turned into the maze.

The cameras were surprisingly easy to dodge as I crept low beneath the small windows of the solitary confinement wing.

Guard closet, here we are.

This was where the magic happened. A few tucks and pulls of a uniform, a change of gait, different posture, and slicked back hair from someone who left out hairspray. No one would look twice. I exited the closet as someone who lacked confidence. He was slightly hunched over, with a scrunched-up face like he was constantly deep in thought.

Yes, yes, that would do.

Thankfully I also had my exit path memorized. I just paid attention whenever they brought me anywhere. And if I got lost, I'd just act like I belonged because my character certainly did.

The hallway split up ahead.

I needed credentials now, something to get me in and out of places. But that was honestly the easiest part of this whole thing.

"Hey, you," said someone behind me.

I hunched further over, turning. I kept eyes on the ground.

"Haven't seen you before. First day?" By the size of his shoes, I'd say he was much bigger than me. Great. But I could still take his keys and credentials.

"Yeah." I shrugged. "Just getting used to things, you know. Trying to keep this job longer than the last one."

"It's a hard one," he said. "Honestly the turnaround is awful."

"I bet," I said.

Now to get close to him. If I attacked him, I would set off the alarm. I needed to do this as stealthily as possible. In and out and go help Rosemary.

I was doing this for her and only her.

Federal Bureau Of Investigation
Transcript Of The Interview Proceedings With

AGENT ROSEMARY COLLINS
SOME NAMES AND LOCATIONS REDACTED FOR SECURITY
INTERVIEW CONDUCTED ON JULY 23
LOCATION OF INTERVIEW: **[REDACTED]**
CASE #: **[REDACTED]**

PROPERTY OF THE FBI

———

SPECIAL AGENT LAUDE: You believed ANTE was trying to create more super soldiers?

AGENT ROSEMARY COLLINS: Supervillains, yes.

SPECIAL AGENT LAUDE: And you gathered this from dreams?

AGENT ROSEMARY COLLINS: Yes. I'm sure my written statement already said that.

SPECIAL AGENT LAUDE: How did you know you could trust these dreams?

AGENT ROSEMARY COLLINS: Did the intel we gathered from them pan out?

SPECIAL AGENT LAUDE: The intel you weren't supposed to be gathering in the first place?

CHAPTER 19

ROSEMARY

JULY 19 – *7:02 P.M. PDT*

Sam thrust his elbows on the table of the base's conference room, looking at me sideways. "I wish I was able to go." His green eyes gleamed with a kind of excitement that was way too inappropriate for the situation.

I checked my weapon. "No, you don't. Trust me, I wish I was staying here working backend too." But I had to go. I *had* to protect people. If not me and the rest of the VIGIL team, who? Besides, they had become my family, and I had their back the same way they had mine. This was why I always pushed through, why I faced the fear, anxiety, and exhaustion. I did it for the people I loved.

"That's just because you're boring. I bet Illuman's excited. Not that this is exciting, but he's ready to punch out some bad guys or...whatever." Sam threw a fist through the air.

"I don't think anyone's excited for anything but the end of ANTE." My eyes dropped down as I took a deep breath.

"Well, just don't die without me." Sam's voice went high for a moment. "Once we get Ironfall back, we gotta still be the dynamic trio."

"Sam!" I smacked his arm. "No one is dying." I hoped. I forced a laugh. "And we're not the three musketeers."

"I get it, I'm the third wheel, but still, I'm part of the OG crew. That must count for something." Good. No more talk of death. I was scared enough of the mission as it was.

Nerves punched my gut.

"Unlike the Safeguarders and VIGIL team who were a thing before we even knew what VIGIL & ANTE Studios was." I rolled my eyes, clutching quivering fingers to my sides.

"Okay but you know what I mean. It was the three of us against the world. Well, the two of us against Ironfall, but we were still a team and now he's on our side. Though the stupid FBI can't see that." Sam said this all in one large mouthful. "Come on, the three of us make such a cool team! A hacker, a spy, and a reformed supervillain!"

"I suppose you're right." I gave him a sly smile.

"And you wish he was here," Sam said.

I blinked. "He'd be...helpful right now." Helpful. Yes, that was it.

"Mm-hmm and the fact that you're in love with him." Why did that send electricity through my body?

"Sam!" He deserved to be slapped about four more times, maybe five.

"Just promise me you'll be okay." For a second he looked forlorn, but then all seriousness dissipated from his face. "I'd hate for my favorite character to die."

"Aw, Sam." I wrapped my arms around him. "I'll be okay."

When I pulled back, he grinned again. Oh no, what was he about to say now?

"If you do die, though, I'll be sure to tell Ironfall how in love with him you are."

I choked. "Then it looks like I'm definitely not dying."

"You are in love with him though."

Heat crawled up my neck, heading for my face. "I am not! Shut up."

"Well if you die I am telling him, so...don't die," Sam chuckled. "And Illuman. Don't forget him! I need him alive so Ironfall and him can start a YouTube channel together. Surprise, this is definitely going to happen."

"Yeah, have fun convincing them of that," I snorted.

"Well, everyone stay safe and all that."

"We will," I said, resolve hardening as my gun slid into its holster. "And we're going to take them down."

JULY 19 – 7:33 P.M. PDT

The helojet rumbled through the night sky like a dark, invisible bullet. The seats lining the walls were filled with FBI, VIGIL (minus Sam), and the Safeguarders.

The red in-flight lights illuminated the scowl Agent Laude wore from across the aircraft.

Movement to my right caught my eye, and I looked away.

Agent Liam rose to his feet, reaching for one of the black straps bolted to the ceiling. "Comm check." He had replaced his normal tieless suit with a combat vest, pants, and boots. We were all padded with armor and black. No skin showed from the neck down to create smaller targets for the Sedator.

"I can hear you loud and clear." Sam's voice pierced my earpiece. Nods all around the helojet, silent, as if answering would shatter the solemn moment.

The helojet began its descent as the white noise got louder. Too bad it wasn't loud enough to drown out my thoughts.

This was it.

Was I ready for another fight? What if someone didn't make

it? My hands shook and my breath turned ragged. I stuck my hands under my thighs hoping to calm them.

"You've all studied the blueprints," Agent Liam said. Nods all around. "We know ANTE bases are rigged to blow, so Cloaker, I want you to go in quietly. Blend in. Turn off the self-destruct system. Then tell us when to move. We don't want to lose any more evidence."

Cloaker nodded, but I didn't see much else as I sank back into my own seat.

Another battle.

Another face-off.

Would my father be there?

Breathe, Rosemary. But deep breaths were so hard when my own chest threatened to strangle me.

"Cloaker, we go in on your signal." Agent Liam spoke again. "Manda, Ver, I want you to stay at the exit. According to the blueprints we have, there's only one way in and one way out. Don't let anyone escape. The rest of you split into teams."

I ended up with Commander Vigil and Illuman. The formula was simple: two people with powers, one agent. Then there was Agent Liam and Degree Surge.

"All right, I'm out of here," Cloaker said. "See you on the other side." And with that, he was gone.

Now we waited for news, the hardest part of the whole thing. The silence was deafening, anticipation thick in the air.

"So...this is cool," Sam said into my earpiece. I assumed everyone else got the same message since we were all tuned into the same system. Ver understood it.

"I can hear you," Cloaker's voice mumbled. "Keep this line clear."

"Right, sorry." Well that certainly shut Sam up.

Someone's phone rang. It was loud, echoing against the metal walls.

Everyone looked around, then glared as Agent Laude picked up.

"Laude." Pause. "He what?" Another pause as my pulse quickened. "How many men can you spare?" Pause. "Well, send as many as you can. I want him found." He slammed down the phone, tugging himself to his feet. "You'll be happy to hear your new best friend just escaped prison."

I glanced at Agent Liam. Ironfall escaped? He escaped. Warmth flooded my chest. He was free. But the look on Agent Laude's face forced me to keep my expression neutral. The FBI would only use this escape to strengthen their case against him.

"If you want my advice, focus everything on ANTE. Ironfall isn't the real enemy here." Agent Liam gave the FBI agent a pointed look.

Agent Laude looked like his eyes might bulge out of his head. "I didn't ask for your advice."

I gritted my teeth.

"He gave us this intel. Cool it." Ver rolled her eyes.

Agent Laude said nothing more, only periodically slammed messages into his phone.

More waiting in that suffocating silence then.

Ten minutes.

Twenty minutes.

Nothing.

I brought my knees up to my chest, hoping to hide the fear that was probably streaked all over my face.

"Self-destruct system is offline. So are their alarms and surveillance systems," Cloaker said.

It was really happening.

As if on cue, everyone stood, checking their weapons. Now wasn't the time to rely solely on powers. Everyone was stocked full of weapons. I checked the gun on my belt and the few knives that I had stored there. Everything seemed to be working. Still, I double-checked just in case my panic-ridden mind had missed something. Anything. Then I tied up my hair, making sure it was secure.

I couldn't miss anything.

Was Ironfall okay?

Inhale. Exhale.

"Self-destruct weapons down at the other ANTE bases. The FBI is waiting on your signal," Sam said through the earpiece. "Sir."

This was it. "Move in."

We emptied off the helojet onto an empty street. The surrounding buildings were dark and boarded up, and any grass or plant life had long since dried up in the desert heat.

A scorching breeze whipped around dirt before settling as our tactical team moved toward a small building at the far end of the street. Two agents pried the door open, and we filed inside. The entrance to the base was disguised as a half-broken book-case which led into a stairwell that took us belowground. At the bottom, the walls widened into a room.

Two guards just inside.

Ver and Commander Vigil rushed in, choking them uncon-scious. Silent. Clean. They handcuffed the guards to the wall before positioning themselves as the new sentries.

I drew my gun, pointing it at the ground in front of me, ready to raise it if I saw anything.

We moved inside, and all the memories from when my parents held me captive flooded back. The flickering lights above. The damp air. The concrete walls and never-ending hallways.

This was very much the same.

Deep breath, Rosemary. Stay calm.

But it was hard to stay calm when we were raiding the place.

We broke off into our teams, one took one hallway, the other took another. Silently, Commander Vigil, Illuman, and myself moved through the corridor. According to the blueprints, this hallway would lead us to a large hospital room.

Weapons raised, we rounded the corner. Empty.

Why was this base so deserted?

I glanced at Commander Vigil and Illuman, but they didn't seem concerned, just focused.

No sound came through the comms system.

It was like everyone was holding their breath.

Around the next corner a guard faced away from us. Illuman silently choked the man out and he slumped to the floor. Illuman pressed a finger to his neck, then gave us a silent thumbs-up. Just unconscious. Another pair of handcuffs, and we moved on.

Just two more hallways until we reached the hospital room. Water dripped from the ceiling every few seconds, echoing through the otherwise silent corridor.

Three more guards rounded the corner, but between Commander Vigil, Illuman, and me, they were also unconscious in a few seconds.

The hall was silent once more.

The hospital doors were just up ahead. They didn't appear to be locked. Could it really be this easy?

I raised my gun again, pointing it at the door just in case. Commander Vigil and Illuman did the same. A second later chaos echoed over the comms. Punching, fighting.

My breath caught. Was everyone all—

An alarm went off, a high-pitched pulse blaring through invisible speakers. My ears.

Commander Vigil rushed forward; her gun raised. "Inside, now!"

"Everyone okay?" I asked over the comm. Just grunting and static.

Illuman kicked through the door, arms raised.

Men lined the beds, lying there, glowing green liquid flowing into their arms. ANTE's super soldiers in the making... A tall man with glasses stooped over one of the soldiers at the far side of the room, but his head whipped up the moment we entered, hand going for something at his belt.

In unison, each man in a bed shot upright. Like they were connected. That wasn't a good sign.

"VIGIL! Step away from your patient with your hands in the air," Illuman shouted. No one moved. "Now!"

The alarm still shrieked, but the men seemed unaffected. The doctor shuffled back, raising droopy arms in the air.

Commander Vigil scanned the room. "Keep your hands where we can see them."

The patients were silent, hands up, tubes coming out through their arm. They were big...very big. And then with powers? There were seven to-be super soldiers in here.

"How much serum is in them?" Commander Vigil turned to the doctor. He was silent. "How much!"

Still nothing from the doctor.

"Control room secured." Agent Liam's voice echoed through my ear. The alarm went silent, relieving my throbbing eardrums. I sighed.

"She asked you a question." Illuman stepped forward, waving a gun at the doctor.

The doctor shuddered, hiding his face. "They've been on the drip for an hour." Was he forced into this? He looked terrified.

"Out of?" Commander Vigil prompted.

Suddenly the doctor's face changed, the hint of a triumphant smile crossing his lips, and he looked us straight on. The helpless terror from moments ago was simply an act. "Enough time for their molecular structure to begin to change."

A man to my left ripped out his IV, standing to his feet. I raised my weapon, my finger hovering over the trigger. *Calm heart, true aim, come on, Rosemary.*

"Don't move!" I said, lining up the sights. Would I have to kill him? Please, just comply.

"We need backup in the lab," Commander Vigil said without taking her eyes off the targets. "We handle this like Moscow."

Moscow? What happened in Moscow? I didn't know this plan, which sent my pulse sky-rocketing.

"Copy that," Agent Liam responded.

The soldier dove to the floor. I fired my weapon, a clang

sounded, but I missed. The other soldiers were rising now, yanking tubes and cords from their bodies. Didn't that hurt?

The lights went out.

Illuman started to glow. Bright, bright, so bright, rays reflected and refracted off him. Bursting with blinding light. I turned, Commander Vigil dragging my arm as we ran through the doors.

"What about—?" I couldn't look back at the blinding light.

The rest of the team met us outside. Degree Surge, Cloaker, and Agent Liam. All safe. Manda and Ver must still have been guarding the entrance and exit.

"The base is secure," Agent Liam said.

Cries from inside. What was Illuman doing?

The light started to fade just a bit. Commander Vigil said, "We go back in in five, four, three, two, one."

We rushed toward the lab and burst inside. The super soldiers were stumbling, rubbing their eyes, screaming. But slowly, they were starting to recover, stumbling to their feet.

We attacked. We nearly outnumbered the super soldiers too. But they were still blinded. Illuman now set off a soft glow, enough to give us light to see. I punched the guy in front of me. He burst with heat, flames just beginning to appear on him.

I roundhouse kicked him in the face, and the flames died out, his eyes rolling back into his head as he fell over. A hand covered my mouth a second later, dragging me back. Adrenaline spiked through my stomach like a knife. I elbowed. A groan, but then nothing. I wrenched around, but I was still dragged back...back out of the light. A pair of glasses dug into the side of my face.

How had someone—? What about Illuman's light burst? I thrashed, but my body still slid away from my team. This wasn't the main exit.

A secret door?

I fought, kicked, but his hand still covered my mouth. I bit down. The hand jerked away and my captor yelped, but we were already encased in the darkness of a secret passage.

I had to get back. I had to.

"Let me go!" I screamed. "Maybe my team will have some mercy."

A soft light flickered up ahead. Some sort of flashlight.

I wrenched and twisted, but his grip was an iron cage. Had he himself taken the glowing green serum? Had he dragged me back here to kill me?

"You're mine now."

Fingers brushed my face and then...

Blackness.

One figure. Unknown location.

"You're putting our mission in jeopardy."

"And how is that?"

"I am seeking justice. She is the reason my wife is dead. My WIFE. And after all we did for her," said the other figure.

The picture blurred, distorting into bright colors and then black-and-white before resetting to its normal disorienting self.

"Your emotions are clouding your judgment."

"You don't understand, she is a threat to this entire operation."

"You don't want justice, you want revenge. Save revenge for later. Right now, we are trying to pick up our broken pieces."

"Who is in charge here?"

"You are, but we have the same goals. We are here to save the world."

"Don't talk to your superior that way!"

DATE AND TIME UNKNOWN

My head was pounding. Pounding. Sleep, I wanted it to wrap me in its loving arms. Where was I? Who was I? It didn't matter. I kept my eyes shut because I wanted to fall back into the throes of sleep.

Yes, sleep.

But my eyes jerked open. Ceiling. Bright light. I squinted. Ow, that hurt, why did my brain feel cloggy? Was that a word? Foggy. It felt foggy.

I turned away.

As my mind cleared, I remembered. The attack. Being dragged off. The Sedator.

A shiver ran down my spine.

I sat up, or tried to. My wrists were tied down to the cot. My hands started tingling with panic. I wanted to scream, but my throat was too dry. I twisted, trying to break from the bonds, but they held firm, unwilling to release their captive.

Help. My dry, cragged throat wouldn't release a sound. *No.* Tears welled in my eyes. This couldn't be happening. I'd told Sam we'd be all right. Told myself. We'd won. We'd almost won. And then that doctor dragged me through the secret passage that wasn't on the blueprints. A passage no dreams had caught.

A door opened and shut. I craned my neck to see who it was but with the lights, the bindings, and the nausea, I felt drugged. I couldn't catch anything more than movement.

I stilled, tense.

My visitor said nothing.

"Wh-what are you going to do to me?" My voice was barely audible. I gulped, holding back tears.

The Sedator appeared at the edge of my vision, still covered in wrappings. I couldn't see any blood or stains where Ironfall had stabbed him. I craned my neck further, making myself dizzy.

Another man. I turned my head.

Dad.

My chest caved. I gasped for air.

"Dad, please." Did he not remember me growing up? Bringing me home from the hospital? Anything?

"You killed my wife."

"No, Dad, please, she was going to...kill me!" And I didn't kill her. Ironfall did...to protect me. "She had her hands around my throat." My mother tried to kill me. And in her own twisted way she thought death was my salvation. Who or what had made my parents this? I'd probably never know...

But this...this wasn't about my salvation. And that scared me even more.

"She's dead, because of you," he repeated. "If you hadn't been born, she would be alive."

"We've taken out all your bases," I whispered. "You have nowhere to run."

He didn't seem concerned. "But I have you. And finally, you will understand what it felt like to lose her."

"Don't do this, please. It hurt me more than you know," I gasped. "I lost my own mother...and my father."

"No!" he snapped. "You don't know."

"Dad, please..."

He held up some sort of needle. It was long. I tried scooting away, but the restraints held me in place. Still, I writhed.

"You see the thing about his power"—Dad glanced up at the Sedator—"is he doesn't just make people unconscious. He can also keep them awake. Through anything." The Sedator's hand gripped my arm, and suddenly everything was clear. I couldn't even close my eyes, my body jittered with awareness.

Pain ripped through me.

I screamed.

Federal Bureau Of Investigation
Transcript Of The Interview Proceedings With

AGENT LIAM BLAKE, DIRECTOR OF VIGIL
SOME NAMES AND LOCATIONS REDACTED FOR SECURITY
INTERVIEW CONDUCTED ON JULY 23
LOCATION OF INTERVIEW: **[REDACTED]**
CASE #: **[REDACTED]**

PROPERTY OF THE FBI

———

SPECIAL AGENT LAUDE: You shut down all the bases.

AGENT LIAM BLAKE: Yes. All in one go. Your department was involved, shouldn't you be investigating them too?

SPECIAL AGENT LAUDE: They have their own procedure. Tell me about what you found.

AGENT LIAM BLAKE: Super soldiers cooking up to full power.

SPECIAL AGENT LAUDE: What kind of powers did they have?

AGENT LIAM BLAKE: They hadn't finished receiving the serum, but one of them could wield fire. Another had telekinesis. All destructive powers in the wrong hands.

SPECIAL AGENT LAUDE: You failed to capture their leader, is that correct?

AGENT LIAM BLAKE: He took Agent Collins hostage. Him and the Sedator got away. And a doctor.

SPECIAL AGENT LAUDE: And how exactly did he take one of your agents? You had the exits covered, did you not?

AGENT LIAM BLAKE: A secret passage.

SPECIAL AGENT LAUDE: Right, because that wasn't shown in the dreams you relied on for intel?

AGENT LIAM BLAKE: There's always an unforeseen element in every mission. You of all people should know that.

SPECIAL AGENT LAUDE: If you were so concerned about a captured agent, you would have gathered more information first.

AGENT LIAM BLAKE: Don't question my level of concern or the validity of my decisions.

CHAPTER

20

IRONFALL

JULY 19 – *11:29 P.M. PDT*

Huh, they never deleted my login. That was convenient. Saved me the trouble of breaking into the base. The door slid open, revealing the Safeguarders plus that awful FBI agent who tried to get me to talk to him.

Agent Laude's mouth dropped open. "What? You…you escaped jail. Why aren't you long gone?"

"Because VIGIL needs my help." I stepped inside, ruffling my hair. "Wrap your thick skull around that." I scanned the room. Everyone was there…except for Rosemary.

"He helped us take down Jasper Emmerling and has been working with us ever since," Agent Liam said. "Apparently, you weren't listening." Was Agent Liam taking jabs at Agent Laude too? I knew I liked him.

"And you trust him?" Commander Vigil never took her eyes from me. "I've been around long enough to know that just because someone does one good thing, it doesn't mean they've changed. Maybe he just wanted to get rid of the competition."

"Or maybe I've seen the error of my ways," I said, still hanging back. "Shocking, I know."

"Well now he has a voice," said the FBI agent. "Something stinks here." Yeah. Him. When was the last time he showered?

"Yeah, I'm not convinced," Illuman said. "You sure gave us a run for our money a few years ago."

Oh, they were asking for it. "Just think, almost beaten by a teenager." I stalked closer. "One who didn't even have the powers he claimed to have."

"Cool it," Manda said. "You don't want to make us regret letting you help us."

"Ironfall, I'm placing you back under arrest," the FBI agent said, his eyes bulging. He didn't move. Arrest me. I dare you.

An icy chill shot through the room, as Degree Surge stepped forward with a hardened look. "You saved us in the theater. Woke us up, healed us. Why?"

"I want to save people, not hurt them," I said. Rosemary still wasn't here. A sinking feeling lodged itself in my stomach.

"Waking you up gave us a better chance against the Sedator. Come on, VIGIL and the Safeguarders against one villain? He didn't stand much of a chance," Ver said. "Even though he got away in the end, but whatever, you get my point."

Cloaker remained silent.

Commander Vigil turned to Agent Liam. "Do you trust him?"

"He passed all the lie detector tests, and he swore he wanted to change," Agent Liam said. Then he looked at me. "Technically, he's clean."

"Technically isn't an answer." Commander Vigil crossed her arms.

"I'm still arresting you."

"Where's Rosemary?" And that's when they looked at each other and I knew for sure that something was wrong. "Where is she?"

"We took out all of ANTE's bases, but they captured her

before we escaped." Agent Liam's brow knitted. "We're trying to find her."

"No," I growled. "If I had been there, maybe this wouldn't have happened."

"Pretty sure you would have joined ANTE," the FBI agent said, spittle flying from his lips. "And then kidnapped her yourself. Now, Ironfall, I'm placing you back under arrest." He brought out an all too flimsy looking pair of handcuffs and I stepped towards him.

"Arrest me and I'll break your arms," I said.

"Stop." Agent Liam narrowed his eyes at the FBI agent. "He's here to help us."

"You can't know that," Commander Vigil said. "That's putting an awful lot of faith in him."

"If I trust him with one thing, it's saving Rosemary. Am I right?" His eyes pierced mine.

"Yes, sir," I said, all sass gone from my voice.

"Then I trust him," Agent Liam said.

My eyes widened, but I quickly masked it.

It was Illuman who finally broke the silence. "Well, that's good enough for me."

"It's not good enough for the FBI." The FBI agent looked like he was about to pull out all his hair.

"We're not the FBI." Agent Liam turned his back on the man. "You're free to leave anytime you want, Laude, but he's helping us get Rosemary back. Besides, there's a supervillain who can put people to sleep and Ironfall's the only one who's immune. He's with us, end of discussion."

I looked at the FBI agent again. "After I save Rosemary, do whatever you want to me."

JULY 19 – 11:56 P.M. PDT

At least the LA base's interrogation room was slightly nicer than the New York one. At this point, interrogation rooms were my new home. I sat back, staring through Agent Laude. He really would look better if he didn't dye his hair that ghastly blond.

I hated red tape. And if we had to go through too much more of it, Rosemary would be dead. I sat back up just as the door opened.

"All right, here's the deal," said Agent Laude. "We give you temporary immunity on the condition that you help us take down ANTE's stragglers."

I crossed my arms, sliding further back in my seat. "And save Rosemary."

"If we can. ANTE is our priority."

"And Rosemary is mine." Gosh I hated this guy.

"Fine, guess you want to go back to jail then."

I sat up, placing both—uncuffed—hands on the table. "Fine. ANTE is my priority. Happy?"

"You must also agree to follow orders and not carry a weapon," he said. "You are also not allowed to kill anyone, steal anything, or break any other laws."

"How am I supposed to prioritize ANTE without carrying a weapon, exactly?" I smirked. *I* could be a weapon, but I wasn't walking into an ambush without something sharp.

"Do you want out or not?"

"I would like to live." I shrugged. "Which I can't do without a weapon. In case you forgot I worked for VIGIL with no issues for months."

"The FBI is in charge now, and we say no weapons."

"Well, I can tell you right now that that's a rule I will be breaking." I relaxed back into the seat. I could tell how much that made this guy squirm. "Any other stupid rules?"

"I'm starting to think you like jail," Agent Laude growled. "Why don't we take a field trip back there now."

"Fine, I won't do anything illegal, and I won't carry a weapon *that you know about*. Now let me sign your stupid paper." I held out a hand. At least he knew I'd still carry a weapon off the books.

Just then, Agent Liam came through the door. "He's not signing anything until you add that he can work off his jail time for us." What? Did he just say that? I thought…I thought he'd be glad to put me in jail once this was all over.

"What are you, his lawyer?" Agent Laude snapped.

"He's a valuable asset." Agent Liam's eyes snagged on mine. "And he's been a great agent so far. I think he should have a chance to work for full immunity."

"I'm with him," I said. "Let me work off my immunity. I've changed my ways. Hey, don't you have a lie detector here too? I'm telling the truth. I have changed."

Laude narrowed his eyes. "You're sure being difficult for having changed."

"Advocating for myself doesn't mean I'm evil." I smirked.

"Exactly." Agent Liam pulled out a tablet. "And look at that, I even brought you some results from the lie detector test." He showed the FBI agent his tablet.

Once more, Agent Laude looked like his eyes were about to pop out of his head. "I need to talk to my superiors first."

"Rosemary's time is ticking away. If you let her die because of this—"

"Go. You have fifteen minutes to get back in here with an appropriate immunity agreement before I let him out and we all go after ANTE and save her. Agreed?" Agent Liam's voice was calm, but firm.

The FBI stooge said nothing, just got up and walked out, slamming the door behind him.

"Why did you do that?" I couldn't help asking.

"Like I said, you're a good agent," Agent Liam said. "You've become part of our team and I think you deserve a second chance at life."

"I wouldn't have done the same. It doesn't make sense. I don't deserve another chance."

"Maybe you don't, either way I want you on this team." Agent Liam stood straighter.

"You do?"

He nodded. "You fit right in."

A small smile played at my lips.

Agent Liam shrugged. "And you're giving this guy such a hard time that you deserve a reward."

"They couldn't have sent someone competent, could they?" I rolled my eyes.

Just then, he was back, brows drawn, and a piece of paper in his hand.

"You win. Ironfall, congratulations, you get to work off your charges." He scowled. "Now, sign here. Or don't. I'd actually prefer that."

"Give me that to read through first." Agent Liam held out a hand. "He does get to carry a weapon, yes?"

"Yes. If he's going to be an agent, he needs one." The FBI agent gritted his teeth. Then he handed over the papers.

I grinned.

"He's smiling. Why is he smiling?" Agent Laude grimaced.

"Do I scare you?" I said, raising my eyebrows and laughing.

Agent Liam handed the document and a pen to me. "Everything's in order. You're good to sign."

I signed.

"Welcome back, Agent Ironfall." Agent Liam shook my hand.

The FBI agent looked like he wanted someone to shoot him. If I weren't a changed man, I'd have been happy to oblige.

JULY 20 – 12:42 A.M. PDT

They took Rosemary. I balled my hands into fists. They took Rosemary. I should have been there to protect her. I should have tried harder to take down ANTE before they got to her. I should have killed the Sedator at the premiere.

My gaze snagged on a picture of her on one of the VIGIL base's screens, and I slammed a fist down on the conference table glass. The pain felt good, like I was doing something instead of waiting for new intel to come in.

I should have seen it coming too, should have known my father had built these bases with multiple hidden exits. I should have been there to stop them from using them.

"We'll get her back," Agent Liam said.

"Yes." I set my eyes on the floor. "We will." Already my mind spun with ways to get her back. Her father wanted revenge on her, a move my father would make too, but I shoved that part aside. He and the Sedator were divided on this much. Which meant emotion clouded Rosemary's dad's judgment. I could exploit that… He also must have another safe house to keep her, but based on how little we knew about ANTE and how hard it was to gather evidence, we might not find it until it was too late. It took us months to find one base—

No. I shook my head.

Rosemary's father would lie low for a while, he wouldn't move too fast, and that meant Rosemary had a chance. Her dad had few resources. Already, Ver and Sam had taken out their network. Financial assets frozen. Communication systems monitored. The man would need money to survive. Unless he had a secret, accessible stash elsewhere, he owned little beyond the mysterious safe house. If my calculations were correct—not that I could afford them to be wrong—this all meant we could negotiate.

Yes, negotiation was our play. But how to contact them?

I couldn't pretend to turn to their side again. Rosemary's father would see right through that. I'd turned on ANTE one too many times.

"We need to negotiate." I said it aloud this time.

"What?" Commander Vigil raised her head up from the file she'd been studying across the conference table.

"Negotiate for Rosemary's release. Finding out where they're keeping her will be almost impossible. She'll be dead before we can make much headway. So, we negotiate." I stood up. "That's our next play."

"We're not listening to the supervillain who broke out of jail and barely got an immunity agreement," said Agent Laude, hiding in a corner not lit up by screens. He was still here.

Agent Liam's arm held me back from clocking the guy.

"He is part of this team and we're getting Rosemary back," Agent Liam said. "We will hear him out."

"We have no way of contacting them." Ver joined the conversation, eyes still glued to her screen as she spoke. "If we did, we'd have a shot at figuring out where they are and get Rosemary out that way."

"We have something better!" Sam shrieked, coming to life again too. "We have a way of contacting everyone."

"What on earth?" Manda said.

"Oh no, no way," Agent Laude said. "This is out of the question. No official statement has been made, but so far everyone believes VIGIL and superheroes are real."

But my brain was already working. "Sam's right. Everyone sees what VIGIL & ANTE Studios puts out. We put something out there and include a message ANTE will understand. We make an offer they can't refuse, and they'll reach out to us."

"This is ridiculous." The FBI agent stomped a heel.

"You can't be suggesting we bargain with terrorists," Commander Vigil said.

"Oh but I am." And nothing she could do would stop me. I was going to get Rosemary out of there, no matter what it took.

"No offense, but we're really trusting this plan from a former terrorist?" Commander Vigil crossed her arms. She liked to do that.

"Supervillain," I corrected, jaw flaring. "And yes. It's our best option."

"I don't care if it offends him. We aren't doing this," Agent Laude said. "Besides, the FBI hasn't decided what sort of statement to make."

"Our secret is out." My fists balled in frustration. "Own up to it and get her back."

"Don't include yourself in this group," Agent Laude snapped. "And like I said, there will be no statement."

"I hate to admit it, but Ironfall's right, it's the fastest way to get them to communicate. ANTE is the best at hiding in the shadows. We need to draw them out," Ver said.

"One agent is not worth admitting the cover-up," said the FBI agent.

"Yes, she is." I gritted my teeth, ready to punch the guy, again. But if I punched him, bye-bye immunity. Which meant I couldn't save Rosemary.

"I agree," Ver said. "Besides, this could be a good thing. Who wouldn't want their favorite movies to secretly be real? We could spin it so the government looked good in this scenario."

"Whereas, if it were leaked that the FBI was trying to cover it all up by letting their new favorite superhero die..." Sam narrowed his eyes. It seemed he was just as intent upon saving Rosemary as I was.

"Is that a threat?" Agent Laude glared at the boy.

"Simple PR advice." Ver grinned. "And seeing as I'm the PR person who helped with the cover-up from the beginning..." Oh, I could hug this girl.

"As owner of BestVIGILMemes, I promise the fans will be excited," Sam said. "They'll think you're heroes for revealing the secret and keeping them all safe all these years."

"Your little blog was shut down," Agent Laude countered.

"Meme site," Sam said coolly. "No one knows the fandom better than me. And do you really think I couldn't get it back up and running this instant?"

"I'm getting tired of your red tape," Agent Liam joined in again. "We're saving Rosemary Collins whether you approve or not. Ironfall, continue with your plan."

"ANTE just lost all their resources," I said. "So this shouldn't be too difficult. Our biggest obstacle is that they're blinded by emotion." And emotion was the one thing that was unpredictable. Threw a complete wrench in my own plans. What would it do to this? Still, it was a risk we had to take.

"So, we make an offer they can't refuse." Agent Liam nodded like he was thinking.

"I can't believe this," Commander Vigil said. My jaw flared. How could she? This was Rosemary we were talking about. Even if I had to go rogue, I'd do this and bring her back. I would do anything for her...

"Now you're suggesting we offer something to these terrorists. I should arrest you right now." Agent Laude's threat was getting old now.

"Come on, we're a bunch of superheroes and spies. Surely we can pull the wool over their eyes and pretend to give them something before stabbing them in the back." Cloaker finally joined the conversation.

"That's very...vivid imagery," Illuman said. "But he's kinda right."

"I'm in," Manda said.

"Count me in too!" Sam said. Of course he was in. Didn't take him much.

"Let's get our girl." Ver nodded.

"We don't leave anyone behind," Illuman chanted. "Just tell me what you need me to do."

"I'm with you," Degree Surge said.

"Fine." Commander Vigil crossed her arms, yet again. "But I still don't like it."

"We can't reveal the secret," Agent Laude said.

"Oh but that's exactly what we need to do," Ver said. "As the official PR person, it's my professional advice."

"Then we're agreed." Agent Liam nodded. "Ironfall, you're running this op."

"Absolutely not," Agent Laude said, but everyone ignored him.

In that moment, my heart swelled. I had a team. A team who cared about each other. Who didn't cut their losses and leave you behind. Except Commander Vigil, but she had come around.

"Yes, sir," I said, raising my chin. *Rosemary, we're coming for you.*

JULY 20 – 1:57 P.M. PDT

Agent Liam shrugged a suit jacket over his shoulders. "You'd better be right about this."

"I am." I picked up a suit jacket of my own. The FBI and their precious press conference dress codes. Was it official? I wasn't sure, but still. "This will work." It had to, and Rosemary's father —if he could even be called that—had better be listening. Because if he wasn't…if Rosemary was already dead…

I could never live with myself.

"After today, nothing will be the same," Agent Liam said. Was he…was he confiding in me? That didn't seem like the wisest choice.

"Sir, we passed that point a long time ago."

He nodded. "The world is officially about to know our secret…your secret."

"A small price to pay," I said. "But it's the right thing to do. And I'm pretty sure they already believe it anyway."

"You really do care about her," Agent Liam said. It was a statement, not a question, and he was right.

"I care about all of you." I nodded. "Though I know you don't believe me."

"Maybe."

"What is that supposed to mean?" I asked.

Just then, a female FBI agent poked her head through the door. "Agent Liam? We're almost ready to start."

"We'll be right there." Agent Liam didn't answer my question, just turned and walked toward the door.

My phone buzzed in my pocket. I picked it up, instinctively thinking it was Rosemary.

Sam: Get her back!!! You've got this.

Sam: The world is gonna flip

Sam: If Rosemary's dumpster fire father doesn't respond I will personally burn him to the ground

Sam: I already have the perfect virus to plant in their computers.

A smile tugged at my lips. He wouldn't be alone in burning him down.

I followed Agent Liam out of the room and into the press conference.

Federal Bureau Of Investigation
Transcript Of The Interview Proceedings With

IRONFALL
SOME NAMES AND LOCATIONS REDACTED FOR SECURITY
INTERVIEW CONDUCTED ON JULY 23
LOCATION OF INTERVIEW: **[REDACTED]**
CASE #: **[REDACTED]**

PROPERTY OF THE FBI

SPECIAL AGENT LAUDE: You escaped from jail, show up back at a government organization's headquarters, and suggested negotiating with a terrorist, is that correct?

IRONFALL: You sound like Commander Vigil.

SPECIAL AGENT LAUDE: Why come back? You knew we'd put you right back in jail.

IRONFALL: Maybe I've changed. Have you thought of that? Maybe VIGIL needed my help.

SPECIAL AGENT LAUDE: They were decommissioned, as Agent Collins told you.

IRONFALL: They were the only people I trusted to take ANTE down for good.

SPECIAL AGENT LAUDE: Let's move into negotiating with terrorists. Under what authority—

IRONFALL: If one of your agents was held as a prisoner you'd cut ties?

SPECIAL AGENT LAUDE: I'm asking you the questions.

IRONFALL: We don't abandon people on our team.

SPECIAL AGENT LAUDE: You seem especially passionate about this. Why is that?

IRONFALL: Because we're friends. She's an agent on our team.

SPECIAL AGENT LAUDE: Just friends?

IRONFALL: I don't see how that's your business.

SPECIAL AGENT LAUDE: You're being investigated by the FBI. Everything is my business now.

IRONFALL: There's no juicy gossip here. We are friends and colleagues. No scandal to be found.

SPECIAL AGENT LAUDE: I see.

CHAPTER

21

ROSEMARY

DATE AND TIME UNKNOWN

I gagged, sinking back into the hard table as much as I could. Pain shrieked through my bones, my joints, my brain. Everything hurt.

Tears wouldn't even form anymore.

Someone save me, please.

The sound of a door opening. I closed my eyes. No, go away. I couldn't take any more.

I opened my eyes. Dad stood over me, face hard. "Please, let me go," I croaked. I knew he wouldn't listen. Wouldn't care.

"No!" he snapped. I flinched.

"Please, Dad. You've already lost. Keeping me won't do any good." VIGIL was safe. The world was safe.

Ironfall...he was...somewhere. What I wouldn't give to see him again...

"But now I have the person responsible to punish. If you had only listened to your mother and I"—he shook his head—"we wouldn't be in this mess."

"No," I said. "That never would've happened. We wouldn't

be in this mess if you and Mom weren't terrorists." What was my life? Why had everything fallen apart?

His face hardened more, and he looked as if he would lash out again, but then his features went blank. "Your friends are holding a press conference."

I said nothing.

"They have to deal with my little mess now. Let's see what spectacular storyline they have for explaining their movies."

"You leaked the information," I said. My fists clenched.

"I'm surprised you didn't figure it out sooner."

"We've been a little busy."

"Yes, but now you have all the time in the world to think."

I gulped, trying one more time to wrench free of the restraints.

"Let's watch together," he said.

Tears pricked my eyes. What did he have planned for this press conference? Whatever it was, it wasn't good. My Dad held up a screen as someone walked on stage. A lower third slide said it was someone from the FBI. I swallowed. *Save yourselves.* That was the only help I could give.

TRANSCRIPT OF THE FBI PRESS CONFERENCE
JULY 20

———

Special Agent Laude: I'd like to thank you all for coming to today's press conference. I'm Special Agent Laude with the FBI.

[Everyone speaks at once.]

Special Agent Laude: Everyone, please. You will have a chance to ask questions in a moment. Our goal is to give you as much information as we can on this developing story. For now, I'd like to welcome esteemed actor and director, Xavier Jay.

Xavier Jay: Thank you, Agent Laude. Two days ago, an unknown subject leaked classified documents allegedly proving that the heroes and villains depicted in VIGIL & ANTE Studios movies are real. They alleged that the organization known as VIGIL exists and that the VIGIL & ANTE Studios actors are its agents. I'm here to tell you that the documents are true.

[Everyone speaks at once.]

Xavier Jay: You will have your time to ask questions. For the past few years, I, Agent Liam Blake, have been undercover as Xavier Jay, and my agents have been undercover as actors in VIGIL & ANTE Studios movies. We are currently investigating the source of the leak.

Reporter: Is ANTE real?

Reporter: Do superpowers exist?

Reporter: What does this mean for the American people? For the world?

[Rhett Wickford steps forward and whispers something into Liam Blake's ear.]

Agent Liam Blake: Yes, ANTE is real. They are a dangerous terrorist organization. Yesterday, VIGIL—in partnership with the FBI—raided their bases, but one of our agents was taken hostage.

Reporter: Who is it?

Reporter: Is it one of the actors?

Reporter: Do they have powers?

Agent Liam Blake: Agent Rosemary Collins was taken during the raids.

Reporter: Do you have a rescue mission planned?

Reporter: Where is she being held?

Agent Liam Blake: We're doing everything we can to get her back. To her captors, we can help you. We have a line of communication open, and we're willing to negotiate for her release. To the ones holding our agent: you have nowhere else to go, and we will find you. We now have time for a few questions.

Ironfall. He was there. He was out. They were trying to get me back. More tears flooded to my eyes.

What was he doing there?

Was he okay?

VIGIL confirmed that everything was real. Why would they do that? How was everything going to turn out okay? And they wanted to negotiate. That was something I needed to jump on, so I swallowed and stared at the paused image, complete with Ironfall in the background.

"Your bases are gone," I said. "Your super soldiers are gone. It's only a matter of time before they find you. You're cornered. If they're willing to negotiate..." I sucked in a breath. "Maybe you can get out of this." Pain shot through my body, but I couldn't tell if it was an aftershock of what my body had just gone through or if it was more pain being inflicted. I winced.

"She's right." Suddenly the Sedator was standing over me as well. "They froze our assets."

Dad cursed, stepping away, taking the picture of Ironfall with him.

"Another reason to punish you," he spat.

"Your little empire is through," I said. "If they're willing to negotiate, you can get something out of it." As much as I hated to say it, it was my best chance at survival. I had to trust VIGIL had a plan as well. "Something that can help you win."

"It's a matter of time before they find our safe house. To stay hidden, we need money and resources." The Sedator sounded fervent now.

"No!"

"ANTE's gone, and that means you're not my boss anymore. Maybe I'll just knock you out and negotiate myself," the Sedator said, standing up even taller than he already was.

"Let me think about it," Dad said.

"They'll give you whatever you want," I said, lying through my teeth. I had no idea how much VIGIL was willing to give, and they definitely shouldn't just hand over whatever he wanted, but in the moment, convincing him was step one. "Dad, please. What am I worth?"

"You killed her." His voice broke. "I don't care who pulled the trigger. She died because of you."

"Dad." My voice cracked. "I'm sorry." I loved Mom too, I wanted to say. And in a weird way, I still loved him.

"You are not forgiven," he snarled. "I should kill you right now."

"James, think about this," the Sedator said, stepping between us. "Let's see just how much she's worth to VIGIL."

"I know that feeling, Dad," I said. "I was so angry at Ironfall for such a long time, and it only turned to bitterness."

"What did you expect from him? He didn't take away the best thing in your life," Dad snapped.

"He still hurt me," I said. "A lot."

"So what, you want us to be buddies now?" my father spat, almost getting around the Sedator.

"No," I said. "I don't think that can ever happen, but you don't need to carry around this weight."

"I don't need your lectures."

"Then listen to mine. Revenge has clouded your judgment. Negotiation is our best chance," the Sedator said. "No money. No resources. We can't run without those. And think, we're the ones with the power here. We have one of theirs. Let's stick it to them."

"We ask for Ironfall," Dad said.

My stomach dropped. No.

Because he'd do it in a heartbeat.

255

"No, please, don't," I wheezed.

A sick smile crossed Dad's face. "I thought you wanted me to negotiate."

"Leave Ironfall out of this," I said.

"He's also part of the reason we're in this mess now that I think about it."

"Please," I pleaded, throat running dry. "Do anything you want to me, just don't exchange me for him."

"Do I detect some strong feelings from you? Is this love?" His voice was mocking.

"No!" I said. "I don't trade lives. Kill me and let him go free."

"He's not that free though," he said.

"But he's alive," I said. "Kill me instead."

"Love, yes, I think that's what that is. And as my daughter, I can't let you have that. You're far too young."

"I'm not in love with him, just take money or something. VIGIL will find you. And if you take Ironfall, I will find you."

"Bold words," he laughed. "But I think I know love when I see it."

"No, you don't," I screamed this time. "I've been on the receiving end of your misguided version of love my whole life."

"Dr. Sutherland," Dad said. "Respond saying we want Ironfall and \$15 million. See just how much they care about my daughter over there."

"Don't touch him or I swear—"

"Shh. My mind is made up. Ironfall is the best way to hurt you."

Federal Bureau Of Investigation
Transcript Of The Interview Proceedings With

AGENT LIAM BLAKE, DIRECTOR OF VIGIL
SOME NAMES AND LOCATIONS REDACTED FOR SECURITY
INTERVIEW CONDUCTED ON JULY 23
LOCATION OF INTERVIEW: **[REDACTED]**
CASE #: **[REDACTED]**

PROPERTY OF THE FBI

———

SPECIAL AGENT LAUDE: You agreed to open negotiations?
AGENT LIAM BLAKE: One of my agents was being held captive. Yes, I did.
SPECIAL AGENT LAUDE: You didn't think of the risks?
AGENT LIAM BLAKE: Of course I did, but saving Agent Collins was top priority. Her life was worth the risks.
SPECIAL AGENT LAUDE: Agents know they're putting their lives on the line.
AGENT LIAM BLAKE: We don't leave a man behind, especially behind enemy lines. You're telling me you wouldn't have done the same thing?

SPECIAL AGENT LAUDE: But I'm not the one being investigated.

CHAPTER
22

IRONFALL

JULY 20 – *5:16 P.M. PDT*

"I got something!" Sam jumped up from his chair. "An encrypted message. It has ANTE's fingerprints all over it."

"We took down ANTE," said Agent Laude. Really? No kidding. It was amazing this guy survived the ANTE raids.

"Um, yeah, of course, but we're missing the Sedator and Mr. Dad of the Year," Sam said. "They saw your announcement."

I ran over to him until I was face-to-face with a computer screen filled with code. It looked like gibberish. "This is what you're talking about?"

"What? You think supervillains use a messaging app?" Sam said. "I promise the line of communication is open." He'd better not mess this up. Rosemary was depending on him. On all of us. On *me*.

I ran a hand through my hair to massage the headache forming.

Rosemary was relying on me.

"What did they say?" Agent Liam stepped forward.

Agent Laude, surprisingly, had nothing to say, he just hovered in the background glaring at nothing.

"They want…" Sam's voice trailed off. "Ironfall. And $15 million." My stomach sank. Of course her father wanted me too.

But why?

"When's the meet?" I stepped forward. My mind was made up. If it was me or Rosemary, I'd choose me every time.

Agent Laude held out a hand like I was a rabid dog that needed taming. "Hold on a minute."

"There has to be another way," Agent Liam said. "They will kill you."

I crossed my arms. I knew that. "And Rosemary goes free. I know these people, they won't negotiate for less." I paused. "I wouldn't."

"Anyone else suspicious of his motives?" Agent Laude said. They would be right to, but they didn't need to.

Rosemary deserved to live, I didn't.

"I know his motives, but I will get slapped for sharing," Sam said. The death glare he received from Mr. FBI expert over there was unmatched.

"Counteroffer $11 million without Ironfall," Agent Liam said.

"They'll only up their price," I said. "I advise accepting their terms as-is."

Never compromise. My father's voice rang out.

"Can you track their messages?" Ver asked.

"The IP addresses are everywhere," Sam said. "I already tried pinpointing their location."

"It was worth a shot," Ver sighed.

"Message sent," Sam said.

Agent Laude threw his hands in the air. "Why is a child sending ransom responses?"

"Hey! I'm seventeen and grew like four inches over the summer," Sam said. "And I can also hack into your bank account in ten seconds, so I'd be careful who you call a child." Go Sam for standing up to this guy. Not that I would ever tell Sam that to his face. It would go right to his head, and we couldn't have that.

"I wouldn't challenge 'the child' to test that if I were you." I side-eyed the FBI agent. "Even if he acts like one sometimes."

"Oh you're one to talk," Sam said. "You should tell them about the pizza eating contest that one time—"

"Back on task, everyone." Manda snapped us all to attention. "You get a response yet?"

"Uh…" Sam looked up, eyes now wide. "It says 'Ironfall and $15 million. 36.5323° N, 116.9325° W. 12:07 a.m. Come alone with a clear duffel bag filled with untraceable cash.'"

"I warned you," I said. "You don't play with these people."

"This is why we have professional negotiators." Who would ruin things, Agent Laude.

"And who trained them? ANTE. Because ANTE was all inside the FBI just a few minutes ago," Agent Liam said. He was right. ANTE knew their tactics because many of them were once the FBI's best agents. "So I suggest not questioning my people."

"Tell them we need proof that she's alive," I said. "If I'm giving myself up, I need something concrete."

"Already done."

And we waited in silence.

A loud ring.

Agent Liam grappled with the phone and held it up to his ear. "Hello?" He knew it was them.

He looked right at me and pointed at the phone. "It's for you." He passed it to me. "Run a trace. Ironfall, keep the conversation going."

"Hello?" I said, not knowing what horrors would meet me on the other end of the phone. All I could think of was Rosemary bleeding out in a chair in a dark room.

Alone.

"Ironfall?" Rosemary's voice came through the phone. My breath hitched.

"Rosemary," I breathed.

"Don't come! Don't—"

She was cut off, replaced by the harsh tone of a man. Not the Sedator. "Come alone. You have our instructions—"

"Wait. How do I know her voice wasn't a recording? I need to ask her something personal, otherwise the deal is off." I kept my tone harsh to mask my terror.

I wouldn't put it past them to kill her after making a recording.

Shuffling on the other end. I pressed the phone closer to my ear as if it would bring me closer to Rosemary.

"Don't do this, don't—" She was back.

"Rosemary." I glanced back at Agent Liam who motioned for me to keep her talking. Keep the phone conversation as long as possible so Ver and Sam could trace it. Trace it and then save Rosemary. "Listen to me. It's going to be okay. I need to ask you…what did I say that night you called me? What is my recurring nightmare? Say it slowly."

More motions to keep the call going longer.

Her voice shook, but she responded. "Your dad would lock you in the basement. And he'd kill you by"—she paused—"slicing your—"

The line went dead.

"Rosemary?" I cried. "Rosemary?" I gripped the phone harder. No. I needed to get to her, but I knew she was alive, at least for now.

I turned.

"I just needed a few more seconds," Ver said. "I couldn't get it."

"We tried."

I set the phone down to keep from tossing it across the room. "I'm going, so get me that $15 million."

"We'll follow you. Once the exchange is happening—" Agent Liam started.

"No. If they see any hiccup in the deal, they'll kill her," I said.

"I go in alone, and no one comes after me." I looked at the FBI agent. "This is what you wanted anyway, wasn't it?"

"They'll kill you!" Sam said.

"Saves tax dollar money by keeping me out of prison." I shrugged. "And Rosemary gets to live. Seems like a fair trade."

"No!" Sam said.

But I turned and left.

Federal Bureau Of Investigation
Transcript Of The Interview Proceedings With

AGENT ROSEMARY COLLINS
SOME NAMES AND LOCATIONS REDACTED FOR SECURITY
INTERVIEW CONDUCTED ON JULY 23
LOCATION OF INTERVIEW: **[REDACTED]**
CASE #: **[REDACTED]**

PROPERTY OF THE FBI

———

SPECIAL AGENT LAUDE: Your own father tortured you, is that correct?

AGENT ROSEMARY COLLINS: Yes.

SPECIAL AGENT LAUDE: Tell me about it…

AGENT ROSEMARY COLLINS: Do we have to talk about this? Can't you read my report?

SPECIAL AGENT LAUDE: You do, and I already have.

AGENT ROSEMARY COLLINS: The Sedator kept me conscious, and the pain…

SPECIAL AGENT LAUDE: Did you divulge any state secrets?

AGENT ROSEMARY COLLINS: No.

SPECIAL AGENT LAUDE: Are you sure?

265

AGENT ROSEMARY COLLINS: Yes, I'm sure.

SPECIAL AGENT LAUDE: He was—

AGENT ROSEMARY COLLINS: Bent on revenge.

SPECIAL AGENT LAUDE: On you? ANTE? The US government?

AGENT ROSEMARY COLLINS: Me. He had it out for the government long before I was even born.

SPECIAL AGENT LAUDE: And yet he chose to complete the exchange. Couldn't be that committed to revenge?

AGENT ROSEMARY COLLINS: Ironfall was to blame too. He's the one who killed my mother.

SPECIAL AGENT LAUDE: Do you blame him for that?

AGENT ROSEMARY COLLINS: He saved my life.

CHAPTER
23

ROSEMARY

DATE AND TIME UNKNOWN

My vision was going in and out as the door slammed shut. I craned my neck, contorting against the iron restraints, but still couldn't see who it was.

"It's your lucky day." The Sedator.

Ironfall accepted the deal.

"No. No," I croaked, struggling again as the metal cut against my wrists.

"Yes. Now get up."

The restraints clicked open, but before I could pull myself off the table, the Sedator threw me to my feet. I stumbled as my vision blurred again. Too...weak...

I caught myself on the table.

One breath.

Two breaths.

The Sedator grabbed my wrists once more and...

...black.

DATE AND TIME UNKNOWN

I jerked awake. Leather brushed against my skin as I sat up. It was dark, but I appeared to be in the backseat of a truck. A whiff of gasoline drifted past. The world spun, then righted itself. Every inch of my body ached. Where was I? The engine's rumble made my head pound. Words…words…they were flying through my head slurred and blurred like there was nothing…

Where was I?

The truck lights shut off, and all was silent. Now, there was only darkness.

My head hurt less, but through the window I could see flickers of stars. We had to be somewhere rural. It was night. That was a start.

The door behind my head opened as something dinged from the front seat.

"Get out." *Dad?* What was he doing here? What was—?

I blinked. *Dad.* It all came flooding back. My pulse quickened. I was a captive. My dad tortured me. *Ironfall.* No, this couldn't be happening.

"I said get out!" Dad yelled more forcefully. I flinched, scurrying away from his reaching hands.

"No," I said, my muscles screaming from the effort. "I won't let you hurt him."

But his arms only pulled me out. I grappled for something—anything—but my hands slid across the slick leather.

"Let me go!" I shrieked as he threw me on the ground. Someone pulled me to my feet and didn't let go. I looked around me, eyes adjusting. There was nothing but dark desert broken only by a long stretch of road. They'd be able to see someone coming from miles away.

You're an agent, Rosemary. I needed to stay sharp, think, not dissolve into a panicked spiral, again. Ironfall wasn't here yet, at least, he wasn't in sight. There were sand dunes everywhere, and mountains in the distance. How long had we driven? How far were we from LA? Were we even in California?

Desert…where was there desert again? My head pounded, blocking out my thoughts.

Ironfall, don't come.

"He's late," Dad growled.

Just as my hopes started to rise, another set of headlights dotted the horizon.

No.

Steel fingers gripped my arm, but I hardly felt it.

"Ironfall, no," I whispered as if he would hear me from a mile away on the straight highway.

The vehicle roared to a stop only a short distance away, the headlights still on as the door opened.

"Leave! Go back!" I couldn't even tell if it was Ironfall from the lights and silhouettes, and my blasted headache, but I didn't care. "Don't worry about me!"

The figure approached, carrying a large bag. He was tall and confident, like this was just any other day for him. I knew that gait, his confidence was unmistakable. Ironfall.

He couldn't give himself up! Not for me. I opened my mouth to yell at him again, but something dug into my side, stealing my breath.

"I have it." Ironfall stopped walking. "$15 million, just like you asked." *No.*

"Come closer." My father beckoned.

Ironfall only tossed the bag toward us. I flinched.

"Give Rosemary to me, then I'll surrender."

"If you want her so badly, you'll come here." My father's tone was hard as steel. "Or do I need to repeat myself, Ironfall?"

"Don't do it." My voice cracked under the strain. "Please, he'll kill—" Sharp. Pain. I cried out.

"I want her unharmed," Ironfall boomed.

The bruises already on my arm screamed as Dad said, "Right, because she's your little girlfriend."

"She's your daughter, and you should be thankful to have someone like her."

"Hand yourself over." My father sneered.

"Hand me Rosemary. We do this like a proper hostage exchange. She walks my way, I walk your way." Ironfall slid his feet apart, relaxed as if this wasn't his first negotiation. "Even you can appreciate the beauty of a hostage exchange, can't you?"

My heart raced.

There was a silence, only broken up by the car still running.

"Fine."

Ironfall nodded, and I was sure I caught a smirk in the dim headlights.

The Sedator spoke for the first time. "Three, two, one." His grip released.

Ironfall stepped forward. So did I.

Slowly, I shook my head, but we walked towards each other. My legs felt leaden as I forced myself forward, praying he had some kind of plan to get everyone out.

He said nothing, I said nothing.

Ironfall, please, don't do this. Don't give yourself up. There was so much I wanted to say, so much I wanted to do, but I couldn't. Helplessness strangled me with every painful step, every labored breath. We moved in rhythm, right, then left, right, then left, his eyes never leaving mine as if to say, "It's okay."

But it wasn't okay at all. I was about to lose the man I—

He was right there, just steps from me.

I stepped again, so did he, and as we passed, his fingers brushed my swollen ones. Warmth radiated up my arm into my chest, throughout my body as everything settled, healed, restored, strengthened. I turned to look at him.

It was as if time froze.

Ironfall.

No.

Why was he doing this?

I couldn't say goodbye.

I couldn't.

Why was he giving his life up for mine?

He turned forward and stepped again, but I grabbed his arm and turned him toward me. Before I even knew what I was doing I grabbed his face and pressed my lips to his. Because it was all I could do. It was I'm sorry and I love you and don't do this and thank you all wrapped into one.

He grabbed my face and kissed me harder, then stepped back.

I shook my head no, but he only nodded, flashing a grin.

"Go," he said, stepping backward, stroking my cheek one last time.

I didn't move.

"So touching." Dad sneered.

Oh no.

"You have what you want." Ironfall turned around. "Now let's go."

"Not just yet…" said my dad.

My stomach dropped.

"Run!" Ironfall shouted at me.

I did. I turned and ran and hated myself for it.

That was when the gunfire started, but it came from in front of me. I threw myself toward Ironfall's car before turning to watch the Sedator and my Dad drag Ironfall behind their truck.

No.

"Stop! Unless you want everyone to blow up." My father's voice echoed. "That's right, I came prepared with a bomb powerful enough to destroy everything within a few hundred yards." *A bomb.*

The gunfire ceased. I peeked up to see two dark silhouettes lying on a sandy ridge, rifles pointed at my father's truck. VIGIL. They were here. They weren't just going to let Ironfall turn himself over. But they were close enough that the explosion would take them out too.

"I didn't know they were here!" I heard Ironfall yell. "I came alone, just like you asked. They just couldn't help themselves from being heroic."

"Good thing I planned ahead. Now I get everything I want." My father's voice rose. "Rosemary, dearest, I want you back now."

No.

But I had to.

Otherwise everyone I loved would die...

I rose, hands in the air, walking back over to the truck, slowly. Then I was right there to the side. It was dark inside.

"Get in." The Sedator shoved me. I couldn't see much, so I had nothing left to do but open the back door of the truck and slide in. "Now let's get out of here."

Once we were all inside, I looked at Ironfall, eyes wide. He laced his fingers through mine, squeezing hard. Was he as scared as I was?

Gears shifted, but the truck hardly moved.

"I think they shot out the tires. We aren't going anywhere." The Sedator cursed.

Dad cursed more, banging a hand on the steering wheel.

One point to VIGIL, but what were we supposed to do outside of that?

That was when I saw the red button in Dad's hand. The bomb trigger.

I glanced over at Ironfall, leaning close. "We have to get that away from him," I whispered into his ear.

"Working on it." His lips brushed my ear. "Side by side?"

I turned to face him, our lips inches apart. "Side by side."

VIGIL was out there with snipers. We were trapped in here with two madmen and a bomb.

"You can't get out of this," Ironfall said to my father. "You don't have a vehicle anymore." I squeezed his hand harder.

"Dad?" I whispered. He truly was trapped, and here we were, trapped with him.

"Shut up! I'm thinking!" He was panicking. He knew this wasn't going to go well for him. And that was what scared me the most. Would he decide that pressing the button was the best option? Just take everyone out. Right now. Including himself?

"Dr. Sutherland, take my daughter at gunpoint. We're confiscating the other vehicle. I'll handle Ironfall. If he even looks at someone the wrong way, I blow us all up. We use them as shields."

I glanced back at Ironfall, who met me with a steady gaze. As our two captors climbed out, Ironfall pressed a kiss to my forehead like everything was going to be okay.

The Sedator yanked me from the truck, gun barrel digging against my side as he pressed himself against my back. I stared to where the VIGIL agents were in the darkness. They held their fire as we made the treacherous walk to Ironfall's car, but then the Sedator raised his gun, shooting towards them. I couldn't see if they managed to get away, but with the gun pointed somewhere other than me, I kneed back. Careful not to let his skin touch me, I snatched his gun, leaping away just as another shot fired through the air.

The Sedator dropped.

VIGIL must've fired.

I looked back at my father gripping Ironfall's arm, the red button in his other hand.

I pointed my gun at him.

"I will use this!" Dad yelled, finger hovering just over the detonator. One press and we were all dead. I kept my weapon trained on him, but he yanked Ironfall closer. I couldn't risk it. My father knew that. Neither me nor VIGIL would risk such a shot.

My breath caught. Would this be how I lost Ironfall?

No, it would not.

He shoved Ironfall forward, and both strode confidently

toward the working vehicle. My gun followed him every step of the way, but Ironfall was still too close.

"In case you forgot, I am the one in control here." His finger once again danced over the red button. I took a deep breath. He didn't sound like he was in control.

"Are you now?" It was the first thing Ironfall had said in a while.

"You can't win, Dad," I said. "Please, just let him go."

"Why? So you can have the very thing you took away from me?" He looked from Ironfall and back to me.

"It didn't have to be like this." I shook my head. "It shouldn't have been like this."

"You're right, it shouldn't. If he had just done his job instead of falling in love with you, none of this would've happened," Dad spat, pointing the bomb trigger at Ironfall.

"She never would have joined you because if there's one thing I know, it's that Rosemary always does what's right, even when it's the hard thing," Ironfall said. "Even when someone tries to make her do otherwise." My eyes stung. "It's not because I fell in love with her, it's because she loves *everyone*. Really, truly loves them to a point where she will sacrifice herself to save them."

I couldn't breathe.

"Dad, this isn't the way," I choked back a sob. "Please."

He held the button up in the air. "I—" He looked around.

Ironfall motioned for me with a small urge of his chin. I did as he wanted, trusting him, stepping farther from the blast zone. Then he twisted, grabbing for the remote, pulling Dad's thumb off as he kicked him back. Dad hit the car, but stood again a second later, yanking out a gun. He was far enough away from—

Bang!

Dad slumped.

Silence.

It was…over.

Ironfall ran for me, wrapping his arms around me as the world turned in slow motion.

It was over.

My father was dead.

I sank into Ironfall's arms, burying my face in his shoulder.

"It's okay. It's okay. You're okay," he whispered, pressing a kiss to the top of my head. "Everything is going to be okay. It's over now."

Everything was a blur. We waited. A blanket was thrown over me. Then the sirens came. Police. FBI. Ambulance.

I stayed in Ironfall's arms, now sitting in a black SUV.

The scene played and replayed in my mind. The fighting. The shots. Ironfall.

I shrank deeper into him.

The kiss.

Ironfall's words.

"Rosemary," he said.

"Hmm?" It was all I could say.

"I love you." He pressed another kiss into my hair. "I love you."

I couldn't look up as more tears flooded to my eyes. "And I love you," I choked.

JULY 21 – 1:07 A.M. PDT

I sighed. It had never felt so good to be back at the VIGIL base.

"Rosemary! Oh my gosh, you're okay! Both of you are okay! What happened?" Before I knew it, Sam's arms were around both Ironfall and me. Our hands were still linked to each other.

Sam pulled back, fast, the wall of screens silhouetting him. "Wait a second. You two are holding hands. Are you—?" A grin broke out. "You finally admitted you're in love with each other, didn't you?"

Despite everything, I couldn't help but laugh. "I don't know what you're talking about." I glanced at Ironfall who had the same mischievous glimmer in his eye. Oh yes, we were definitely going to hold this over Sam too.

"Oh, no, you have the look of two people who totally have kissed and not because they're acting," Sam said. "I can't believe this is happening! Starfall is real!"

"Okay, fine, maybe we did," Ironfall said. "But you can never post about it."

"I promise nothing." Sam smirked.

I smiled again. "It's good to see you again, Sam."

"The gang is back together." He hopped on the spot. "It was lonely without you."

"Yeah, yeah." Ironfall rolled his eyes.

"Is ANTE…?" Sam's voice trailed off.

"The Sedator is dead. And so is…"

"Oh." Sam looked at me. "I'm sorry." He shifted as if he didn't know what to say.

"I'll be okay." I forced a smile. "We won. VIGIL won. No more ANTE."

"Yeah," Sam said. "But what happens next? The whole world knows. It's not like we can just keep a secret and keep making movies or whatever other cool things VIGIL does from the shadows."

I looked at Ironfall as if he would have an answer, but he shrugged.

"I suppose we're at the mercy of that awful FBI agent," Ironfall said.

"You don't have to go back to jail, do you?" My breath caught.

"Immunity deal." Ironfall smiled down at me.

"Yeah, thank goodness he got one," Sam said. "He escaped

out of jail and then came to find you, but you were kidnapped so...yeah."

"Oh." I nodded, relief flooding through me. "Okay." So maybe...things could be normal...one day, though nothing would ever be the same. But maybe that was good? I didn't know, I just knew that I needed to sleep for about three weeks.

"Rosemary!" Ver burst into the room. I broke away from Ironfall to wrap my arms around her. "I was so worried! Then the FBI was everywhere and I couldn't get to you."

"It's okay." I smiled faintly. "We won."

She hugged me again. "Yes, we did."

"We made a big mess, but we did win," Sam agreed.

"Shut up, Sam," Ver laughed. "We'll see about the state of this PR nightmare though."

"None of you are going to 'see' about anything." Agent Laude's voice filled the base. He was followed by Manda, Agent Liam, and a slew of other agents. "VIGIL is shut down until we do a thorough investigation of the situation. Congress is going to want to hear about this too."

I took a deep breath. We just got back, couldn't we have one day? Or like an hour? Or something? Anything?

Ver turned to us. "It's going to be fine. You'll see."

Agent Liam moved toward us, but Agent Laude blocked his path. "I'm sorry, but I have to separate all of you until you can be thoroughly debriefed."

We stepped away, and I sighed.

We were safe. The whir of computers enveloped me.

I didn't have to worry.

But all I wanted to do was grieve.

Federal Bureau Of Investigation
Transcript Of The Interview Proceedings With

AGENT LIAM BLAKE, DIRECTOR OF VIGIL
SOME NAMES AND LOCATIONS REDACTED FOR SECURITY
INTERVIEW CONDUCTED ON JULY 23
LOCATION OF INTERVIEW: **[REDACTED]**
CASE #: **[REDACTED]**

PROPERTY OF THE FBI

SPECIAL AGENT LAUDE: So you're saying if you hadn't agreed to the exchange, we wouldn't be in this position?
AGENT LIAM BLAKE: If I hadn't agreed to it, one of my agents would be dead and the remaining ANTE stragglers would still be free. That's what I'm saying.
SPECIAL AGENT LAUDE: Anything else you'd like to add for the record?
AGENT LIAM BLAKE: We're on the same side. Remember that.
SPECIAL AGENT LAUDE: Hmm.
AGENT LIAM BLAKE: You don't sound convinced.
SPECIAL AGENT LAUDE: Well, Liam, you certainly put up a good fight.

AGENT LIAM BLAKE: It's my job to protect this nation.

SPECIAL AGENT LAUDE: But that isn't your only job, now is it?

AGENT LIAM BLAKE: We all took the same oath.

SPECIAL AGENT LAUDE: We're shutting VIGIL down, Liam.

AGENT LIAM BLAKE: No. You can't. You need us. ANTE may be gone, but the world still needs us.

CHAPTER 24

IRONFALL

AUGUST 31 – *4:03 P.M. EDT*

The tape player stopped in the Department of Defense committee room as the chairman leaned into the mic. "That concludes recorded interviews with the primary parties of VIGIL. Let the record show that little information was redacted and will be provided to committee members who hold the proper security clearance."

The room was large and filled with desks, freshly polished with a particularly potent cleaner.

A small cough echoed throughout the chamber, but no one noticed.

"Thank you, Agent Laude. Were each of these interviews taken under oath?"

He leaned toward the mic. "Yes. They were also put through our rigorous FBI lie detector exam."

"You would say they are each accurate, is that correct?" another committee member said. He was older, probably in his late sixties and more unaware of the technology. A bit concerning, actually.

"Accurate to their perspective, sir," said Agent Laude. "There is a certain degree of difference, but that's to be expected."

"Noted," said another one of the committee members.

"What about Ironfall's story?"

I straightened at my name. This was the perfect opportunity for Agent Laude to send me right back to jail.

"I find him credible, in this instance."

Cameras flashed, but I hardly noticed as I let out a breath.

I glanced over at Rosemary sitting a few seats away. Her brown eyes twinkled as she gave me a reassuring nod. She trusted me. The team trusted me. And that meant more than all the power in the world.

Attention shifted to me.

"As you will remember, Ironfall, you are under oath to tell the whole truth and nothing but the truth," said the chairman. "What do you have to say?"

I cleared my throat, looking around at the staring faces. Strangers, all curious, though some still seemed afraid. Some excited. "I took another oath too, as an agent of VIGIL. I vowed to protect the United States of America. My past may have been...misguided..."

"Why should we honor your immunity agreement? You pose a national security threat."

"There's a threat if I don't help. Do you know how many enemies the people of the United States have? How many people with powers do you have defending it?" I said. "If there is one more person to add to the fight, I suggest you take it."

"And you have, what, your friends here to vouch for you?"

"I helped take down ANTE with the rest of VIGIL." I said straightened again. "That might boost my credibility, don't you think?" I flashed a grin before bowing my head again.

A low chuckle rumbled through the room, but the chairman raised a hand to silence them.

"Yet because of VIGIL, multiple national security secrets have been revealed, especially the government's use of highly powered individuals. To be frank, VIGIL blew it, Agent Liam," said a committee member.

"With all due respect, ANTE blew it, sir," Agent Liam interrupted. "They are the ones who blew VIGIL's cover. What we did after was for the good of the country, and we succeeded."

"But it's causing quite a scandal. The world's eyes are on us and our exposed black ops operation now. There is no legal precedent for superpowers, and we had freedom before. Why shouldn't we shut you down for good?"

"Now that the world knows, this isn't something you can sweep under the rug. Our enemies are watching…waiting. You need us more than ever to protect you from threats you haven't even known about," Agent Liam said.

"Not to mention," I interrupted this time, "the world kinda likes us."

"Agent Collins, we haven't heard much from you," said another committee member, a petite woman with hair almost as red as Rosemary's.

"You're right. This is a mess, but it's something we must deal with," Rosemary said. "ANTE had sleeper agents embedded inside the government for years. They have been FBI agents, congressmen, actors, businessmen. You didn't even know about them until we found them, and it took a villain, a random teenager, a couple hackers, and two agents to take them down. We may be an unlikely team, but it's what the world needs. So sure, dismantle us, but let's see how that works out for you. Because together"—Rosemary looked straight at me—"we will be heroes."

BESTVIGILMEMES.BLOGGINGLIFE.COM

FEATURING THE BEST VIGIL & ANTE STUDIOS POSTS
(DON'T @ ME)
– UNAVERAGEVIGILFAN2002

USERNAME:

FORGET COMIC CON...WHO LISTENED TO THE CONGRESS THING?! LIKE WHAT?! OBVIOUSLY WE NEED VIGIL AND THE SAFEGUARDERS PROTECTING US

———

cloakerstan:

Talk about a mic drop moment

———

StarfallShipper3:

Starfall. That's it. That's the post.

———

saveVIGIL:

#LetVIGILdoitsthing

———

fandomfighter2006:

VIGIL & ANTE STUDIOS FANDOM RISE UP! DON'T LET VIGIL GET SHUT DOWN!!!

CHAPTER

25

ROSEMARY

DECEMBER 12 – *5:03 P.M. PST*

Ironfall squeezed my hand. "You ready?" I looked out through the car window at the oncoming crowd. The red carpet. The flashing lights. The world looking up to us as heroes.

I smiled as nerves fluttered in my stomach. "Let's hope this one goes better than the last one."

"I know it will," he said. "And if it doesn't, it's probably the safest place to be with the newly reinstated Safeguarders and VIGIL agents."

"You're right," I said, still grinning.

He leaned in to kiss me.

"Um...guys?" Sam said from the other side of the limo. "I love me some Starfall, but in moderation. Please."

"Unless you want everyone to know the identity of your celebrity crush, I suggest you stop," Ironfall said.

Sam's face turned white. "What? I don't have one!"

Mia's eyes darted from Sam to Ironfall as she burst into laughter.

I giggled. "Then you have nothing to worry about." Beads of sweat had already started forming on his forehead.

"Out of *courtesy*, I will stop," Sam said.

Ironfall's gaze met mine, shining with amusement. "Blackmail, you mean."

"I'm being nice, Ironfall." Sam grinned. "I'm allowed to be nice."

"You're going to have to watch them together in the movie, Sam," said Mia, playfully touching his shoulder. "If my predictions are correct, that is."

"My lips are sealed," Sam said. "But only because my contract says so."

I took Ironfall's hand. "And because we get to share your secret if you don't."

Sam gasped in fake offense. "You're taking *his* side?"

"Right, right." Mia grinned, smoothing out her dress. "I can't believe I'm actually here with you guys about to walk the red carpet."

Sam wrapped an arm across her shoulder. "We are totally the coolest extras in history."

"Yes, Sam, you are," I said. Ironfall only rolled his eyes, but I knew he loved it.

The limo slid to a stop at the beginning of the red carpet.

"All right, gang, let's do this," Sam said.

And then the door opened, letting in the breezy winter air. Ironfall got out first, offering me a hand. Chants of *Ironfall* and *Rosemary* filled the air. Because we were here as ourselves now. The world knew and it all felt fresh and new, like it was always supposed to be this way.

Sam and Mia followed us out of the car, and as a pack, we made our way through the crowd, signing autographs. (Sam tried to sign autographs too, but no one knew who he was or believed that he was VIGIL's tech guy.)

Ver rushed towards us, arms wide to pull us in for hugs. "You guys look amazing!"

"So do you!" I laughed, embracing her.

She stood back, pretended to brush away tears. "My movie star, all grown up." She looped her arm through mine as the three of us walked together down the carpet.

The first reporter in the lineup motioned me toward her, and security prompted me to follow.

"What's it like being both a VIGIL agent and an actress?" she asked.

"Oh my," I laughed, brushing a strand of hair behind my ear. "It's been a whirlwind. Before we had to take a filming break, I had filming all day and missions pretty much all night."

"It's safe to say you lived off caffeine then?" said the interviewer.

"I actually try to stay away from caffeine, but everyone else certainly did." I nodded.

"I think I speak for the rest of the fandom when I say we are so glad VIGIL was reinstated. The world is a much safer place, especially with someone so talented in its service."

I smiled, true happiness surging through me. "Thank you so much." VIGIL was back, and people wanted us.

Before I knew it, I was inside the theater with the other VIGIL agents, my new family. We hugged and laughed and just…were. No fear. No mistrust. We were together, waiting to go watch our movie. Like how it was supposed to be.

Like we were heroes.

"Thank you," Ironfall whispered in my ear. "For all of this. For giving me a second chance."

I looked up at him. "And thank you for giving me one."

His lips brushed against my cheek before we walked further inside, hand in hand. Not as enemies, not as friends, but as something so much more.

ACKNOWLEDGMENTS
(A.K.A. THE END CREDITS)

We Will Be Heroes was finished in the midst of one of the most challenging times of my life. I moved away from home, started a full-time job, and struggled with debilitating anxiety. Honestly, the fact that this book even exists is a miracle. Words cannot describe how grateful I am for everyone part of finishing The Vigil & Ante Files, but I will try my best.

First, I have to thank Micheline Ryckman for believing in me. Micheline, without you, We Will Be Heroes probably wouldn't have been finished. Thank you for encouraging me and pushing me to continue writing when I was struggling. You have been so understanding, kind, and flexible through this process. I am forever grateful that you took a chance on Rosemary, Ironfall, Sam, and The Vigil & Ante Files. It is an honor to call you my publishing Mom.

Thank you to my family: Mom, Dad, Savannah, Grammy, Grampy, and Uncle Brian. Thank you for always being there for me and praying for me. You are truly my biggest fans, and I love you so much.

Thank you, Natasha, for being the big sister I never had. I am so thankful that God brought you into my life. You are a fierce warrior for Christ, and you constantly challenge me to draw closer to Him. I love you so much.

Micaiah, you are such a great friend. Thank you for always being down to bounce ideas back and forth. I look forward to the day when you release a book! Yes, this is forever in writing, so you're obligated to finish editing that manuscript.

Thank you to Christina and Lucy for all of your work in producing and marketing this book. Both of you have stepped in when I haven't been able to, and I am so grateful. Whimsical is so blessed to have each of you.

And thank you, reader, for reading the final installment of Rosemary and Ironfall's story. I am truly grateful for your support.

Last, but certainly not least, thank you to my Lord and Savior Jesus Christ. You gave me the words to finish this series when I had none. This book, and all my future ones, are yours.

P.S. Sam wants it to be known that he owes everything to Micheline Ryckman. Without her, he wouldn't exist.

ABOUT THE AUTHOR

Megan McCullough wanted a superpower, so she picked up a pen and became an author. Living in Florida, the theme park capital of the world, only fuels her love for storytelling. When she isn't writing, you can find her designing a book cover for someone else's literary masterpiece, fangirling over the Marvel Cinematic Universe, or wishing she was at Disney World. Join Megan's adventures through her Instagram @meganmccul-loughbooks or at meganmccullough.com.

Made in the USA
Las Vegas, NV
22 August 2024

94268167R00176